ANDRE GONZALEZ

Warm Souls

To my dad, Larry. You may not remember, but you were my very first reader in 2002.

"With endless time, nothing is special. With no loss or sacrifice, we can't appreciate what we have."

-Mitch Albom

Contents

1

Chapter 1

It had rained every single day since they pulled Isabelle Briar's remains from the lake. Martin had shed tears as he watched the dive crew jump into the water in search of his long-lost daughter. An hour later, they emerged with a pile of bones and Martin's heart sunk as the gray skies cried heavy tears over the small town of Larkwood, Colorado.

His ex-wife, Lela, had already been taken into custody by the local police. Martin was forced to watch old pictures of his family flash by on the news and internet. The story was all anyone talked about, and he soon refused to show his face in public—especially with his new girlfriend nearby, who didn't need the harassment of the limelight during her first week in 2018.

In 2018, news stories were posted online for viewers to watch at their leisure. These same stories were shared to social media for the entire world to watch, judge, and even leave their opinions in the form of a comment.

There were thousands of thoughts and prayers for Izzy, and this touched Martin as he scrolled through the comments.

There were even dozens for Martin directly, people trying to step into his shoes and imagine their spouse murdering their child. But, as always on the internet, ugly, cruel people also crawled out of their dark corners and accused Martin of being a neglectful husband. Why wasn't he home that night? Was he out at the bars? Having an affair?

Get fucking real, he thought, reading these ludicrous theories. He wondered why people bothered reading articles online if they were only going to form their own story.

Despite the trolls, the overall support from the online community helped Martin through a difficult week. So did Sonya.

Sonya had learned over their six months together in 1996 how to handle Martin's emotions: when to insert herself into the situation, when to back off and give him space. This particular week was a balanced mixture.

Martin's cell phone rang constantly from relatives and friends all around the country. Sonya still gawked in amazement every time he spoke into the tiny device.

"What can I do for you?" she had asked the night after the body recovery.

"Just *be* here. Please don't stress about doing anything. We can order takeout for every meal, I really don't care. Just being by my side is all I can ask from you right now."

Seeing Izzy's bones pulled from the water had fucked with his mind; part of him had expected her body to still be somewhat intact.

"Unfortunately, people litter this lake, making it more acidic," a member from the forensics team had told him. "That accelerates the decomposition process."

Martin had spoken with a handful of forensic team members, and each of them spoke in the same tone: flat and emotionless.

He thought of these events as he stared at the casket, its perfect black gloss still glimmering on the gloomy day. The prior night was the rosary service at the church, an event he still couldn't remember. Before arriving to the cemetery was the funeral service at the same church, also a fuzzy memory. All he could do was stare at the coffin and allow the burden of regret to settle on his soul.

Sure, he received the closure he had sought by learning what exactly had happened to his daughter after 22 years of wondering. But what he really wanted was one final hug, one last kiss on her forehead, a final whiff of her scent to hold in his lungs and heart forever.

He never encountered her when he had traveled to 1996, always keeping a safe distance to watch her from afar like a guardian angel, terrified to tinker with the past before learning how it worked. Only guardian angels weren't supposed to stand helplessly outside the house while the one they protected was murdered inside.

Thinking of those few minutes of hell made him clench his fists and tremble with rage. Chris, the old man, the keeper of time or whatever the fuck he was, had knowingly set him up for failure. There was no situation where Martin could have barged into the house and saved the day; he had no reason to believe that Izzy's demise would come from inside.

God damn it all.

The priest droned on in the background as Martin kept his eyes fixed on the casket. His daughter was in there, never able to laugh or sing again. Martin's mother sat on his right, hugging his arm. A gathering of roughly fifty friends and family came to show their support for Martin and Izzy. When the story became widespread news, Martin was asked if the funeral would be open to the public, which he promptly rejected.

The priest finally stopped speaking and many of the guests visited Martin in the front row to offer him hugs and hand-shakes, wishing him the best in his recovery. He mindlessly returned the hugs and mumbled a quick thanks as people moved down the line.

After fifteen minutes the cemetery had cleared out, leaving Martin alone with Sonya and his mother. The funeral director prepared to lower Izzy into the earth. He didn't want to watch, but felt comfort in knowing where she was.

"Do you feel up to grab some coffee?" his mother, Marilyn, asked. "My treat."

"Sure." Martin just wanted to leave the cemetery.

They all walked slowly to the car, Marilyn struggling up a slight hill to the parking lot. Sonya handled the driving on this emotional day and took them to the nearest coffee shop in a silent car ride.

When they arrived, Martin grabbed a table while Sonya and his mother went to order the drinks. They had gotten along well despite just meeting a few days ago. Marilyn hadn't asked where they had met in the midst of all the commotion, and he was glad because they hadn't yet discussed a story to tell people when asked that very question.

They joined Martin at the table.

"Martin, I need to tell you something," Marilyn said, a sudden shift in her already solemn tone. "I know this isn't the best day, but it really can't wait any longer."

"Mom, what's wrong?" he asked, a pit forming in his stomach.

She forced a smile as she stared down to her coffee cup,

running a finger nervously around the brim.

"I've been diagnosed with Alzheimer's."

Martin's jaw dropped and Sonya seemed to shrink into herself. Welcome to 2018 with Martin Briar, where kids get buried and mothers contract deadly diseases.

Chris, he immediately thought. *That motherfucker.* He'd been waiting for something bad to happen; the old man had told him it would when he least expected it.

"I. . . I don't know what to say," Martin replied.

"There's nothing to say," Marilyn said flatly. "It's not in the early stages, either. The doctors said I have two to four years to live, and that the symptoms will start progressing any day now."

Not realizing he had any more left, tears formed in Martin's eyes. "Have you already been suffering?"

His mother, who seemed to have aged twenty years in the last five minutes, nodded gently as a tear rolled down her cheek. "I've been forgetful with silly things: where I put my keys, what I was looking for in the kitchen. I didn't think anything of it until I got in the car to go to church and couldn't remember which way to go."

The church was only a mile from her house, the same one he had seen burnt to ashes on his trip to 1996.

"Mom, I'm so sorry."

"I know. And I wanted to tell you before I get any worse. I don't know when that will be. My mind still feels clear, and I don't know what exactly it's going to do."

She fell silent. They all knew how this would progress and eventually end.

"I've made arrangements with a senior home that special-izes in Alzheimer's. It's just over in Grant."

Martin shook his head aggressively. "No. I'm not letting you go to that home."

"Marty, it's okay. You'll be able to visit—it's only a fifteen-minute drive."

Martin's face had turned bright red as tears and mucus flowed from his eyes and nose, pooling together on his chin.

"No. I'm not gonna let you rot away in a home while you forget every detail about your life. You can stay with me."

"Marty, there's no room for me in your apartment—"

"I'm moving," he interrupted. "I've come into some money and am going to buy a house."

He wasn't lying, but he also wasn't sure exactly how much money was waiting for him in his investment account, either. That would have to go on the to-do list for tomorrow.

"Money from what?" his mother asked.

"I've done some investing, and things have exploded for me."

"You never mentioned this."

It felt like it had been six months since they last met for dinner after their quick trip to the mysterious store, the *Wealth of Time*, which it had been for Martin, but in reality it had only been a week. Martin didn't keep much from his mother, so her surprise was warranted in this scenario.

"It sort of took off over night. Caught me by surprise as well."

"Well that's great news, Marty. I still don't want to burden you. The toll this disease can take on the family shouldn't be questioned."

"I know it'll be hard, but I'm going to step away from my job. I've come into that much money."

He didn't know if this was for certain. Yes, there should be a good sum of money to at least live off for a couple of years. It was also possible that his investments changed the route of history and saw the companies flop. Maybe he would have to go back to his miserable job at the post office, but his bad fortune had to turn around at some point.

"You're living with me, Mom. You don't have a say in the matter."

He almost said *us,* but caught himself. His mother wouldn't have an issue with Martin and Sonya living together, but he wanted to avoid the topic at the moment.

"I love you, Marty. That's the main thing I wanted to tell you now before I forget who you are."

She resumed crying as if she flipped on a switch.

"Why would you say that?"

"Because it's going to happen. I've accepted it. I've taken all the pictures of you and your brother, and your father. I wrote on the back of every single one who is in the picture and who they are in relation to me. I don't want to forget, but as you said, I don't have a say in the matter. I love you, Marty, and I'm proud of you. I knew one day you'd be able to get your life back on track after Izzy, and it looks like that's starting to happen."

She shot a quick wink to Sonya that made her blush.

"I love you, too," Martin said. "Now let's get out of here. We need to get ready to move."

2

Chapter 2

The gray clouds disappeared the next morning, and the sun shone into Martin's apartment for the first time since he arrived back in 2018. The heavens knew the gloom was necessary, and with Izzy now properly buried, the world returned to normal.

It was Friday, and Martin refused to wait until Monday to learn what waited in his investment account. Waking up in his apartment without a hangover was a new sensation, but having Sonya cuddled up next to him was something he wouldn't trade for all the alcohol in the world.

His feet hit the ground at six o'clock and he wasted no time making a quick breakfast. He had slept like a log the night before and felt ready to tackle the day ahead. Butterflies flapped wildly in his stomach as he pondered the prospect of becoming rich in the next few hours.

He didn't expect it to happen so quickly, but Martin already felt at peace with Izzy's burial. After so many years, it was only natural for the brain to accept her death, no matter how hard the heart refused to believe it. The news of his mother's

Alzheimer's also helped overshadow some of the emotion, as did the pending excitement of what would soon happen at the investment center. The past few days had been an abstract painting of emotions.

Sonya joined him in the kitchen a few minutes later, her hair a frazzled mess, but still beautiful with its subtle streaks of silver mixed in with gold.

"Good morning," Martin greeted her as he flipped an egg in the skillet.

"You seem awfully chipper today," she replied with a wide smile.

"I'm hoping today's a great day. Do you care to join me downtown this morning? You can explore since it's changed so much since you've last seen it, then we can grab lunch when I'm done with the investment people."

"I'd love to. I've always enjoyed downtown—can't wait to see what it's like now."

"Perfect, I'm planning on leaving here at eight to head down."

"Works for me," she said, crossing the room with her silk nightgown flowing behind. She had visited the local department stores to rebuild her wardrobe while Martin spent hours at the police station to conclude Izzy's decades-old case.

She wrapped her arms around Martin's waist from behind and rested her head on his shoulder. "Are you sure you're doing okay? This whole week has been absolutely crazy. I can't imagine what you're going through."

Martin nodded, keeping his concentration on the stovetop. "I'm doing okay. I'm sure this will be a process. Some days will be good, and others will be bad. Yesterday was extremely difficult, but I hope to leave it in the past. All I can do is look forward and control what I can."

Sonya kissed his back before setting the table. "I'm glad to hear the positive outlook. I'm here for you on the good days and bad, don't forget it."

They sat down for breakfast, laughter and life filling the apartment for possibly the first time ever.

* * *

Martin debated wearing a suit, but settled for slacks and a polo. There was no dress code to enter the investment center, but he needed to look the part of a wealthy man stopping by to pick up his funds.

During the drive downtown, they found themselves on the same stretch of highway they had driven during their mission to Columbine High School in 1996. That memory felt like it really had happened two decades ago, and Sonya never acknowledged it after seeing the entire school in flames on the nightly news.

Within thirty minutes they parked in a garage underground from the Sixteenth Street Mall, an outdoor mall spanning a mile long through the heart of downtown Denver.

Businessmen and women filled the sidewalks on their way to work in one of the many skyscrapers. Sonya gawked at the city that had nearly doubled in size from what she remembered in 1996.

"When did Denver become so big?" she asked, more to herself.

"Don't get lost this morning," Martin said as he led them

toward the investment firm.

They crossed one block before reaching the sparkling golden sign that read: THOMAS AND LEONARD INVESTMENTS.

"Well, this is it. I have no idea how long this will take, maybe an hour. Go grab some coffee and walk the mall, I'm sure everything has changed since you've last been here."

"Yeah, you could say that," she replied, admiring the buildings that kissed the clouds.

"Meet me here in, say, one hour. If I'm not here, just come back every half hour. We really need to get you a cell phone. That will make this all easier. If you find a phone store, maybe take a look. Tell the sales people you're just browsing, otherwise they'll harass you into a $1,000 phone."

"A thousand dollars for a *phone*?" she gasped.

"Yeah, you'd be surprised. Does that all sound like a plan?"

"Yes. I'll even find a spot for lunch."

Martin pecked her on the lips and entered the building.

He had chosen to invest with this firm simply because he knew it still existed in 2018. Many firms had gone under during the recession in 2008, but he remembered the massive golden sign on the mall, inviting those with the deepest pockets to enter its doors.

Their offices were on the lower level of an eight-story building, and the gold theme continued all the way inside with golden walls, chandeliers, and a fish tank in the lobby's floor.

This place is obnoxious.

"How may I help you, sir?" a young African-American man asked from behind the front desk.

"I was hoping to withdraw some funds from my account today. Is there someone available to help?"

"Certainly," the man replied, typing on his keyboard and

splitting his stare between the screen and Martin. "Give me one moment to track someone down for you."

"Thank you."

Martin took a seat in one of the heavily cushioned lounge chairs in the lobby. A door— with a golden handle, of course—was the only other thing visible aside from expensive artwork hanging on the walls.

The door opened and another man appeared, much older than the enthusiastic kid behind the front desk. He locked eyes with Martin and started toward him with a hand extended, his perfectly tailored suit moving precisely with each step.

"Good morning, sir," he said in a most formal voice. "I understand you're looking to draw funds today?"

"Yes, sir," Martin replied, shaking the man's firm hand.

"Perfect, I can assist. What is your name?"

"Martin Briar."

"Oh," the man said abruptly, and scrunched his brow. "Please come this way, Mr. Briar."

Martin met the man's puzzled face and his heart drummed a bit faster. *Do they know something about me? Why would he look at me like that?*

"My name is Edward Clarence. Let's get situated in my office and we can discuss your account."

"Okay." Martin's nerves throbbed in his fingertips as his palms started to moisten.

He followed the man, whose pointy features reminded him of a weasel, through the door and into the silent office space where finance professionals moved millions of dollars every day for their clients. Behind the door was a long hallway that branched into other hallways. Offices lined the hall, each with a name painstakingly etched on the glass doors. The work spaces resembled the prestigious lobby with polished oak desks, golden nameplates, and more abstract art on the walls.

They walked three doors down, and to the left entered the office of Edward Clarence.

"Please have a seat, Mr. Briar. I'll be right back."

Martin situated himself in the chair, less comfortable than the loungers in the lobby.

Edward returned a couple minutes later with a stern-faced woman in a pantsuit.

"Mr. Briar, this is our vice president, Karen Grabble."

"Good morning, Mr. Briar, it's a pleasure to meet you," Karen said as she sat behind Edward's desk and logged into the computer

"Likewise."

Karen had bright red lipstick and curly black hair tucked behind her ears. Martin imagined she had been attractive in her twenties, but life in the finance world had clearly taken its toll on her in the way of wrinkles and bags under her brown eyes.

"Mr. Briar, I'm here because we have some questions," she said, crossing her hands on the desk as she stared at him. Edward had closed the door and stood awkwardly in the corner of the room.

"Is there a problem?" Martin asked, fighting to keep his voice calm.

"Not a problem, just some curiosity. We've been trying to get in touch with you for the past few years with no success."

"What exactly were you trying to get in touch with me about?" He tried to play it off cool and felt like he was succeeding.

"Well, sir, you made some investments in 1996 and haven't touched your account one single time since. As your balance grew, this caught our attention and we wanted to reach out to make sure you were okay. We even searched through death records to make sure we hadn't missed something."

"I'm sorry about that," Martin said in a forced voice of gratitude. "I've been out of the country for the last few years. I honestly forgot about this account until recently, and that's why I'm here today."

Karen stared into his eyes, clearly trying to fight back the urge to say something.

"Very well," she said. "How much were you hoping to withdraw today?"

"I don't even know what my balance is. Could you tell me that?"

"Of course."

She turned to the computer and drummed on the keyboard.

Martin had invested $30,000 in 1996 into various technology and health companies that he knew still existed in 2018.

Please be a million. A million would be so perfect.

Karen continued on the keyboard, and Martin wondered if she was dragging out the process for whatever reason. She seemed like the kind of lady who got hers kicks from pissing off people.

"I show your current balance as $12,750,000."

Holy. Fucking. Shit.

"Excuse me?" Martin asked, his heart going from a rabid, caged animal to a frozen snowman in the matter of one second.

"Twelve point seven five million, sir."

How the hell did this happen? I'm not rich. I'm filthy *rich.*

The tension in his body had reached its peak and Martin

wasn't sure if he should laugh or cry all the way to the bank. He could buy his new house and car and never have to work a day again.

"That's a lot more than I was expecting," he said with the slightest waver in his voice.

Karen stared at him, unimpressed.

"Can I withdraw all of it?" he asked.

The vice president scrunched her eyes at the screen, as if looking for some loophole that would not allow this random bum off the streets to take home $12 million. She pursed her lips tighter with each scroll down the screen.

"Yes, you can. Please know that we take a 1% cut from all withdrawals."

"Not a problem. I appreciate you taking the time to track me down."

Martin knew they were hoping he would turn up deceased at some point. There were no beneficiaries listed on the account and all of that money would have become their own.

"Please give us a few minutes to cut you a check. Is there anything else we can do for you today?"

"No, just the withdrawal will do. Thank you, you've been a great help." He hoped she could sense the sarcasm in his voice, but her poker face left him clueless.

She offered a quick grin that likely hurt her face before standing and leaving the office.

"Well, that was interesting," Edward said as he returned to his rightful spot behind his desk, and they both let out relieved laughter.

Edward made small talk with their famous client while they waited for the check to be delivered.

Twelve million dollars, Martin thought. *I'm gonna marry*

Sonya.

3

Chapter 3

Martin stepped outside to find Sonya pacing circles outside the investment firm. She stopped when she saw him and jogged over.

"How did it go?" she asked.

"We need to get to a bank right now," he said. He had folded the check and slid it into his pocket, not removing his hand from the pocket in the process.

"What happened?"

Martin looked over his shoulders in both directions and whispered. "Twelve million dollars."

Sonya's eyes bulged. "You're shitting me."

"I'm not, let's go right now, my bank has a branch on the mall."

He walked as she followed along his side.

"Martin, what on earth are you going to do with all of that?"

He walked faster.

"I have no idea. Apparently I'm buying a house for all of us to live in. Maybe I can buy us each a house on the same block." He chuckled. "I'm still shaking from when they handed me the check."

"We need to sit down and budget this money. I don't want you blowing through it all before Christmas—that can happen."

"That's not gonna happen. I'm gonna put it in savings while I figure out what I'm gonna do. I really do want to buy a house. My apartment is miserable and harbors lots of bad memories. That's all I really want. I suppose we can travel the world."

"Travel the world or travel through time?"

"I told you to not bring that up yet."

"We could do both. Travel through time and see the world. Imagine the Renaissance Era. We could live like royalty."

Martin had hidden his canteen of the Juice in the back of his liquor cabinet. He explained to Sonya the terror he felt wielding so much power, and the guilt of knowing he had caused his mother's Alzheimer's due to his selfish decision. He could have taken the original offer and lived the rest of his life like an emotionless zombie. Instead he would spend every night crying as his mother forgot the face of her own son.

How's that for a fair trade?

The bottle was stored away in hopes of being forgotten. As soon as Martin had arrived home with it he immediately regretted his decision, overwhelmed to know he could go to any time. He could visit the triceratops that used to roam Denver, or go to the year 3000 and get struck by a flying car, assuming the world still existed.

Having a history buff for a girlfriend didn't help, either. She wanted to live out her life's work: witness the construction of the pyramids, be a fly on the wall during the Civil War, and a whole list of things he'd never have a desire to do.

All he wanted was to get the check deposited, and if it didn't bounce, know that this wasn't a dream.

Still, the Juice pulsed in his mind like the heart beat from Poe's *Tell-Tale Heart.* It tugged at him with a mystical force, begging him to drink it and go on a new adventure.

Who do you want to go try to save today? it asked. *Fall into my trap where you are most vulnerable. Remember Columbine? Do you want to try to stop 9/11 next? Maybe the Oklahoma City bombing? We can have a grand time.*

They reached the bank, deposited the check—in which the teller did a double take at the figure—and were back on the mall within five minutes after what ended up a non-climactic encounter. He'd obviously never deposited millions of dollars, and didn't know what to expect, soon learning it was treated like any other transaction.

"Let's go eat lunch," he said as the first wave of relief took over. "I need a drink."

* * *

"Our life is going to change forever," Martin said as he took his first sip from the Jack and Coke delivered to their table. Sonya had decided on the first restaurant she spotted with an outdoor patio, a concept rare to find in 1996, but standard in 2018.

"Outdoor patios and rooftop decks are all over the city now," he explained to her.

The restaurant was deserted as the lunch rush was still an hour away at noon.

"I want to make one thing clear, Martin: all of this money is yours. I don't expect a penny of it. If I need to get a job to help contribute, then I'm happy to see what the teaching world has to offer here."

Martin threw his head back and bellowed laughter.

"Sonya, I just deposited a check for an amount I can't even wrap my mind around. I'm not working another day in my life, and neither are you. All we need to figure is out how we can stretch this to last for the activities we want to do."

Sonya stirred the straw in her soda and smiled. "Marty, you really don't need to be so generous."

"How can I justify wiping my ass with hundred dollar bills while you go work some job for twelve dollars an hour?"

She giggled, and Martin used the moment to soak in her beauty as the sunlight glowed on her face and lit up her blue eyes.

"Well, thank you. I'll help you with whatever you need, even taking care of your mom."

The topic was still sensitive, and Martin winced at her words.

"So how does this magic juice work?" she asked, knowing she needed to change the topic immediately.

Martin chuckled. "Magic juice? I guess we can call it that. Apparently it works just like the pills, only I have a lot more of it than one pill for each trip. Chris said all I have to do is think about where I want to go—er, *when* I want to go—and drink the Juice. Then I fall asleep and wake up where I want to be."

"Do I still get to come along?"

Martin nodded as the waitress returned with their food. "Yes. That works the same way. As long you're touching me, you'll come along for the ride."

Tell her now, before it's too late.

Martin could still hear Chris telling him that Sonya continued to age regardless of how much time they spent in the past, compared to him, who wouldn't age until he returned to his present time in 2018. She went through time as a form of property, apparently having her own set of rules.

"You should know something," he said.

She looked up to him curiously as she took a bite of her sandwich.

"I love you."

She chewed with a smile, mumbling that she loved him back. He couldn't tell her, not with the obvious look of joy on her face. She already had enough on her plate with trying to figure out life in 2018, and he couldn't justify adding more to her well-hidden stress levels.

"So tell me," he said. "If you could go to any era in time, where would you go?"

Sonya stared to the table and took a sip of her drink.

"Honestly, I would go back to the 20's."

"What's in the 20's?"

"My grandfather," she replied coldly. "He's always been a mystery in my family, but it's my family's fault. They shunned him. I don't know why."

"Really? Your grandmother never mentioned anything?"

Sonya shook her head. "Nope. She was the one who started the rule about never speaking his name. I don't even *know* my grandfather's name. That's how bad it is."

"What *do* you know?"

She shrugged. "I've heard that he was an English spy, captured and persecuted by the United States. I've heard he was an outlaw on the run, robbing banks for the Irish mob. I've also heard he went crazy and was admitted into the asylum. I have no idea which of them is true, but I'd love to find out."

"How would we go about finding him if we don't know his name or what he looks like?"

"My grandma has a storage unit. It was filled with all of her things when she passed. I'm convinced there has to be a trace of my grandpa in there."

Martin nodded. "Well, if you can get strong research together on how we can go about finding him, I'll go with you to the 20's."

"Really?" Sonya slapped her hand on the table, rattling the silverware and glasses in unison.

"Well, jeez, if you're that excited, how can I say no?"

"Martin, this is huge. I'll start researching tomorrow. You have no idea what this means to me." Sonya stood and crossed the table to give Martin a kiss.

"The Roaring Twenties," he said. "Do you know how far our money will stretch in that era? Twelve million is like a billion dollars in those days. We can live like actual gods."

"Martin, we're not taking all of that money. Are you trying to get us killed? We can't just show up out of nowhere as a random rich couple."

"We can tell everyone we come from oil in Texas and wanted to escape to a more laid-back city like Denver."

"No, that's not happening. That was a time of not just the mafia, but also bandits running rampant. You could shoot someone in the middle of the street and get away with it because there wasn't the technology to track down a murderer like there is today. If we show up with all that money we'll be robbed and murdered within two months. Word gets around fast, especially about new people in town."

"Okay, okay. You're scared of the gangsters and cowboys. Fine, we don't bring the money, just enough to get by on.

But I need you to have a complete plan. I went back to 1996 without a clue what I was doing, and it was absolutely painful at moments trying to figure things out on the fly."

"I can do that." Sonya couldn't contain the overflowing joy brimming in her voice.

They ate their lunch, making plans to buy Sonya a cell phone as soon as they finished. And lingerie.

4

Chapter 4

Martin stood outside the Adams County Courthouse on Monday, angst and excitement brewing. The weekend passed in a blur as he and Sonya spent Saturday and Sunday looking at houses with a realtor.

Today, however, wasn't about him, Sonya, nor their future home. It was about justice. Lela Briar had her scheduled arraignment. The news channels had touched on her story throughout the week, with one legal analyst suggesting her team of attorneys plead guilty to save the taxpayers time and money. She had already confessed, and there was no use in trying to fight it with an insanity plea. The entire city knew she had done it, and insanity would be impossible to prove twenty-two years after the fact.

Despite the dozens of opinions swirling around, no one had any insight as to what would actually happen. The final piece of Martin's closure was to see Lela locked behind bars for the rest of her life. *The cherry on top,* he thought, reminiscing on the night he had witnessed his wife toss their deceased daughter into the lake like a fish.

Rumors spread that Lela had made a request to attend Izzy's funeral, but the judge promptly shut it down. True or not, it was an idea that disgusted Martin. A murderer who went to the funeral of their victim was a new level of twisted.

Martin entered the courtroom and hid in the back row of the gallery. He had spoken to her for the last time at her kitchen table when she confessed to ruining their lives. How she lived with such a dark secret for more than two decades was beyond his comprehension. Maybe she was psychotic, after all.

"All rise for the Honorable Ernesto Garcia!" the bailiff shouted from the corner of the room. A tall, lanky man of brown complexion appeared from the secret door behind the judge's bench.

"Thank you, you may be seated," he said in a booming voice that could strike fear into the bravest men. "Please bring in the defendant."

A side door swung open to reveal Lela, her orange jumpsuit baggy over her thin body, handcuffs snug around her wrists. Her hair was tied into a messy bun, something she had always done when in a hurry. Black bags hung below her eyes.

A police officer led Lela across the courtroom to her position at the defense table where two attorneys nodded to her.

"Will the defendant please stand."

Martin watched as the judge spoke in a tone that tolerated no bullshit.

Lela rose from her seat and kept her head down as the judge prepared a stack of papers.

"Lela Briar, the state of Colorado hereby charges you with murder in the second degree of Isabel Briar. Do you have a plea offer today?"

Lela broke into hysterical sobbing. Martin believed she

hadn't meant to kill Izzy. It was an innocent affair that turned for the worse when she was called out by their daughter. Maybe she hadn't done so well over these last twenty-two years after all.

Lela's attorney, an older man in a basic suit, stood beside her, handed her a tissue and spoke on the defendant's behalf.

"Your Honor, we plead not guilty to the charges," he said. Groans and murmurs waved through the gallery as Martin sat frozen and attentive.

"Are you planning to enter an insanity defense?" the judge asked, scribbling furiously on a sheet of paper.

"No, Your Honor," the attorney replied while Lela continued to wipe at her face. "We are willing to plead guilty to a charge of manslaughter."

The district attorney who sat across the aisle from Lela and her team jumped out of his chair. "We will need a couple of days to discuss, your Honor." He was a large man with muscles that filled in his suit, certainly not a man you'd want to cross on a bad day.

The judge nodded while keeping his focus on the notes he was writing.

"We will reconvene on Wednesday," Judge Garcia said. "If the state would like to revise its charges to manslaughter, this will need to be decided by then. There will be no extensions. Court is dismissed."

The judge banged his gavel and disappeared.

Martin stayed to watch Lela, the one-time love of his life. She had finally stopped crying, but kept her head down, nodding as her attorney leaned over and whispered to her.

Martin had brushed up on Colorado law and knew the plea for manslaughter was nothing but a desperate attempt at a shorter sentence—six years maximum compared to twelve years for second-degree murder. Lela would unfortunately have no path to life in prison or the death penalty, as those were punishments strictly applied to first-degree murder. The district attorney had assured he'd pursue the harshest punishment available.

Lela was taken out of the courtroom by the same police officer who helped her in. Martin left, hoping she'd get the maximum twelve years.

* * *

When Martin returned home, Sonya sat at the kitchen table with a laptop open and papers spread messily across the table. He had shown her how to use the modern computer and the new (to her) search engine called Google.

"What are you up to?" he asked, knowing damn well what she was looking for.

"I found him," she said. "I actually found him."

"How?"

"I came across a website that lets you track down your family tree. All it asked was for certain information on at least two prior relatives. I was able to give three: my mom, dad, and my grandmother. Then it shows the info it has. All it gave me was a name and a date of birth, but I've been trying to dig more with it."

"What was his name?"

"Charles Heston. It was confirmed through the marriage certificate from when he married my grandma in 1912. I just can't find much else. No death certificate, no mention of him being an outlaw, mental patient, or any of the other wild stories I've been told."

"Is it possible that all of the stories are false?"

Sonya nodded slowly. "It is. My mom claimed my grand-mother never told her anything about my grandpa. Most of the stories I overheard were between my mom and her cousins speculating when I was little. Even the storage bin full of documents might just be another myth."

Martin slung his arms over her shoulders, embracing her warmth. "Look, I know how badly you want to find out the truth about your grandfather, but you've got to understand it may not be easy, even with the Internet."

"I know that. I've kept my expectations low and tried to not get overexcited when I found his name. But that's more than I've ever known about him. I just know somewhere—or someone—has the answers."

"You know, in all this time we've been together, you've never once mentioned your family, aside from the fact that your mother died when you were young. What do you know about your dad?"

Sonya closed the laptop and stood from the chair to meet Martin at eye level. "I think of myself as a pretty open book, but when it comes to my family history, I'd rather not talk about it. My father was a bad man, and I'll leave it at that. I loved everyone else in my family very much, except for him."

"And there's no one that would still be alive today? Or even back in 1996?"

"I'm sure I have some distant cousins somewhere, but everyone else passed on. After my mom died, my dad obviously raised me. Let's just say I moved out of the house on my sixteenth birthday because I couldn't take it anymore."

"I'm sorry you had to go through that by yourself." Martin pulled her in, wanting to provide the comfort she deserved. "Whatever you want to do, we'll do it. Just say the word."

They stood in silence for a moment before Sonya spoke. "I want to meet my grandfather. Even if I don't tell him who I am. I want to meet him and know who he really was."

"We can do that."

"And I don't want you to ever bring my dad up again. I'll talk about him when the time feels right, if there is such thing."

"Of course. I certainly understand that feeling."

Sonya hesitated as if she wanted to say something, so Martin nodded to her to continue.

A lone tear rolled down her cheek. "One last thing," she said. "Please don't make me see that old man ever again. I've had nightmares about him. I need him out of my head."

Martin tensed up at the mention of Chris, but calmly said, "Don't worry. We'll never see him again."

5

Chapter 5

"First you give my mom Alzheimer's, and now you're fucking with Sonya's mind." Martin spoke to himself as he sped through town for a return visit to the Wealth of Time store. "You're gonna tell me everything I need to know, then I'm gonna choke the life out of you."

He laughed nervously as he passed the church, only two blocks away from the antique store that was tearing apart his life. The memories sent chills down his back as he recalled his brief encounter with the priest at the burned down church in 1996.

He turned into the Wealth of Time's parking lot and felt the world fall silent as the blood froze in his veins.

The building was gone. Not gone like the church, which had been a pile of rubble, but gone like it had never existed. It wasn't a matter of Chris closing down shop and moving out, leaving a vacant building. There was no building, just an open field as if there had never been anything constructed on this specific plot of land. Tall grass sprouted from cracks in the random patches of concrete.

"What the fuck?!" Martin screamed, driving further into the deserted lot. "You motherfucker!"

A figure appeared to be walking toward the empty lot from the surrounding neighborhood. It could have been someone out for an afternoon stroll, but Martin sensed the person was headed straight for him, even from a quarter of a mile away. He put the car in park and waited.

He's definitely coming here, Martin thought as the figure drew closer, and was able to make out that it was a man. He took confident steps like he was on a mission and had no time to waste. He was dressed in jeans and a t-shirt, and puffed on a cigarette.

Martin stepped out of his car, compelled to encounter the man.

"Mr. Briar?" the man shouted, now fifty yards away. Martin could make out black wavy hair slicked back with lots of grease.

"Who wants to know?" Martin asked, now regretting leaving the comfort of his car.

The man popped the cigarette between his teeth and grinned as he took the final steps to reach Martin.

"Mr. Briar, my name is Mario Webster. Chris told me you'd be here today, sorry I'm late."

What the hell is going on?

"You're probably wondering where the store went. Chris likes to move it shortly after giving someone new the Juice."

"Who are you?"

Mario grinned again and flicked the cigarette away after a final puff.

"I suppose you could call me a travelling secretary of sorts. Chris isn't able to be in multiple places at once, even though it seems like he always is." Mario chuckled at himself.

Martin debated trusting this random stranger, but who else would know exactly where he would be?

"Why are you here?" Martin asked.

"Well, Chris knew you needed to speak with him, but he's unavailable. I guess you could say I'm filling in for him."

"Do you know things?"

Mario smirked. "I know *everything*."

"Good, because I came here for answers. Everything has been fucked up since I got back."

"Well, that was part of your agreement, was it not?" Mario asked mockingly. "For something bad to happen in exchange of the Juice. Chris feasts on emotional pain, and that's what he's getting from you."

"How can he get it if he can't even show his face?"

"He has his ways."

Within a matter of seconds, Mario morphed from a friendly person into a face Martin wanted to punch. How dare this man come to Martin and spew nonsense.

"I just need answers before I even consider taking a sip of that Juice."

"That's funny, because we know you've already made up your mind. Going back to the Roaring Twenties? One of my favorite times."

Martin dismissed the comment. Chris had always shown the capability to know what he was thinking and didn't want to get into it with this new messenger.

"So what is it you want to know? I'm not as secretive as Chris, I promise. He gets his kicks watching people figure things out on their own."

"When I take my girlfriend with me, what happens to her in the current world?"

Mario's grin returned, as if he expected the question.

"Well, she's already left her current world, so she disappeared."

"Can we go back to 1996? What would happen?"

"You can go to any time you want. When you take a person through time as an object, they completely vanish. Their body travels through time, leaving no trace in their past. You know the missing person reports, right? Grown men and women who go randomly missing and we wonder how on Earth someone with a family and friends can just vanish. This is how."

"But no one knows she's here besides my mom."

"Well then, you have nothing to worry about. You can come and go as you please with her, since she's essentially unaccounted for in 2018."

Martin stared Mario in the eyes and noticed that they looked black. Yet, behind that grin, he sensed a secret.

"What is it you're not telling me?"

"You're good, Mr. Briar," Mario said, chuckling. "Very good indeed. Chris was right about you being a perfect fit."

"A fit for what?"

"For the Juice. You see, we don't just give this stuff to any random Joe off the street. People are carefully scouted and observed for years. We chose you because you have a hunger to make things right. Even in your darkest days, Chris saw the light in you, knew you'd be the perfect candidate to do big things."

"Then why does he travel to the future to watch wars like it's a spectator sport?"

"You have to understand there a billion things happening at once for Chris. Like I said, he can't be everywhere. Besides, he doesn't get in the way of the world. He lets life carry on as it would normally. No interference."

"Except for giving my mom Alzheimer's, right?"

Mario's grin vanished into pursed lips.

"You made an agreement. Don't try to make us feel bad about what that agreement led to. You were warned it would be painful, and you haven't even experienced the truly painful part yet."

"What else can you tell me?"

"I can tell you to stay cautious everywhere you go—and with everyone you meet. The Road Runners are out in full force and will stop at nothing to get every glowing person they can find."

Martin had forgotten about the subtle, golden glow that radiated from the skin of those who had been blessed with time travel. He studied Mario's arm and saw it immediately.

"No matter what era you decide to travel to, or even what part of the world you go to, for that matter, it's imperative that you remain alert for the Road Runners. They have grown considerably with their brainwashing of innocent time travelers."

Martin remembered watching them burn down the liquor store in 1996 and murdering his acquaintance, Calvin Yoshiki. He didn't need an explanation on why they should be avoided.

"And how can I tell if someone is a Road Runner?" Martin asked.

"You can't. That's the problem. They'll approach you to strike up a bond, because hey, you're both time travelers, and why shouldn't you be friends? If you fall into that trap, it's already too late. They'll poison your mind."

"Why do they do this?"

"They want to rule the world. I think they're just evil people trying to stop others from doing good during their travels. Your friend, Calvin, did nothing wrong. You met him—he was doing research to try to make his present time a better place. And they came and wiped him off the map. It's best for you to simply not get close to any other time travelers should you meet them. They are spread all throughout time: past, present, and future, as well as all around the globe."

"You guys ask me to avoid people, but sometimes I need information and I never know where to find you."

"You know enough now, my friend. Just stay out of the way of the Road Runners. Go do what you need to do and keep a low profile. The more exposed you are to the public, the easier they'll find you."

"How can I find you?" Martin asked.

Mario's grin returned. "We'll find you, Martin. We're all over the place, and we'll know when you're truly in need."

Martin nodded and extended a hand. "Thank you for all your honesty."

Maybe these people aren't as bad as I thought.

"The pleasure is all mine, Mr. Briar," Mario said as he returned the handshake. His flesh was cold and clammy. "We'll see you around."

Mario turned and walked with his same confident pace back toward the neighborhood, disappearing as quickly as he had arrived.

Martin watched the sun glowing orange above the blue mountains. He had never felt so small in the world.

6

Chapter 6

On Wednesday, Martin returned to the courthouse for the pros-ecution's decision. Things could progress quickly depending on what occurred today, and he needed to be the first to know.

The gallery was filled with more people than the initial hearing on Monday, likely due to the press coverage received in the two days since. The silence deafened the room when Lela entered, shortly followed by Judge Garcia.

The orange jumpsuit looked good on her. It had been hard at first to see his former wife in such a predicament, but she had asked for it. Everything would have been handled much differently had she come clean on that fateful night. It was the cover up that irked him into having such vengeful thoughts and wishes. She would have gotten away with it had Martin never met Chris. Maybe there was some good that came out of this situation that otherwise grew more regrettable every day.

"How will the prosecution proceed?" Judge Garcia asked in his intimidating voice.

The district attorney stood and brushed off his suit. "Your Honor, the state would like to drop the charge of murder, and press a charge of manslaughter against Lela Briar."

Lela's defense attorney nodded as if he expected the decision.

"And does the defense have a plea to this charge?" Judge Garcia asked.

The defense attorney stood. "Your Honor, we plead guilty to the charges of manslaughter."

"Very well. Court will be in recess until this afternoon when we will convene for a formal sentencing. Please note this will strictly be handled by the court. There will be no testimony or jury required since the plea is guilty, so no need for the attorneys to prepare any statements."

The judge banged the gavel and chatter immediately erupted like a busy high school cafeteria. Martin stayed in his seat and wouldn't leave until he knew Lela's fate.

* * *

They kicked everyone out of the courtroom for the four-hour break, so Martin had called Sonya to inform her of the news. She wouldn't let her new cell phone go more than two minutes without checking it, even though he was the only one who had its number.

Martin had lunch in the court's cafeteria, sure to keep his head down to avoid harassment from any reporters who might be in the crowd, before court resumed and he settled into his seat in the back row.

"Will the defendant please rise?" Judge Garcia boomed.

Lela stood in slow motion, bracing herself. Martin saw her

hands shaking from across the room and knew the rest of her body trembled beneath the baggy jumpsuit. Lela wouldn't last in prison, where there were no manicures and pedicures available. She had a feisty personality but lacked the toughness to survive against women who would be twice as strong as her.

Will you be having such angry thoughts if she actually gets killed in prison? Martin asked himself. Even prisoners didn't take kindly to inmates who had harmed children, leaving a high probability that Lela would, in fact, face some dark days ahead.

"Ms. Briar—" Martin shuddered as he heard the judge address Lela by her married name, which she clung onto after all of this. "After reviewing previous rulings, I've decided to impose the maximum sentence of six years in prison. In addition, you will be forced to pay a fine of $500,000 and have four years of probation upon your release. If I could add more years I would, but the law doesn't allow me to do so. No one who kills a child should be allowed to see the light of day. Our bailiff will assist you with some clerical matters before you begin your sentence. Now please leave my courtroom."

The judge rose from his bench with a snarl and exited to his chambers. He must have been having a rough week, or he genuinely hated Lela, which was fine with Martin. He smiled to himself in the back row and stood to exit.

"Mr. Briar! Martin!" a woman's voice shouted as soon as he stepped out of the courtroom into the main hallway. It was a reporter, one he recognized from TV on one of the local news stations. "Mr. Briar, may I have a word?"

Almost made it out, he thought as the short woman ran to him with a microphone in hand.

"Alright," he said flatly.

"Thank you, Mr. Briar. I'm Dani Fisher with Channel Nine."

She stuck the microphone in his face, and he remembered her as the field reporter for the evening broadcast. She seemed to always be trotting around town, her skinny frame and short hair always in someone's business. Seeing her up close reminded Martin of a raccoon the way she stared at him with such desperation above her tiny nose. "Mr. Briar, what did you think of the sentencing?"

"I would've liked to see a longer sentence. I thought the DA was going to pursue second-degree murder no matter what. Apparently he has more important things to tend to."

Martin had learned the art of giving short responses after being interviewed numerous times in the days following Izzy's recovery from the lake.

"Are you happy to see your ex-wife go to prison?"

"I'm happy to see justice delivered, but still wish it could be longer."

"Will you move back into your old home now that she'll be in prison?"

"Absolutely not. That home is where my daughter was killed. I have no interest in going there for any reason."

"Will you visit your ex-wife in prison?"

What kind of stupid questions are these?

"Of course not. I've made my peace with her already and have nothing further to say."

"What's next for you?"

"I'm going to live my life in peace and try to put all of this behind me."

More reporters gathered around with microphones and recorders held out to catch a statement from the defendant's ex-husband. He felt like a celebrity with the bright camera lights blinding him.

"Are you going to stay in Larkwood?"

"I haven't decided yet. I'm currently in the market for a new home."

"Who was the woman you were holding hands with at the funeral?"

"My—" Martin caught himself before saying *girlfriend.* The press would have a field day if they knew he took a new woman to sit with him at his daughter's funeral while Lela sat in a jail cell. "She was a relative. No more questions, please."

Cameras snapped and reporters barked various questions in what sounded like group mumble. He had no interest discussing his personal life with any of these people and perhaps had already said too much. The fact that they had seen Sonya disturbed him, and knowing that they had been hiding at the funeral—whether from a distance or blending in with the crowd, he'd never know—disgusted him. He pushed his way through the mob like a running back trying to plow through a defensive wall as they all shouted one last desperate attempt. Martin kept his head down and darted toward the exit.

His cell phone buzzed in his pocket.

"Hi, Mom," he said.

"Marty, I just saw you on the TV, wanted to make sure you're okay."

"I'm fine. These reporters are like bloodhounds. Hopefully that was the last time I ever have to deal with them."

"You looked good on there. Are you happy with how it turned out?"

"It's the best we could have asked for given the situation. I wish the DA would have put up more of a fight for the murder charges instead of jumping for the plea."

"It's probably for the best. This way it doesn't have to be dragged out for a trial and everyone can get back to their lives, especially you. Did I ever mention that I never liked Lela? Always thought there was something off about her."

Martin chuckled, the tension starting to leave his face. "Yes, Mom, you've mentioned it hundreds of times since we got divorced."

"Okay, good, just wanted to make sure you knew."

Martin wrapped up the call with his mom and wanted to leave this whole situation behind. It was ugly business, being reminded about Izzy's murder on a daily basis. Perhaps his mom was right about there not being a full trial. That would only lead to hearing testimony and details about the day that ruined his life. All he wanted was to pretend it had never happened.

7

Chapter 7

"I want two things done within the next couple of weeks," Martin said to Sonya when he arrived home from the courthouse. "We need to have a new house picked and ready to move into, and a concrete plan for what we're going to do in the past. And when we're done with our business in the past, I need a vacation, and one that doesn't involve following people around. I need a beach and an unlimited supply of frozen drinks."

Sonya had not removed herself from the laptop aside from eating and bathing.

"Well, do you wanna help me do research then?" she asked. "I've been on this computer all day and can't find anything on my grandfather."

"You need a break from the research. How about we look at houses for a little bit? Help clear your mind. Daydream about our future home. Then jump back into your research with a clear mind."

Sonya nodded and kept clicking the mouse.

"I don't know anything about real estate in 2018. All of these prices look outrageous to me, but I also don't know if it's normal."

"It's normal. Houses don't cost $100,000 like they used to. Those same houses are probably selling for $300,000 today. Remember, we have a lot of money now. We won't be outbid."

"I know, but a million dollars for a house is absolutely wild."

"Then wild it is. I don't really care at this point. I just want the house that I'm going to live in for the rest of my life."

"Martin, some big mansion isn't going to magically change your life."

"I know that, but I need a change. I'm literally getting a second chance at life and a fresh start. I want to build a life with you. Is that not what you came here for?"

"Of course it is."

"Well then, find some houses where we can do that. I'm not expecting a mansion, but I don't want another apartment, either."

"Okay, you've made your point. I'll look at houses."

Martin wanted to tell her about the press, but decided to leave her out of the drama. They were all obnoxious maggots, as far as he was concerned, and he didn't want to frighten her by revealing that they had seen her at the funeral. She had enough on her plate.

* * *

Sonya had arranged three house tours and one open house visit the following day. She had apparently thrown her reservations to the wind as the houses were in wealthy areas like Cherry Creek, Washington Park, and even one in their old stomping ground in Littleton.

How ironic if we end up the Klebold family's neighbors, Martin thought, the idea actually giving him goosebumps instead of a laugh.

Each house was beautiful by its own right. The one in Cherry Creek faced the Rocky Mountains straight on and had the most up-to-date appliances and interior. It was truly the house of a filthy rich person. The house in Washington Park was historic, probably built in the early 1900's, but had its own natural beauty that no modern home could compete with. And lastly, the home in Littleton and soon-to-be winner of Martin and Sonya's brief house hunting adventure, was the biggest of the three, yet the lowest priced. The tri-level home had seven bedrooms, five bathrooms, walk-in closets, and a finished basement that opened to a beautiful backyard complete with a basketball court and swimming pool.

Martin watched her as they walked through the house, her eyes growing bigger with each new room and section of the house they explored. He wanted a home they could live in until Father Time took them from the world, and they found it, but thinking about the future made Martin's stomach churn in guilt.

You have to tell her, he thought. *She has to know that she won't stop aging like you. If you go back to the 20's and live there for even a year, that's one more year she'll be older while you remain frozen at 54.*

Martin shook the thoughts out of his head, living in the moment instead of dwelling on the future.

"I think we should live here," Martin said when they finished the tour. "I think we should buy this house right now."

Sonya couldn't keep the wide grin off her face and jumped

toward Martin, into his embrace. "I never imagined living in a place like this. It's magical. There's so much room for all of us."

The house provided plenty of distractions to keep Marilyn's mind occupied as she clung to every last memory that tried to flee her ailing mind.

"It's perfect," Martin said. He called his realtor and asked for the paperwork to be drawn up for an offer of $1.2 million.

* * *

Not even Martin had realized how quickly the real estate process now moved. The offer was sent and accepted within an hour, and they already had a move-in date set for two weeks after inspections and other tasks were complete. His realtor assured him this was the norm, seeing as he hadn't purchased real estate since his and Lela's house almost thirty years ago when it took months to complete the process.

Martin only needed two days to pack up his tiny apartment. Sonya had tried to make it a sentimental event—he had lived there for eight years—but all he could really remember were the late nights drinking on the patio, drinking on the couch, drinking in the kitchen, and even drinking in his bed. The apartment walls had witnessed Martin at rock bottom, and he wanted to take none of those memories with him into his new home.

His mother's house required a lot more assistance. She had lived there over forty years, and the process was indeed sentimental as they helped pack up memories that had lasted a lifetime.

Cleaning out his mother's closet, Martin found a dusty, worn-down shoe box filled with decades-old family pictures. Seeing portraits of him and his brother playing in the backyard made his stomach churn.

This is all because of you, he thought, the images of Daniel slithering into his house where Lela waited to take him to bed playing in his mind. Martin had never taken the time to reflect on this specific incident, considering what happened a few minutes afterward, but the sight of his brother filled his soul with a hot rage.

"Thank God you're out of our lives," Martin said, staring at the portrait of him and his brother at age eleven and nine, their thigh-high shorts showing all the leg scrapes and bruises that accompanied childhood. He packed the box away and continued digging through the closet where he came across a chest that housed all sorts of mementos from his late father: handwritten letters, post cards, and random gifts from the various places he had visited.

Martin lacked memories of his father. His old man had worked in both the military and later as a traveling salesman for one of the most successful nutritional companies in the country.

"Your father just can't stand to be home. He doesn't believe in home," his mother had told him and his brother when they were teenagers. "He loves you very much, and insists he does this so you can live a comfortable life, but we all know he needs to be on the road, living out of a suitcase in a different city every night. I think your father wishes he were a rock star."

Marilyn had never told them about the drug addiction he fought, or the dozens of women he had slept with, but Martin had grown to suspect these things after having more adult conversations with his mother. He sensed that she hated the man, but didn't want to say anything to tarnish his reputation as the head of the family. She had shouldered a lot of pain when the boys were teenagers in need of a man to guide them, and essentially raised them on her own.

Looking back, Martin wouldn't have it play out any differently. Marilyn Briar was the hardest working person he knew, and her constant display of fighting through every day is likely what kept him alive during the barrage of suicidal thoughts in the years following Izzy's death.

Martin didn't even cry when his father passed away. At the funeral, it felt more like a distant relative lying in the casket instead of the man responsible for giving him life. He had so many questions he wanted to ask his mother about him, but always held back, noting the obvious pain that swelled behind her eyes every time his father's name was mentioned.

He imagined a family running through the halls of his new, massive house. Kids gathering around the dining room table for dinner every night. It was the best way he could imagine what kind of home it truly was. And it was perfect, everything he could have asked for thirty years ago. But today, Sonya was beyond her child-bearing days.

There would be no kids to fill the bedrooms, no family gatherings to fill the living room, but it was a home, and exactly the start of a new life he needed with Sonya.

8

Chapter 8

When October arrived so did the moving trucks, ready to pack up both Martin's and Marilyn's lives and move them across town to Littleton, Colorado. Martin never thought he'd have the opportunity to pay for professional movers, and took great pride in watching them haul loads of boxes without him having to touch a damn thing.

"As soon as we get unpacked and settled in I want to sit down and make a clear plan. We need an exact date for when we'll be going back, along with where we want to try to live, and what our story will be for anyone who asks. We also need an escape plan in case we get spotted by those Road Runners."

Martin explained this to Sonya in his empty apartment as the movers took the last box out and journeyed two blocks down to his mother's house that would take a lot more than the twenty-five minutes needed to pack up his tiny apartment.

"I'm having a hard time finding anything on my grandfather," she said. "But I'm pretty sure he's still in Denver in 1919. It was never mentioned that he went—or was sent—anywhere else."

"There's got to be something we can at least follow as a lead. We'll find it."

Martin and Sonya left his apartment for the final time and drove to his mom's house.

When they arrived a couple of minutes later, they found Marilyn sitting outside on the front porch crying as the movers ran in and out of her house with boxes and furniture.

"What's wrong, Mom?" Martin asked, hurrying over to her. "Did the movers break something?"

"No," she sobbed. "My mind is the only thing that's broken. It's starting to get worse. I was on the phone with a friend and she asked where we're moving to, and I couldn't remember. I still can't remember. You've told me a dozen times and I just don't know."

Marilyn rubbed her forehead in frustration as if trying to press the thoughts back into her skull.

"Mom, it's okay. Don't put so much pressure on yourself. We're moving to Littleton."

"Littleton. That's right."

Martin could see the light in her mind turn on as she remembered. The fact that there was still a light in her head was a good sign.

Marilyn leaned in to Martin and whispered. "I'm so sorry, dear, but I've forgotten your girlfriend's name. I think she's too new for me to remember."

"That's okay. Her name is Sonya."

"Sonya, okay... that's a pretty name."

There was no look of remembrance to this information.

Sonya hung back a few steps away from the porch, leaving a path for the movers.

"Mom, I'm going to buy you some puzzle books. Things like

49

crosswords, word searches, and those hard Sudoku ones you like. You need to try and do these every day. They say it helps slow the decline of Alzheimer's. So does reading, so I'll get you a library card when we move so you can stock up as many books as you need."

"Thank you, that's very kind."

Marilyn's tears slowed down, her son comforting her with a strong embrace. Sonya served them all a glass of lemonade as they watched the movers pack away the rest of the house over the next two hours.

* * *

The movers finished unloading everything into the new house by four in the afternoon. Martin ran to his new liquor store, sure to introduce himself to the staff, and bought an expensive bottle of wine, something he rarely drank but knew Sonya and his mom would enjoy.

Sonya ordered pizza for dinner and they all sat on their new deck overlooking the Rocky Mountains, drinking merrily and stuffing their bellies. Life was perfect and Martin looked forward to plenty more evenings just like this one.

Marilyn pulled him aside after dinner, while Sonya cleaned up, and thanked him for letting her move in with them.

"It's going to be ugly, and if it gets too hard, feel free to admit me into a special home—"

"Mom, I'm not doing that; stop with that nonsense. You dedicated your life to me; this is the least I can do."

Martin kissed her goodnight and watched her disappear

down the long hallway to her new bedroom suite, complete with its own bathroom and small living room to lounge in.

When he returned to the kitchen, Sonya put away the final dish.

"Are you ready?" he asked.

"Ready for what?"

"To plan our trip."

"Already?"

"I want to move quickly, possibly even leave tomorrow. I have an idea to help my mom with her disease, but I want to do this first."

For Martin the math was simple. He could leave tomorrow—or even tonight—spend a few months in 1919, and only ten minutes will have passed in 2018. Then he could travel to the future in search of an Alzheimer's cure—there had to be one.

All that would see only twenty minutes pass, even if he spent ten years in the future seeking a cure. He'd leave Sonya behind for the trip to the future, unsure of how long he'd need to stay. He wanted them to spend their lives in the new home they just bought, not in some unknown future.

"Take out the laptop, so I can dig into your grandfather's past. There's gotta be something we can use."

Sonya obliged and put the laptop on the dining room table.

"What all have you searched for?"

"Just his name."

"Sonya, you're never going to find anything that way. You have to be more specific."

He wanted to tell her she had been wasting her time, but having such a powerful search engine was a new concept for her, so he let it slide.

"Google will give you whatever you want, so you've got to give it more details. Let me show you."

Martin opened the search engine and typed in *Charles Heston.*

"Look at how ridiculous this is. It pulled 1.5 million results in half a second. It even tells you that."

He pointed to the small gray print that showed these statistics as Sonya peered over his shoulder.

"You're not going to find anything that way. It's a virtual needle in a haystack. This entire first page is all about an old actor named *Charlton* Heston, and I'm sure there are hundreds of pages all about him."

"I'm so sorry, Marty, I didn't know. I was going to click through all of these pages until I found something."

"It's okay. Let's see what happens when we narrow our search terms."

Martin entered *Charles Heston Colorado* and hit the enter key.

"There we go, only 330,000 results came back by adding that one word—a bit more manageable. Let's try others."

Martin opened multiple tabs and Sonya watched as if he were performing a magic trick.

"You said there were theories that he was an outlaw, a spy, and a mental asylum patient?"

"Those are the rumors I know of."

"Let's try those."

Martin entered *Charles Heston spy, Charles Heston outlaw, Charles Heston mental asylum* into each of the tabs.

"Still a lot of results on Charlton Heston, but these should be easier to skim through and find something that might stand out."

Martin clicked around as Sonya pulled up a seat beside him. He clicked through the numerous tabs, adding *Colorado* to each search term for the best results. Sonya remained silent as she kept up with his fast scrolling down the pages.

After ten minutes of silence, Martin exclaimed, "Here we go!"

He clicked on a link and waited anxiously for the page to load.

An old newspaper clipping from *The Denver Post* filled the screen. The article's image was a mugshot of man with a deranged appearance: bulging eyes, wild hair, and a wide grin as he held the letter board in his fingers.

HESTON, CHARLES

10 14 1919

They both studied the letter board and looked from it to the man's face.

"It fits the time frame. What does the article say?"

Martin read aloud.

"Denver, Colorado. A suspected English spy, Charles Heston, has finally been captured after a four year run from the law. Mr. Heston is suspected to have lived multiple lives across the country under different aliases. He has fathered children with at least four known wives around the country. His most recent wife, Maryanne Heston (nee. Bowman) reported her husband to the local authorities after learning of his secret identity. He is set to stand trial in December and is pleading an insanity defense."

"Maryanne Bowman. That's my grandmother. I never knew her as Heston, and now I know why."

"Sounds like *all* of the rumors you heard were true. He really was an English spy, and an outlaw on the run. And I'll bet he somehow won his insanity plea and got sentenced to an asylum."

"I can't believe I'm related to this man," Sonya said, holding her hand to her open mouth. "Four different families that they know of. What a scumbag."

"So what exactly do you want to do if we go back to 1919?"

"Oh, we're going. And I'd love to stab him in the dick."

Martin giggled. Sonya rarely showed an angry side, but when she did, made sure it counted.

"I need more than that before I can agree to go. This doesn't need to be some game of revenge."

"I can get revenge without getting my hands dirty. What if we're the ones who turn him in? We can go back, live in the city for a while, and spill all the facts to the police. Then we can be there to watch him get arrested, and even stay for his trial and see what happens. I think back then the asylum was a harsher punishment than going to prison."

Martin tried to put himself in her shoes and thought if that was worth the trip one hundred years back in time. He didn't enjoy the thought of having to follow people around, but what else would ever be an option when traveling through time? If they wanted to change a part of the past, there would always be a need to follow someone.

After the botched attempt of saving Izzy's life, this proposed trip seemed tame in comparison. Besides, it was only ten minutes to him, and he could live like a king in that era.

"Okay, let's go. If he gets arrested in October, maybe we should plan to get there in August or September, what do you think?" Martin asked.

Sonya stared at the screen blankly, clearly concentrating on her thoughts and not the computer.

"Let's say early September. Do you get to decide which day we arrive?"

"I honestly don't know. All he told me was to think of the time I want to go to and drop the Juice on my tongue. I suppose I can think of a certain date and see what happens."

"Let's say September first. It could take a couple weeks to find him, then we can figure out how to get him to confess."

"Okay, that's fine. Now where should we plan to live? What's our story for 'moving' to Denver in 1919?"

"We don't need to explain anything to anyone. If anyone feels the desire to ask, tell them the truth: you're a postal worker."

"I don't know if that's going to work in this era. People know each other. They know who their postman is. It's not like today where you'd never know if the Pope was dropping off your mail."

Sonya nodded. "You can always say you're a writer covering stories in Denver for Colorado Springs. Who says you have to be from a different state?"

"I like the writer angle, but I'm still gonna go with a different state. I don't want to risk anything. We could meet someone from Colorado Springs, and they could throw all sorts of doubt our way. I'll pick some remote place like New Hampshire. What are the odds of meeting someone from there? I never have."

Sonya shrugged. "I don't know much about the landscape in 1919, but I think we should stay in a central place near the capitol. If we get spotted by the Road Runners, it's easier to lose them in a crowded space instead of a secluded one."

"Makes sense. How are we supposed to know what these people look like?"

Martin had never told her about the golden glow around his skin, figuring it was best to not have her in a constant paranoid state of staring at everyone's skin. He didn't even know if she'd be able to see it since she wasn't a time traveler.

"We don't have a way of knowing for sure," he said. "All they warned me was that they will try to be overly kind to try and lure us in. So it's important to be careful who you become friends with. In fact, it's best if we don't really become friends with anyone. I'm not saying to not speak to anyone, but we have to be careful about accepting invitations for dinner and things like that."

Sonya crossed her arms, clearly unsatisfied with the terms, but Martin had rules to uphold if they didn't want to end up in the wrong hands.

"It's not as thorough as a plan as I would've liked, but there's only so much we can prepare for. We'll have to take another day when we arrive and really set something in place. I say we leave tomorrow."

"I've been thinking about the money," Sonya said dismissively. "We can't take any with us because the bills won't look the same. Did you even think of that?"

Martin's brow drooped immediately at the thought. No, he hadn't thought of that, and she was absolutely right. The currency was different in 2018 compared to 1919, and that was something they would surely consider counterfeiting and throw them in prison for.

"Is there anywhere we can get old currency?" Martin asked, nodding to the computer.

"Not for an even exchange. Those old bills are rarely seen in circulation any more. It would have been easier to get some in 1996, but I've looked it up already and you can only find them from collectors. And they don't even have that much for us to take."

Martin nodded. "Well, I was hoping to not have to do it again, but it works. Betting on sports is how I made all of my money in 1996. I already knew the results because I looked them up and made bets with bookies when I was visiting."

"Well, we're gonna need something. We can get jobs that pay like twenty cents an hour."

Martin laughed. "No, we're not going to do that. Besides, that puts us at a greater risk by encountering more people. It's too risky."

"And dealing with bookies isn't risky?" Sonya snapped at him.

"It is in a different way, but that's usually only when you lose and don't pay up. I think I'll play it much differently this time, lose some bets on purpose to keep them less suspicious. In 1996 I was so excited to win sure money that I wasn't thinking straight. The bookies were getting very suspicious after I won a couple of questionable bets."

"If you think it's safe, then I don't see why not."

"Perfect. I'll do some research on games to bet on, and tomorrow you can go buy at least one of those older bills for us to take. We'll need something when we arrive to stay in a hotel for a couple of days until we can get everything figured out."

"Tomorrow? You sounded like you were ready to leave first thing in the morning."

"I'd like to, and we still can. We should probably head to bed for the night, we need to bless our new bedroom, if you know what I mean."

"Martin Briar," she gasped. "Your *mother* is in this house."

"Yeah, on a different floor on the opposite side."

Sonya smirked as she grabbed his hand and pulled him away from the kitchen table. Life felt normal, and the thought of traveling back in time one hundred years was the furthest thing from their minds when they made love that night.

9

Chapter 9

The night dragged for Sonya. She had no problem falling asleep, but wished she never had. Her mind brewed a horrendous barrage of nightmares and dark thoughts on the eve of their trip to 1919.

Her first dream sequence took her to Colorado Springs, to the cemetery where her mother was buried. Only instead of a green, welcoming cemetery, the grass was dead, the trees bare and black as if charred by a fire, crows cawing from high up on the charcoal branches.

All of the tombstones lay flat on the ground between dead flowers. Except for one.

She walked slowly, the lifeless grass crunching with each step, and as she approached the only visible tombstone, she smelled the lingering odor of smoke.

Am I in hell? she thought as the crows laughed in chaotic unison.

"You're not in hell. *I* am," her mother's voice cackled from the tombstone.

"Mom?"

"Yes, Sonya. I hope you're happy. You sat by while your father killed me. Did you think I'd forget?"

A hand appeared atop the tombstone, fingers splayed out like a high-five, only the hand had gray skin, and random spots of flesh missing to reveal the bone underneath. It grasped the top of the stone, blending in with its grayness, before the rest of the body to which it was attached appeared.

The corpse had the characteristics of Sonya's mother: high cheek bones, round nose, and eye brows stuck in a furrow. Her once brown hair was now thin streaks of white on a mostly bald head. The gray face drooped as if it might fall off the skull like a perfectly cooked rack of ribs. There were no eyes in the sockets, just two black holes that stared into Sonya's soul.

Sonya tried to speak, but her throat clenched shut with tension. She tried to turn and run, but her knees locked, and her eyes refused to look away from her dead mother.

The corpse put both hands on top of the tombstone and glared down to it. It was cracked down the middle, splitting the text that read: *In memory of a most loving mother, Gloria.*

The corpse managed a grin through the loose flesh, revealing yellow and black teeth. "You see that?" the voice croaked. "A most loving mother."

Sonya remained frozen, heart thudding against her chest like a trapped person banging desperately on a locked door.

"I spent all those years raising you to be a woman, only to watch you stand aside while your father killed me. You didn't even flinch! Tell me, *Sonya*, was it worth it?"

"Mom, I'm sorry!" she managed to shout with a sharp crack in her voice, tears pouring down her face.

"All I get is a 'sorry'? Why don't you come give your mother a kiss?"

60

The corpse reached out its arms, and this time the flabby flesh *did* fall to the ground in a *gloop!* sound that pushed Sonya to the brink of vomiting. Her mother smooched her lips before laughing like a madwoman.

The ground trembled, causing the crows to flap away and return to their depths in hell. The tombstone completed its collapse by splitting down the middle and falling to each side, and Sonya's mother remained standing, howling at the skies turning black, making everything invisible.

The tension left Sonya's body as the world changed in front of her, even though she couldn't see it happening. It reminded her of a stage play when the crew would hurry and change the set during a brief moment of darkness. When the ground settled, she heard nothing but her heart pounding in her ears. Sweat formed heavy beads on her back, but she didn't notice; all she wanted was to wake up.

"She's over there," a voice whispered from behind, and she whipped around to see nothing but more blackness. "Sonya," it whispered again, then more whispering voices joined a chorus repeating her name, echoing in the silence. "Don't be afraid. Don't be afraid."

The whispering grew louder, and she became convinced all of the voices were somehow coming from within her head.

"Don't be afraid. Don't be afraid."

The voices repeated this a dozen times before fading back into silence.

"Sonya," an older man's voice came from behind her. She turned around to a flash light pointed right at her, blinding her as her arms shot up to shield her eyes. "It's me."

It was the old man from the antique store and she broke into immediate goose flesh at the sound of his voice.

"Get away from me!"

The flashlight turned upward to reveal the old man's grinning face and blue eyes staring at her. "Now, now, Sonya. I need Martin. If you dare take him from me, you'll have hell to pay! I'm in no mood for negotiations. Leave him alone. You'd disappear in the night if you knew what's best for both of you."

"You don't control us!" she barked, rage brimming to her surface. "You have no right to interfere with my life, or Martin's life."

"I would never violate our agreement, but I have to defend what is rightfully mine. You've gotten away with so much, but it ends here. Leave Briar to me."

Chris giggled, eventually howling as the world rumbled like an earthquake. A black cloud swirled around Chris, making him invisible as darkness spread across the skies.

Sonya looked up and shrieked.

* * *

She didn't wake up screaming, but the sheets clung to her sweaty back. Her heart thumped in her ears as she panted for breath like she had just run a marathon.

Martin snored next to her, undisturbed by her quick trip to hell and back. He had no clock on the nightstand, so she checked her cell phone to find it was only 11:30. She hadn't been asleep for two hours and it felt like a whole two days had passed.

Everything had moved so quickly from the time Martin asked her to join him in the future. *Too* quickly. It had all been part of the plan, but not expected several months ahead of schedule. It would all work out, regardless. They always made adjustments on the fly.

On a personal front, it became clear what she needed to do before going back in time with Martin.

I need to visit my mom's grave.

She would drive to Colorado Springs in the morning, but for now had to find a way to fall back asleep. She stared at the ceiling, listening to the steady whooshing sound of the ceiling fan, unable to close her eyes, fearful of all of her regrets and guilt waiting on the other side of her eyelids.

10

Chapter 10

The next morning Sonya rolled out of bed at eight o'clock. She had played around on her cell phone to research her English spy grandfather, but came up with nothing further.

By the time she stepped foot on the ground, Martin was already five pages deep in a small notebook of baseball scores from the 1919 season. He hadn't mentioned what awaited after they returned from this trip, but it was definitely driving the urgency in him to complete every task promptly.

She had volunteered to go buy the rare currency to use when they traveled back. Colorado Springs was about an hour away from Littleton, but she could make it in good time and be back before lunch with a clear mind and a crisp hundred dollar bill.

She dressed quickly and quietly, not wanting to draw any attention, and when she strolled to the living room, Martin was writing in his notebook with the laptop on his legs.

"How's it going?" she asked.

"Good. I completely forgot 1919 was the year of the Black Sox scandal."

Sonya stared at him blankly, having no idea what he was

talking about.

"The Chicago White Sox were the best team in baseball, one of the best teams in the game's history. They were paid off by the mob to throw the World Series and let Cincinnati win. They were huge favorites, so the payoffs for anyone who bet on the Reds were enormous. What I'll do is make some decent money off the games during the end of the regular season, of course losing some on purpose, before placing a big bet on the Reds to win the World Series. Why not stock up on this old currency while we can? In case we decide to come back for a luxurious vacation one day."

"I think after this we'll definitely need a vacation. So what's the plan for today?"

Martin put the laptop aside and stood from the couch, looking over his shoulder to the hallway toward his mother's room.

"I think we should leave after lunchtime. Make sure my mom is fed and content, maybe have her relax with a movie."

Sonya nodded. "Okay. That'll work. I need to go buy this currency."

"Do you want me to go with you?" he asked.

"No, that's okay. You stay here and make final preparations. I know where I'm going. I couldn't sleep last night, so stayed up exploring the map on my phone. It's pretty cool how you can drop yourself into the middle of the street and get an up close view of everything."

"Is everything okay? Are you nervous about this trip?" he asked.

She was nervous, but for reasons she could never explain to him.

"I'm a little nervous. My grandfather was always spoken

about like an old myth, on the rare instances he was actually mentioned. It's like he was Santa Claus, and all I ever wanted was to know him. I'm still in shock by what we learned last night."

"Yeah, I can imagine," Martin said, crossing the room to embrace her. His scent was bitter, but she had grown to love it. She wanted desperately to tell him the truth she had kept buried since meeting him. She was the best at her job, but had never made the mistake of developing real feelings toward one of her subjects. Daydreams had started popping into her head during their summer together in 1996. She toyed with the idea of running away with him, having him dump his special Juice down the drain and run off to a remote island with his millions. But there was no escaping her life. They would find her and force her to return.

"Well, I really should get going if we want to stay on schedule. I'll be back in a bit. Is there anything else I should get while I'm out?"

"No, I think we're all set. I'll order the lunch, so don't worry about it."

She kissed him, a faint taste of milk from his bowl of cereal still on his lips.

"I love you," she said, meaning the words for the first time.

* * *

The drive to Colorado Springs had light traffic and she made it there in fifty minutes, leaving her ten minutes ahead of schedule. She turned into St. Michael's Cemetery, underneath a stunning archway decorated with sculptures of angels and flowers. Cemeteries always created a sick feeling within her, a grim reminder of what the finish line looks like, no matter how far away it may seem. A directory stood near the entrance. This was a map of the multiple loops and plot numbers. Beside the map was a bundle of laminated pages with the listings of every name currently resting within the grounds, alphabetized by last name.

Even though it had been years since her last visit, she still knew the way, driving directly to loop B. Her arms trembled when she stepped out, and her legs felt like giving out if any more nerves built up within them.

She spotted the tombstone from forty feet away and enjoyed instant relief when she saw it had no crack down its center. The only damage was a couple of chips around the edges that likely came from years of weather.

Sonya stopped in front of the grave and studied the rest of the stone. The same quote was inscribed from her dreams, and this gave her a brief moment of goosebumps before she fell to her knees. She wept uncontrollably, tears sinking into the soil below. What always made her sick—and perhaps hesitant for visiting and getting her final closure—was knowing her mother's body wasn't actually buried in the ground, instead sunken to the bottom of some river across town. Maybe that's why she had a different connection with Martin, considering his daughter had also been tossed in a body of water just like her mother. The gravestone was merely a tribute to a life lost too soon, a dirty throbbing secret that only her and her father knew about.

How many others have visited you, Mom? she wondered. Their family in Denver was scarce, only a couple of cousins that she could think of. Everyone else lived out of state. There was a good chance Sonya was the first visitor to this grave since the funeral ceremony in 1952.

"I'm so sorry, Mom," she cried. "I should've said something."

"You can always go back and save her," a familiar voice said from behind.

Sonya pivoted around, ready to swing at the old man, but decided it best to not cause a scene in the middle of a cemetery.

"What are you doing here?" she asked, her sorrow vanishing and giving way to an instant rage.

"Why such anger toward me?" he asked, cracking that fucking grin.

"Anger? You *disgust* me. I don't know what kind of game you're playing, but you better cut the shit out. Martin seems to believe you and your thugs, but I'll get the upper hand. I always do."

"You have it all wrong. We have a deal, you and I, and you've not been following it. You're supposed to leave my recruits alone, but you've only been helping yourself to all of them. I haven't been too upset and have let you continue living your free life, but I can't help but surprise you like that night at the restaurant. You and Martin were having such a lovely evening until I showed up as your waiter, it's too bad."

"I get it, you get to play God and think you control everything and everyone you give your nasty Juice to. We're getting very close to creating our own juice, so we won't even need to steal your mindless recruits."

"That's not very nice, dear. You only see the surface of people, and that's your problem. Sure there are plenty of duds, but every now and then I get to meet someone like Martin. My knowledge goes beyond that of time. You can learn a lot about people when you have the capability of going through time and seeing the person they once were. A person's formative years are so crucial."

"You don't know what you're talking about."

"Angelina, dear, I always know what I'm talking about."

"Fuck you—don't call me that!"

Chris winced at her shouting, but his grin remained. "My, my. You should know such attitude is frowned upon in 1919. If you act like this they'll have eyes on you around town."

Sonya gave up. She couldn't stand arguing with this old piece of shit. "Crawl back into your hole and don't ever show your face to either of us again. And don't send your goons, either."

Chris winced again. "Mario would not like to hear such hateful talk from a lady. I'll be sure to let him know you called him a goon. Don't let the Road Runners eat you alive, it might hurt."

Chris blew her a kiss and turned to leave the cemetery.

Sonya had forgotten where she was or what she was doing. She turned to the gravestone, rage boiling to the top of her head. "I'm sorry, Mom."

She left the cemetery with no closure.

11

Chapter 11

Martin packed the notebook into a briefcase. He also put on a suit, realizing no one in 1919 walked around in jeans and a t-shirt. The world was still very much formal and he'd suggest for Sonya to wear one of his mother's older dresses to help her fit in with the times.

He started to wonder what was taking her so long when she finally rolled into the long driveway. The garage hummed as she pulled in and he met her at the entrance, splaying his arms out to act like a 1920's entertainer.

"Everything okay?" Martin asked after she parked and got out. "What took so long?"

"I drove to Colorado Springs first."

"The Springs? What for?"

"I had a dream about my mom last night, and I figured I should go visit her grave before we go back into the past."

"Are you okay? You didn't have to go alone—I would've joined if you asked."

"I'm fine. I needed to go by myself. I had my moment there, but now I'm ready for our trip." She stopped and examined his attire. "Why are you wearing that?" she asked with a grin.

Martin laughed. "It's my outfit for the 20's. What do you think?"

He spun in a circle to model his three-piece suit.

"I think I like it. I've never seen you in a suit before. We might just have to stay in the past if this is what you're gonna wear every day."

"Very funny. It's your turn. My mom has some outfits you can wear."

"I'm not wearing your mom's clothes, that's absurd."

"You wanna show up in 1919 like this? Wearing sweatpants and a baggy t-shirt? They'll think you're homeless or a cheap hooker."

"Well, good thing we need money, right?" Sonya said with a hearty laugh.

"Sonya Griffiths, cracking a joke? I never thought I'd see the day."

"Well my mind is all messed up right now, so you're getting a weird version of me today, sorry."

"Oh, no, it's fine. No need to apologize, but you really should change. At least wear a long dress if you have one."

"I have exactly one."

"Perfect. We'll need to blend in, not a good idea to stick out on our first day. All the men wear suits when they go out and about, and the women wear long dresses. No skin."

"What time are we trying to leave?"

"My mom already ate. I think she's in her room working on a crossword puzzle. So I was thinking we can have lunch, then get out of here."

"Okay, that works."

Martin had fought nerves all weekend, but speaking about

the trip in such a nonchalant manner helped relax him. He still hadn't retrieved the bottle of Juice from the basement bar, uneasy at the thought of drinking it.

Sonya disappeared to their bedroom, leaving Martin at the top of the basement stairwell.

Just grab it and bring it up, no need to stall at this point.

Martin ran with his brief moment of inner courage and walked down the stairs with his head held high. It was just a bottle of liquid, what was there to even be afraid of?

The bar stood in the back corner of the basement, overlooking the large party space. Cabinets lined the wall, and he pulled one open to rummage through the alcohol, bottles clinking together as he reached into the back. He could feel the Juice's presence in the cabinet, and when his fingers found the bottle they clenched it, pulling reluctantly to bring it back into the open.

I wonder what happens if someone else drinks it? he thought. Knowing Chris, it would probably cause the person an eternity of emotional pain for him to feast on.

With the bottle in hand, Martin studied its contents—purple liquid flowing, tempting with its secrets—for a brief moment before running back up the stairs. His appetite for lunch had vanished, but he needed to force something down.

Just one drop on your tongue, he remembered Chris explaining. *Just like taking medicine. Nothing to it.*

His reassurance carried him to the top of the stairs where Sonya had settled at the kitchen table for lunch. Martin had ordered Chinese takeout and immediately regretted not getting something even heavier like barbecue. The kitchen smelled of fried rice and egg rolls as Martin placed the bottle on the table with a heavy thud.

"Are we taking that with us?" Sonya asked.

"Well, you want to be able to come back, right?"

"Duh. But we shouldn't take that whole bottle. It could break, and then what? Pray to your beloved Chris to come save you?" She said this with a visible amount of sarcasm. "We either need to move it to a plastic bottle that won't break, or take a small amount in a container. Do you have a flask?"

"What do you think?"

"Of course, silly question. I'd say fill a flask with it, and that can be your travel container. That way it can't be damaged, and we just need to worry about keeping it in a safe place."

"Do you think the Road Runners will try to steal it?" Martin asked.

Sonya glared at him for bringing up the mysterious people they were supposed to blindly run from.

"No, I'm not worried about the Road Runners. I'm worried about people thinking this is some kind of moonshine. Remember, we're entering the era of Prohibition, and people will pay a premium for alcohol. They'll also steal it if they think they can get away with it."

"Prohibition, huh? Not cool."

"You'll live. And we'll find a speakeasy—it's not like alcohol just vanished from the world."

"What a time to be alive. Let me get the flask, I might as well bring another with booze – maybe we can sell it for a few bucks."

"Not your worst idea."

Martin left the bottle with Sonya and ran back downstairs to get his flasks, returning a couple minutes later with one empty and another filled to its brim with whiskey.

"Were you gonna eat?" Sonya asked him.

"Oh, yeah. I should."

"Eat real quick and I'll fill the flask."

Martin obliged, forcing the food down his throat as he watched Sonya fill the silver flask.

"So this is it? You just take a swig of this stuff and off we go?"

Martin nodded. "Not even a swig. A drop."

"One drop? This stuff will last you forever. Literally."

"I know, it's like a lifetime supply in that bottle. Are you stalling?" Martin asked, and Sonya looked to him with big eyes and raised eyebrows.

"No. Why?"

"Well, you've taken the lid on and off from that bottle at least ten times now. You're either stalling or nervous."

Sonya looked to her hands as if they had betrayed her. They had indeed been fidgeting with the bottle. "Maybe I'm just nervous."

"Well, it's time. Everything is ready upstairs. I figured we'd just lay down in bed and I'll take my drop."

Martin rose, threw the empty takeout boxes in the trash, and started for their bedroom upstairs, grabbing the bottle in a tight fist. He was also nervous, but wouldn't tell Sonya since she was having her own doubts. It wasn't the traveling that made him antsy, but the barrage of warnings from Chris and his team. Why wouldn't they just tell them specifically what to look out for, instead of these vague statements?

Chris had issued no warnings when Martin first swallowed the pill to return to 1996. Instead, he let him know the only rule was to not encounter his past self. And when he had, by accident, Martin had felt like his head might explode right off his neck.

It was important to follow Chris's advice, but fair to remain skeptical about his motivations. All they could trust was his word, but now they had a little more knowledge for this journey back in time.

Martin entered the bedroom where his briefcase waited on the bed. Sonya lay down, her blue dress splayed in every direction.

"Ready?"

Sonya nodded silently, thoughts clearly plaguing her mind.

"Alright, I'll see you on the other side."

Martin twisted the lid off of the bottle and held it to his lips.

"Bottoms up," he said, sticking his tongue out and letting the drop fall on his tongue. It had no flavor, might as well have been water, but it did tingle his tongue while his lips instantly turned numb.

Martin placed the bottle on his nightstand and slid onto the bed, his briefcase clutched in his left hand, and Sonya's hand in his right. His mind started to spin from a strong sense of fatigue as he stared at the ceiling and thought, *September 1, 1919. September 1, 1919.*

He repeated this like a child counting imaginary sheep to fall asleep. Within seconds, blackness took over and he was falling.

12

Chapter 12

"We should've done this from a hotel room downtown," Martin said as he sat up on the dirt. Sonya joined him in staring at the open space that stretched into eternity.

In 1919, Littleton was nothing more than a small town. The area where their 2018 house stood was in the middle of a dirt field. Homes wouldn't be developed for another seventy years. There were no roads or buildings in sight. A journey to Denver proved challenging since they had no car and no way of calling a ride from their phones. They were alone, left to scrap for resources on their own.

"We should probably start walking," Martin said. "There's gotta be civilization around here. I think downtown Littleton is six miles away from our house. We should start there."

They used the mountains as their compass, knowing they were always to the west.

"Six miles will take three hours for us to walk," Sonya said. "There has to be a better way."

"Yeah, it's called running, and I don't exactly want to do that in this suit."

Martin judged it to be roughly the same time of day as when they had left 2018, shortly after noon.

"We'll get into town around dinnertime, find somewhere to eat, then call a cab to take us downtown," he said.

Sonya shook her head, clearly not pleased with their current situation. If they had gone to a hotel downtown, they'd already be there to settle in right away.

"Do you wanna tell me what happened in your dreams?" he asked as they dragged their feet through the dirt.

"Not really. I don't wanna relive it anymore. It has a lot to do with my past haunting me, and I'll leave it at that."

Martin sighed, wishing she'd open up about the nightmares so he could help, but if she wanted to hold that burden for herself, then he couldn't stop her. Now that they were in 1919, Martin decided it was time to tell her the truth.

"Can I tell you something?" he asked nervously.

Sonya walked with her head down to spot the random holes and bumps that might cause a broken ankle.

"Sure." Her voice came out depressed, and he debated if this was actually the right time.

"There's a bit of information I recently learned about you and traveling through time."

Her head perked up like a dog who just heard a whistle in the distance.

"What? From your friend Mario?"

Martin nodded. "Yes, from Mario, and he's not my friend. He told me that you'll continue to age as you travel through time. There's no stopping of aging for you. So if we stay here for ten years, you'll be in your sixties both here and when we return to 2018."

Sonya shrugged. "Are there people who don't age?"

77

Oh, boy.

She stared at him, eyes burning his face to get a read.

"Martin," she said calmly. "Are you telling me that you don't age when you travel through time?"

He nodded slowly, refusing to show any emotion. They kept walking and she remained silent, Martin growing increasingly uncomfortable with each step they took.

"So?" he finally asked after ten minutes.

"So what? Do you want me to congratulate you?" She made zero effort to hide her sarcasm.

"No, of course not. I just want to know what you think."

"I think we need to hurry up and *not* spend ten years here. It's not really fair, but I guess I was aging regardless, either way, right? Have fun watching me grow old."

"Sonya, I didn't tell you this to upset you. I didn't even know about this until Mario mentioned it. It was already too late by then. We were here—well, in 2018—already."

She waved her hands in the air. "It's fine. Nothing we can do about it now. Stop worrying so we can get out of here and go back our lives."

"We're here for you—I just wanted to make sure all the facts were out on the table."

"Yes, Martin, I know what we're here for, thank you. I still plan on handling that, then we can leave."

Martin fell silent. They continued walking, having covered at least a half-mile since they arrived. There was still no sight of life anywhere, and the thought made Martin uneasy. These weren't quite the Wild West days, but the scenery reminded him of an old Western movie. There was actual tumbleweed blowing along the ground, dirt kicked into their faces from the random spurts of wind, and surely people riding around on horses somewhere. They just needed to find them.

* * *

Four hours later they finally saw a building on the horizon. As they approached it, they saw even more and realized it was the beginning of a neighborhood. Small houses lined up neatly next to each other, all ranch-style, as multi-level homes still weren't a concept at this point in time. Even though they were both exhausted after hours of walking on rough terrain, they sped up at the sight of life.

"Thank God," Sonya muttered under her breath. Their discussion earlier had taken a back seat and they were able to converse about their plans of this particular trip, and ideas Sonya had to spruce up the new home when they returned to 2018. Martin still sensed a sort of resentment from Sonya, but she didn't exactly make it obvious.

Martin's mind remained occupied with a trip to the future to find medicine for his mother. It probably wasn't fair to Sonya to be so distracted with that thought when they had business to tend to here in 1919, but he couldn't help himself.

He had every intention on taking his special, solo trip once they arrived back to 2018. It would only be a quick ten minute nap as far as Sonya was concerned.

Back with the Alzheimer's cure before dinner is even served. Martin smiled at the thought.

Aside from that trip, he didn't have much of an interest to travel to another time without her. It was becoming their pastime, but Martin would like the solo trip to the future to truly learn all of the rules and nuances of time travel. He suspected there were thousands of small details he didn't know, and would probably never know, no matter how hard he researched.

* * *

Forty-five minutes later they reached the neighborhood where all of the houses looked similar: two wide windows with a door in the center, brick exterior, and green lawns all covered by generous shade from the many trees that lined the block. The leaves were starting to fall and peppered yellow and orange marks across the grass.

"Honey, we're home," Martin said with a small cackle to himself.

"This definitely looks like early suburban life. There were no suburbs until the car was invented—people would never make it to work on time—so it's safe to assume anyone who lives here has a car, which means they have money." Sonya spoke in her history teacher voice, poised and informative. He could listen to her talk all day. She had a way of lulling him into a deep comfort regardless of what she was talking about.

Martin had brushed up on the era on Wikipedia. Aside from Prohibition beginning, women were in the middle of fighting for their rights to vote, World War I had ended the prior summer, and the worst Depression the country would ever see loomed around the corner in the next decade. And somewhere on the other side of the country Babe Ruth was smacking home runs at a rate that made people believe he was superhuman. Maybe he was also from the future and came back to become the first celebrity athlete.

"Should we knock on someone's door? Ask to use their phone for a cab?" Sonya asked.

"No, of course not," Martin said. "We look like shit. We're covered in dust and dirt, and I'm pretty sure I stepped in horseshit. We can't go into some stranger's house like this."

The neighborhood was quiet. All of the men would have been at work downtown while the women stayed home with the kids. School would be in session, so many of the women likely spent their days cleaning the house and preparing a massive dinner for the family to chow down whenever Dad got home from work.

Life was simple, and while he didn't agree with the gender-specific roles of the era, it kept the chaos to a minimum, something that had all but vanished in the new century.

"If there's a neighborhood here, then there's got to be a restaurant nearby. Or even a small grocery store. Something." Martin spoke as if he knew the area well, but had no idea where he was in relation to modern-day Littleton.

"We can go for a little bit more, but we'll have to stop at some point. We're not walking all the way to Denver," Sonya said, her voice a bit more hopeful than before.

It only took them ten more minutes before they found what was downtown Littleton, a block of shops and restaurants.

"The promised land!" Martin shouted, giggling at the sight. Sweat dripped down his back, his shirt clinging to his back while his kneecaps burned like they were on fire.

They settled on a restaurant called The Cottage, a small diner with a window table that faced the main road. There were a couple of families walking around the town, but it remained rather quiet.

They entered and were given the window seat, relieved to have survived the first half of the day in 1919.

13

Chapter 13

The owner of The Cottage was a short Italian immigrant named Milo. He had lived in the United States for forty years, moving with his parents from Italy when he was a teenager in 1882. Life was hard when he had arrived during his developmental years, trying to fit in with American kids in high school, all while learning English and the new culture.

It was a culture shock in every sense, and when the American kids started calling him names like wop and spaghetti slurper, Milo would return home to cry in his room until dinner was served. He had hated it, and after six months had decided that taking his life would be more bearable than facing the racial slurs thrown his way all day by the American assholes.

One cold night, Milo ventured down to the railroad and lay on the tracks. It would probably hurt, might even make his eyeballs gush out of their sockets, he supposed, but it would be quick and over without a second thought.

That's when the old man had approached him.

"You don't need to do this, Milo," he told him. "You can be anything in this country, didn't they tell you that?"

Milo had refused to get off the tracks and spoke from his lying position.

"It's a lie!" he cried. "You can be anything if you're an *American*. They hate everyone else."

"I don't think that's true now. You're in the land of opportunity, my friend. That's why your parents chose to come here."

"No," Milo snapped back. "They came here so we didn't get killed. It's no longer safe at our home. I wish they picked somewhere else."

"Milo, what would you say if you had the opportunity to go back and change everything? Would you do it?"

The old man's voice was cold, yet filled with temptation.

"Yes. I'd change it all. I'd take my chance in Sicily, or maybe just move north where it wasn't so bad."

"I see. What if I could give you that opportunity?"

At this, Milo sat up, but it was too dark to make out any of the man's features besides his white hair, the color of snow.

"Who are you?" Milo asked.

"I'm Chris."

"How did you find me here?"

"I was out for a walk. Beautiful evening, don't you think?"

"What do you want from me?"

Chris grinned, his white teeth revealed in the dark pit that was his face.

"I only want to help. Call me crazy, but anyone lying on the train tracks isn't having a good day. So tell me, Milo: do you want my help?"

Milo's mind had raced with so many thoughts that it didn't occur to him until this moment that he never gave his name to the old man. His arms and back broke into chills at the realization.

"I can give you opportunity, both in this country, or back at home should you choose," Chris said.

"What kind of opportunity?"

"If you get off those tracks and come with me, I'll show you. All I ask is that you trust me. A train will be here in twenty minutes, so I suggest you decide quickly."

Milo stayed on the tracks and dropped his head. "Okay," he mumbled. "Where are we going?"

"I have a store. I do all of my work from there—I even sleep there. I can show you what I'm working on. If you think it's a fit for you, then great. If not, you can leave, but at least I kept you off the tracks, right?"

Milo thought about the kids calling him a wop. "Sure, I guess."

Milo went with the old man that night and never looked back.

* * *

After reminiscing on that cold night in 1882, Milo smiled when the couple walked into his restaurant. Chris had asked him to keep a close ear on their conversation, wanting to know their plans for the year 1919.

Milo greeted them as he would any customer. The woman was beautiful with glowing skin and a heart-melting smile. The man was nothing special and his suit looked like he pulled it from a dumpster in the alley. He must have had money to land a lady like the one in the flowing blue dress.

"Good evening, you two, and welcome to The Cottage," Milo said as he approached their table, a gentle smile greeting them.

"I haven't seen you around before, are you new to town?"

The man nodded while his lady friend stared at him nervously.

"Yes we are. My wife and I just moved here from Texas and we're checking out the area for a place to live," the man said.

"Oh? Well, in that case, welcome to Colorado," Milo replied, a most distant Italian accent buried in his speech. "Do you nice folks know what you'll be having for supper?"

"I think so," the woman said.

How strange the woman speaks in public. What kind of man would allow this? Milo thought. Women never spoke unless directly asked what they were ordering. These people must certainly be from the scary future where women voted for who ran the country. What were they going to ask for next, to *work* in the government?

"I'll have the turkey sandwich," she said, ordering first in a power move that made Milo question every bit of the man's dignity.

"And I'll have the burger, with a soup on the side," the weak man said.

Milo stared at them both, debated calling out the man, but decided to not make a scene. Chris had made it clear to not be memorable to the couple from the future.

"Perfect, I'll get those orders started for you right away."

Milo left them for the kitchen to prepare their meals. The entryway to the kitchen allowed for the restaurant's sounds to carry in with perfect clarity. Milo used this to his advantage, often times being the only one working, as he could hear when a customer needed something or had a complaint. He could beat them to the punch, making him appear like a spectacular waiter who deserved the best of tips.

Today, however, the acoustics allowed him to spy on the couple. Milo had met plenty of people from Texas, and these two didn't have one trait of a Texan. He didn't appreciate the obvious lie.

As he threw the burger and turkey on the grill, Milo took a step back to soften the sizzling sound and focus on the couple's conversation. They were the only ones in the restaurant, so he could hear them as if sitting at the table beside them.

"This is a cute place," the woman said.

"Yeah it's nice. Do you think he's a Road Runner?" the man asked.

Road Runner? Milo thought. *Why would they think I'm one of those assholes?*

"Martin, you can't go around assuming everyone is a Road Runner. You're paranoid."

"We just need to eat as fast as we can and get to Denver. Something's not right about this place."

The woman sighed. "Is this how our entire trip is going to be? You living in fear of everything and everyone?"

"No. I have my reasons for my suspicions. Just trust me."

Milo heard frustration in Martin's voice. They sat in silence for the next few minutes, so Milo peeked around the corner to see what they were doing. The woman was staring out the window while Martin fidgeted with his silverware.

Milo flipped the meat and filled two glasses of water.

"Here you are, folks," he said as he stepped back into the dining area. "Your supper should be ready in a few minutes." He placed the waters on the table and watched them with the curiosity of a child. "What are you folks doing after dinner tonight? Any big plans?"

"I think we're gonna head downtown to find a place to stay.

That's where we want to live, and need to start looking at places tomorrow." The man spoke as the woman turned her attention to Milo. Even though she had spoken out of turn, Milo felt a kindness radiating from her, something rare for people from the future.

"And what do you do for work?" Milo asked, knowing the man wouldn't have likely prepared an answer.

"I'm an author," Martin responded quickly.

"Oh? Anything I would know?"

Milo hadn't touched a book in years, but wanted to play along.

"Probably not. I write children's books. For young kids just learning how to read."

Perhaps you're smarter than you look, Milo thought as Martin seemed to have an answer ready for any question.

"What part of Texas are you from?"

"Dallas," Martin said confidently.

"Ahhh, the big city. No wonder you want to live in Denver."

Martin nodded as a bell chimed from the kitchen.

"Ah! Appears your dinner is ready. Let me get it all together for you nice folks."

Milo disappeared into the kitchen and listened.

"What are you doing?" the woman asked in a hushed and hurried voice.

"I'm saving us."

"We never agreed on a final plan for our backstory. I hope you're remembering everything you're saying because you'll need to repeat it to anyone else we meet."

"I know that. We're doing fine, stop worrying."

Now the man seemed to have control of the conversation.

Milo put their food on plates and returned to the table where he interrupted an apparent stare down between the couple.

"*Buon appétito*!" he said cheerily as he slid the plates in front of his customers. "Is there anything else I can get you?"

"Not right now, thank you," the woman said.

Milo nodded and let himself back into the kitchen.

The couple remained silent as they ate, not speaking one word to each other until the food was gone. Milo debated calling Chris, but didn't have much to offer.

When he cleared their table, the man asked, "May I use your telephone?"

Milo had expected the question, and knew Chris wanted him to do anything to slow the couple down.

"I'd say yes, but my telephone has been out of service for the last week, I'm afraid. It takes a while to get someone out this way and take a look."

"Is there anywhere around here that might have a phone to use?" Martin asked.

"Most places will be closing down for the day in the next few minutes. I'm the only one who stays open past six in case anyone wants to have a late dinner."

Milo knew about the payphone two blocks further down Main Street, but it intentionally slipped his mind in the moment.

The woman looked at Martin in an unsettled way and Milo knew he had thrown off their plans. "I suggest you folks get going and start asking around before everyone turns in." Milo grinned at them as he dropped off their bill.

The man rummaged through his pockets and retrieved a crisp twenty dollar bill.

Wow, they are good, Milo thought, the currency one of the small details people usually overlooked. Whenever the snobby people from the future came into his diner and tried to spend their futuristic money with gigantic faces on them, Milo took great pleasure in calling the police on them for attempting to pay with counterfeit money. Watching them squirm as they were questioned, and lie about receiving the money from the local bank, brought warmth to Milo's soul.

But not these two. They were on top of their shit and likely had every fine detail accounted for. It explained why Chris was so insistent on keeping the man on their side. Milo would never mention it to the old man, but he had been making some highly questionable mistakes in who he was giving the Juice to. Granted, Milo didn't get to meet anywhere close to all of the newcomers, but the dozen he had met in the last five years have been complete busts and traitors. He wondered if the Road Runners' sales pitch had improved in recent times because it never used to be so simple for people to disobey Chris and change their allegiance.

This was all beyond his knowledge and paygrade to worry about such things, but he wondered nonetheless.

The couple tossed the money on the table and stood from the booth.

"You folks have a pleasant evening, and come back and see me sometime."

"Will do," the man lied, and they left the restaurant in a hurry.

Milo gathered the money and studied it, admiring its crispness, before flipping the sign on the door to Closed and going to his back office to call Chris.

14

Chapter 14

"I think he was one of them," Martin said as they hurried down the sidewalk.

"One of who?" Sonya asked, her arm interlocked with Martin's.

"Road Runners. I think our waiter was one."

Martin didn't want to share the knowledge of the glow he had seen on the man's skin, but might have to if danger kept presenting itself.

"He was friendly," Martin continued. "Chris said to look out for people who are overly friendly, trying to trap you in their trust."

"Oh my God, Martin, stop it with the nonsense. I don't give a shit what Chris says. He's a delusional old man."

"I'm just saying we need to be cautious."

"Of *friendly* people? Are you shitting me?"

"Can I ask you something?"

Martin knew Sonya hated being asked if she could be asked a question. *Just ask the damn question!* she would yell, but she only nodded this time.

He rolled up his sleeve and stuck his arm out in front of her. "Do you see anything?"

She examined his arm, clueless as to what she should be looking for. "Looks like your arm. Do we really have time for this?"

"Look closer. Really look. Do you see a glow?"

Sonya put her face a couple of inches from his arm and squinted, turning her head in different directions.

"Martin, are you feeling okay?"

He could see his glow as clear as daylight, but he knew what he was looking for.

"So you don't see anything?"

"No, all I see is your arm. What are you getting at?"

"Look, I know that waiter was at least another time traveler. Those of us who are have a glow to our skin. I guess you could call it a side effect. He had the glow, and I'm sure he saw mine. That's why when he started acting too friendly, I knew we had to get out. I've never been so uncomfortable during a meal."

Sonya stared at him blankly.

"Your skin isn't glowing, and neither was that man's, so what do you want me to believe? I'm looking at your arm as closely as I can."

"I don't know if you're able to see it. I don't know how any of this works. I just know that I can see the glow on myself and others. I learned of this in 1996 from the liquor store owner."

"The guy who was killed in that fire? He was a time traveler?" Sonya's voice had risen.

"He was. And he was a good guy, doing research to help save his future. He taught me a couple of details about time travel, the glowing skin being a main one. He also warned me about the Road Runners, said they were after him. Then I watched them murder him and burn his store to the ground. So, yes, I believe Chris when he says they should be avoided, and you should too."

"Just so I'm clear, the Road Runners really are bad and you can tell when someone is a time traveler, but I can't?"

Martin nodded as he stared at the ground in deep thought. "That's why it's important we keep a low profile. We just don't know what to expect from the Road Runners. I'm pretty sure our waiter was one, or else he would have acknowledged my glowing skin, right? I don't know their game except for that they'll act nice to lure you into trusting them. Was he supposed to let us go so easily tonight? Is he going to pop up again later, maybe run into us on 'accident?' It's best we don't speak with anyone unless we have to."

Sonya nodded, staring at Martin with her seductive eyes that had never lost their pull on him. He only hoped she would put her negativity toward Chris aside and realize what they were dealing with. The old man pissed him off plenty, too, but it was clear he didn't want any unintended harm to befall Martin.

"We really need to get downtown," Martin whispered, and started walking again.

The sun approached the mountains, casting orange across the sky. They'd only have another ninety minutes at best before the darkness would creep in.

After walking two more blocks, Sonya spotted their way out.

"There it is! Look!" she cried out, pointing like an anxious child to a toy on the store shelf.

Martin followed her finger to the glass phone booth that he had passed over just moments ago, mistaking it for a store kiosk of some sort. It stood right below a high arching sign that read WELCOME TO DOWNTOWN LITTLETON.

They locked eyes with each other, grins forcing their way onto their faces, and ran to the phone booth. Martin pulled open the door and they both squeezed inside. Martin couldn't recall having ever seen an actual phone booth. There had been plenty of payphones downtown, even a couple still in 2018, but never an actual glass box to stand in for privacy.

He pulled the phone from the cradle, popped in a nickel, and turned the rotary dial to zero.

The phone rang twice before a woman's voice answered. "How may I direct your call today?"

"Yes!" Martin said, excitement nearly leaping out of his throat. "I need a taxi to come to downtown Littleton."

"One moment, sir, and I'll connect you with a cab company."

The phone cut to silence with subtle clicking sounds. Martin thought the operator might have accidentally hung up, but was relieved at the sound of the phone ringing again.

"Thank you for calling Denver Taxi, my name is Chris, how can I help you?" a man's voice greeted him.

Martin froze.

"Hello? Is someone there?" the man asked.

"I'm sorry, yes," Martin snapped out of it, realizing it wasn't *the* Chris that kept his girlfriend up at night. "I need a taxi in downtown Littleton as soon as possible."

"And your final destination?"

"We'll be going to downtown Denver, looking for a hotel."

"Okay. I'll have a driver head out now. He should be there in thirty minutes. Your total trip should cost around two dollars. Meet him on Main Street right on the corner of the strip mall."

"We're already there."

"Perfect. We'll be there shortly. Have a good evening."

Martin hung up and found Sonya hanging on to every word

94

after doubting they would make it out of Littleton tonight.

* * *

Dozens of cars drove by while they waited. The men working downtown would have finally made their way home. Martin watched in amazement as the clunky boxes of steel passed by them.

Sonya sat on the sidewalk, citing soreness in her knees from the long walk all day. She planned to take a warm bubble bath whenever they checked in to a hotel.

The sun had set for good when the taxi arrived, an all-black box that looked like a hybrid of a future Jeep and the past's horse-drawn carriages. There was no sign on the roof indicating its purpose, but when the lights flashed at them they knew it was for them.

Martin led them to the car and opened the door for Sonya to slide in first. They settled in the squeaky leather seats.

"Good evening," the driver said, turning to look over his shoulder at his new passengers.

Martin immediately examined the man's skin, not seeing any glow.

"Good evening, sir," Martin said.

"My name's Thomas. How do you do?"

"We're doing well. I'm Martin, and this is my wife, Sonya."

"Ma'am," Thomas said to Sonya with a nod.

Thomas looked like he couldn't have been much older than twenty-one. His face was youthful, glowing, and his brown hair slicked back with plenty of grease.

"Where can I take y'all tonight?" he asked.

"We were hoping you could tell us," Martin replied. "We want to stay downtown, but don't know any hotels. Is there anywhere you recommend?"

Thomas drove away from Main Street and stared at Martin in the rear view with a thoughtful expression. "What kind of hotel you looking for? I know the fancy ones, the average ones, and the ones where you can take a street lady into. I've seen it all since I started driving this taxicab two years ago."

"How about a fancy one?"

Thomas nodded. "Sure. The fanciest are the Oxford and the Brown Palace. The Brown Palace is where the rich and famous stay. President Taft stayed there a few years ago when he was in town."

Martin should've remembered these two options, seeing as both hotels remained in operation in 2018, still welcoming the high-class members of society.

"Let's do the Brown Palace then," Martin said.

"Alrighty," Thomas said as he led them through the outskirts of Littleton.

Martin noticed the engine's steady puttering and thought back to the BMW he wanted to buy in 2018. It was going to happen, dammit. After all the shit he had endured in 1996, the least he could do was splurge some of the money he had wisely invested.

"You folks new to the Denver area?" Thomas asked as they approached an on-ramp for the freeway.

Sonya stared at Martin, deferring to him to keep their fake story going.

"Yes, we just arrived here from Dallas," Martin said.

"Dallas, huh? I've heard that's a good place." Thomas spoke

in an emotionless voice that made Martin wonder if the young man was depressed or just bored.

"Yeah, we heard Denver is a fun place, and wanted to see it for ourselves. How long have you lived here?"

"I've lived in Colorado my whole life. Grew up on the eastern side of the state. My papa runs a ranch, but I wanted to go to school and got the chance here in the city. He wasn't happy that I didn't wanna continue the ranch life with him, but my mama talked some sense into him."

"What are you going to school for?"

"Business. I don't know what I wanna do, just that I wanna work for myself. Like Mr. Brown, the owner of the hotel you're staying at—he owns everything in this city. I just started my senior year, so we'll see how it goes when I graduate in May."

"Well, good luck to you."

"Thank you, sir."

Martin stared out his window at the blackness of the night. There were no neighborhoods, no commercial buildings to provide the glow of a city at night.

"How often do you drive?" Martin asked, breaking a prolonged silence.

"I drive five days a week—or should I say nights. Wednesday through Sunday. During the week I drive from six 'til midnight. Saturday I go until two, but that's prob'ly gonna change when Prohibition goes live—no more drunks to pick up. And Sunday I drive from lunch 'til dinner time, an early night for me."

"And are you mostly in Denver?"

"Yep, I'm only in Denver. Only time I'm not is when someone requests a ride elsewhere, but that's not too often."

"We may need some rides around town in the next couple months. Would we be able to request you?"

Thomas nodded, staring from the rear view to the road with quick flicks of his eyes.

"Yessir. Just ask for me when you call, if it's during those hours. If I'm available, I'd be happy to give y'all a ride."

"I'll keep that in mind. Thank you."

"My pleasure."

Martin sunk deeper into his seat, relieved. Thomas had passed his first test and didn't realize it as they drove closer to downtown. The young cab driver didn't ask what they were in town for, why they would need rides, or why they insisted on having him. It was simple yes and no answers with the kid, and Martin appreciated it. They now had a local with plenty of knowledge of the geography and happenings in Denver. He didn't know how often they would need him, if at all, but it was a tremendous resource to have in their back pocket.

Buildings appeared in the near distance, many of them lit and glowing a soft golden light to contrast the black night. It was nothing like downtown in the next century, but it was downtown Denver just the same. And they had finally arrived.

15

Chapter 15

The Brown Palace looked no different from how Martin remembered it in 2018. He had never been inside the luxurious hotel, but the exterior apparently went undisturbed over its century of existence. Its brick facade towered eight stories tall, one of the bigger buildings in town at the time. The street-level windows provided a glimpse into a packed bar of patrons—mostly men—enjoying the last days of alcohol before the government took it all away. Signs on the building advertised a spa, along with times for serving tea throughout the week. Martin felt like he was trapped within an old black and white photo of the historic hotel.

Thomas had dropped them at the main entrance, but they walked down the block to get a feel for the area and their bearings, wanting to know exactly how much had changed since they were last downtown to collect Martin's millions of dollars in 2018.

Sonya gawked at the building. "I've been here before, but look how pristine the building looks in this era. All of the future chaos of downtown is gone, and this is clearly the place where the highest class people hang out."

"Well, this is where we're going to be tonight and maybe the rest of the week."

"I just can't believe I'm going to stay at the Brown Palace when it's still a new hotel in the city."

The same street names were in place, but downtown was still in its early years and lacked the towering skyscrapers and constant bustle of a major city. A few homeless people rummaged through trash cans on the deserted sidewalks. One in particular walked by them mumbling to himself about a spaceship landing on his brain. Apparently, some things never changed.

They completed a lap around the hotel and Martin remembered a bit of history he had learned about the Brown Palace. There was supposedly an underground tunnel that ran from the hotel to a brothel across the street. This gave the upper-class businessmen a chance to sneak over and live out their wild fantasies. Rumor had it that even Presidents who stayed here took advantage of the secret tunnel. Martin recognized the whore house right when he saw it, a two-level house directly across the street. All the lights were off, every drape closed, and the front door had its window covered up, too.

Martin would confirm if this longstanding rumor was true on his own time.

"Shall we?" Martin asked when they arrived back to the entrance, a set of heavy double doors with shiny golden handles.

"Please, I'm exhausted."

Martin leaned into the bulky door as the hotel's lobby welcomed them with the soft tune of a piano in the background. Chairs and tables filled the open space ahead with hotel guests enjoying a late dinner as the pianist played from the corner of the room, his fingers gliding like angels over the keys. Granite walls towered over them, lanterns hanging on each pillar. They looked up to see the square shape of the lobby stretch to the hotel's ceiling, the hallways for the eight levels of rooms appearing maze-like from the bottom.

Across the lobby Martin spotted the front desk, and led them to it, slightly embarrassed at their raggedy appearance as everyone in the dining area was dressed in pristine suits and dresses while they sipped expensive champagne and ate steak and lobster dinners.

A tall man with thin complexion and pale features stood behind the counter dressed in a black-and-white suit and a top hat. He smiled at them as they approached.

"Good evening, and welcome to the Brown Palace," the man said in a stern voice. "Do you have a reservation?"

"No. We were hoping you might have a room open."

The man looked Martin up-and-down, not bothering to hide the disgust in his eyes. His eyes jumped to Sonya and made the same judgmental path along her dirty clothes. The man, whose name badge read *Carson*, sniffed and looked down to the guest book on his desk.

"I'm afraid we have no open rooms," Carson said after a few moments. He looked at Martin blankly.

"Are you sure about that?" Martin asked.

"Certainly."

Don't cause a scene, but don't be pushed around, either.

"Well, sir, I think you're lying."

"I most certainly am not lying."

"You're assuming I don't have money because of the way we look. You're making a mistake."

Sonya tugged on Martin's arm. "Let's just go."

"No, we're not going."

Martin rarely caused a fuss, but felt compelled in the heat of the moment. His legs were practically numb after walking all day, even after dinner and the long cab ride. All he wanted was a drink and a hot shower, and if this skinny asshole behind the counter was trying to stop him, then he was going to hear about it.

"Sir, money is not the issue. I have no rooms to offer."

"Is there a manager I can speak with?"

Carson scoffed and turned away, disappearing into a back room behind the desk.

"What happened to keeping a low profile?" Sonya muttered under her breath.

"I'm not putting up with this guy's bullshit," Martin said, emphasizing *bullshit* so the word would carry into the room where Carson had gone.

Three minutes passed and Martin wondered if Carson was simply hiding in the back and waiting for them to leave. As someone who used to spend eight hours in the same spot on the couch, drinking and smoking, Martin welcomed the challenge.

Two more minutes passed before another man walked out of the office and approached the desk, a wide grin revealing polished teeth.

"Good evening, folks, what seems to be the problem?" the man asked. He stood eye level with Martin, and appeared slightly younger than Carson. He wore the same suit as every other staff member in the hotel.

"I feel judged by the gentleman who was just helping us. I just want a room for my wife and I. We've had a long day if you can't tell—that's why we're a mess."

Martin pulled his wallet out and rummaged through it, slapping a crisp hundred dollar bill on the counter.

The manager's eyes bulged at the sight of Mr. Franklin staring at him with his usual pursed lips.

"Like I explained, I have money. I'm sorry I don't *look* like the rest of your guests right now, but I just need a room so we can clean up and stay in town for a few days."

Martin felt Sonya's leg bouncing beside him, and nudged her to stop.

The manager flipped through the book, searching for anything that Carson may have missed.

"What is your name, sir?" he asked casually, as if there had been no issue at all.

"Martin Briar."

"Mr. Briar, we can make arrangements for you to stay as long as you'd like. I do apologize for any inconvenience so far."

Martin wished he could laugh in Carson's face. *That* would cause a scene. He had always fantasized about being rich, having that rare opportunity to push his way through any situation with the power of a dollar, acting entitled, knowing the world owed him everything because of what was stashed in his pockets. And it worked. And he liked it.

Martin never thought money would change him, but then again, he never had money like he did now in 1919.

The manager completed checking them in to a room and handed over a pair of two brass keys that jingled. "You'll be in room 619. It will be $30 per night, but I'll waive the first night for the trouble we've caused you today."

"Thank you," Martin said in his best *I'm-rich-and-entitled* voice.

"Please let us know if you need anything at all during your stay."

Martin took the keys, grabbed Sonya by the waist and left the front desk with a quick nod. They rode the classic elevator to the sixth floor—stairs weren't an option for their exhausted legs—and proceeded down a narrow hallway to room 619. Old Western paintings decorated the hallway, as they passed them in a blur, gaining speed as they approached their room door.

Martin jiggled the key into the lock and twisted until he heard a click. The door creaked open to the room already lit up from a floor lamp in the far corner. Their legs were useless as Martin's knees tingled from the throbbing pain. Without saying a word to each other, all stress had disappeared as they stepped into the room, relieved to have made it to the end of the day that seemed to never end.

16

Chapter 16

"I'm not gonna lie, I could go for a shower right now," Sonya said when they entered the hotel room. "I'm pretty sure my brain is running on fumes, but I am *not* getting into that comfy bed covered in dirt and sweat."

"I agree, but I just need a second to lie down," Martin replied, lunging for the bed and splaying across the comforter decorated with a pattern of large, obnoxious flowers. The curtains over the windows had a matching design that made Martin feel like he had indeed traveled back one hundred years. He took a moment to admire the repeating hexagonal pattern running along the carpet, and the small cushioned chair and ottoman that appeared to be for someone half his size. "How about you get started and I'll join you in a bit?"

"I've heard that one before," Sonya said, rolling her eyes. "I'm gonna get out of the shower and you'll be snoring in that same spot."

Snoring never sounded so appealing, the ultimate sign of a heavy sleep in Martin's opinion.

"Whatever you say. I just need five minutes," Martin

mumbled, already feeling sleep's tight grip around his mental throat.

Sonya wandered into the bathroom, closed the door, and had the water running within seconds as Martin rolled on his back and stared at the ceiling.

Here we are again, he thought. *Back in the past with no clue how this will turn out.*

A knock banged from the door, causing Martin to jump off the bed and stumble to catch his already wavering balance. *Did they forget to give us something at check-in?*

There were no peepholes in 1919, just a solid door to leave the surprise of who stood on the other side. But with Sonya in the shower, and Martin alone for at least the next fifteen minutes, he already knew who was knocking. The very thought of the old man sent fresh adrenaline throughout his veins, even with his body fatigued beyond belief.

Martin pulled open the door.

"Fancy finding you here," Chris said, grinning in his usual black suit.

The quickest way to get rid of him, Martin had learned, was to listen and do whatever he asked.

"What do you want, Chris?" Martin asked, trying to sound authoritative, but too tired to make it believable.

"I heard you were staying here. A good friend of mine owns the hotel, and told me he spotted you checking in."

"You're friends with Mr. Brown?" Martin asked, raising an eyebrow.

"Certainly. Mr. Brown chose to use his Juice to create businesses in sites that will thrive in the future. He's made billions throughout time and all around the globe. The savviest man I know."

"So why are you here?" Martin asked again.

"I know you had a long trip today, so I'll make it brief. May I come in?" Martin stepped aside and let the old man enter.

Chris plopped down on the chair next to the window, and grabbed his chin before he spoke. "I have some news about the Road Runners. It appears they've made you a top priority.

"The Road Runners know you're in this year and plan on hunting you down," Chris continued. "That's why I'm here—to warn you."

"And what exactly am I supposed to do about it?" Martin asked.

"Do exactly as I told you. Be aware of anyone trying to be extra kind. You can look for the glow, but they keep it concealed with long sleeves, gloves, and anything that will help cover their skin. Some have even found a way to conceal the glow. I'd advise you don't go out at night. That's the only time they'll snatch you off the street. During the day is when they'll try to lure you with smooth talk or something that seems innocent. If you know you've encountered one, it's important that you lose them. Change locations because they'll be following you all over town until they find the right moment to take you."

"What do they want from me?"

Chris shrugged.

"They think you'll betray me and join them. It's unfortunately something they've succeeded at in recent months. You don't have any plans on joining them, do you?"

"Of course not. After I've seen them in action at Calvin's store, and all the stories I've heard, why would anyone want to join them?"

Martin had a list of questions to ask about the Road Runners, but the quick burst of adrenaline had already worn off. His eyes felt like boulders in his face trying to pull his head down to a pillow.

He didn't need a reminder about how dangerous the Road Runners were. The old liquor store in 1996 was probably still smoking. His old friend, Calvin, would have turned into a pile of ashes within minutes.

"I wanted to warn you about the severity of which they will be following you," Chris continued. "I have my own people around town keeping an eye on you, as well. For security. If they notice any Road Runners tailing you, they'll be quick to interject. These encounters can turn violent quickly. But we have to do whatever we need to defend ourselves and what we stand for."

"And what exactly is it that you stand for?" Martin asked, his body refusing interest, but his mind demanding answers.

Chris stood and paced around the room, stopping to stare at the bathroom door where the steady sound of running water continued.

"We encourage a free world where people can roam through history and make the world a better place."

"And making those same people sell you their souls in exchange?" Martin hadn't expected to be quick on the draw with a snarky comment.

"There's a price to pay for everything," Chris said calmly, as if he'd heard this hundreds of times. "Even those who wish to do good in the world have to pay. Nothing comes free."

Martin could have continued his argument with the old man about the morality of his "fees", but had no energy to do so.

"You always come here and tell me to be aware of these people, but you never seem to give me any advice on what to do if I encounter one," Martin said. The room started to spin and he wanted to go to bed. Why couldn't have Chris come in the morning?

"There's not much you can do besides run," Chris said. "Keep in mind these people don't have any special powers—aside from the Juice, if you consider it a power. If you hide, they have to find you like anyone else would."

"So I can fight them off?"

Chris waved a hand at Martin. "I wouldn't take any chances. The ones they send out to hunt people are highly skilled in combat and stealth. Ninjas, essentially."

"Why do they exist?" Martin was finally getting answers. If Chris wanted to talk, then why send him away? He'd been waiting forever to learn this information. "If you're the keeper of time, then how did these people end up with the power?"

Chris nodded. "I gave them the same Juice as you. There was a time when they were good and wanted to make the world a better place. Sometimes power corrupts people. A handful of them revolted, upset by the price they had to pay to obtain the Juice. They made it their number one goal to get revenge on me."

"They want to kill you?"

"Kill me?" Chris chuckled. "That would be nice. They'd love to *torture* me. Pick me apart limb by limb. The funny thing is they'll never catch me. I have people all over watching. I know where the Road Runners are in different parts of the world and in different eras of time. They've grown into quite the organization, I must say. There are thousands of them, all trying to recruit people to join their angry cause. But I have an army. They're no match for me."

"If you have so much manpower, why not just wipe them out?"

Chris chuckled, a sound that sent chills down Martin's spine as the clock ticked away on the wall, approaching midnight. "Despite what you think about me, I don't just go around killing people. I'd like to capture the Road Runners and speak with them, try to get them to see things the way they did before their brain was corrupted by their bitter counterparts. We've only killed when pushed to those limits."

Martin took two steps forward and stood directly in front of Chris, staring into his deep blue eyes, wanting to see his soul, if there was one. The old man reeked of stale cologne that nearly made Martin gag.

"Is there a problem?" Chris asked, his familiar grin returning.

Maybe it was the irritability, but Martin had an urge to choke the old man and save the Road Runners some time. He'd had enough of the random visits and vague explanations. *Why did I ever accept this bullshit?* he wondered. *Why didn't I just say no and continue on with my shitty life? I would've pulled the trigger eventually and ended it all so easily.*

He thought back to his mother, sitting in their new house in 2018, her mind slowly fading into the darkness of dementia. It was her idea to go into the antique store—she would never pass one up. That one decision led to all of this. If Martin would have just waited in the car that day, would he be in this current mess? Sure, he had Sonya now, the brightest light in his life since Izzy, but was it worth it if they both ended up dead in an unknown place, far away from their current lives?

"What will they do if they catch us?" Martin asked, his last question.

"They'll try to convince you to join their group, that's always their main objective. They'll give you some time, too. They'll work hard to convince you. You could call them the world's best salesmen, because they sure do convert many."

Chris paused and cleared his throat.

"And if you don't agree to join their pact, they'll kill you."

Martin chuckled, slap-happy by this point in the night. "I suppose that's a bold strategy."

"You won't be laughing when they catch you. You need to take this seriously."

"I *need* to go to bed."

Chris sighed. "Very well. Just know that if you think you're being followed, it's because you are. We'll have our eyes on you, for protection. Carry on with your business and stay alert. Even though we're close, we may not necessarily be fast enough."

"Gee, your guys must have trained under JFK's Secret Service detail."

Chris shook his head. "It's your funeral. I'll see you around."

The old man pivoted and left the room, shutting the door quietly behind him.

Martin lay on the bed, the water still running in the bathroom. As he dozed, he imagined the world as it must have truly been: thousands of people all with a special ability to travel through time, jumping from century to century as effortlessly as boarding a bus.

There was a war of sorts between Chris's people and the Road Runners. A war that had gone on for how long? A few months? Years? Thousands of years? Martin could have asked questions for the next six hours if he had the energy. Was everyone who got sucked into the world of time travel forced to pick a side in this war, or were some neutral and allowed to carry on with their business? He wanted to stay neutral and not involved. If they wanted to protect him, then that was their choice. He was here to help Sonya quickly so he could plan a trip to the future to save his mother's ailing brain.

17

Chapter 17

They woke at noon, groggy and needing more sleep. Yesterday was filled with an absurd amount of exercise and stress. Martin faintly remembered hosting Chris in the room a few hours ago, the encounter feeling more like several weeks in the past. Part of him wondered if it was a dream. Even if it was, everything Chris had told him was still true, and he'd be sure to not let Sonya know about the special visit.

"I think we missed breakfast," Sonya said with a loud moan and stretch. They stayed under the sheets, their bodies aching everywhere. "I've never been so tired in my life."

"I wouldn't mind a relaxing day, honestly," Martin said. "What is the plan regarding your grandfather? What did you find in your research?"

"Not too much. Looks like they were in Kansas before coming to Denver. They should be getting here sometime within the next two weeks."

"Then why don't we go to Kansas and find them?"

Martin wanted to get as far away from Denver as possible after Chris's warning, but knew better than to come out and say it.

"We're not going to Kansas. Why would we put ourselves in the line of danger? They had guns, and they used them."

Martin felt sick. A long journey awaited trying to find someone by sheer luck, wandering around town until they either bumped into them, or met someone who knew them. How easy it must have been for criminals to stay on the run in these old days.

"Then what should we do today?" Martin asked, ready to concede.

Sonya shrugged. "I think we should walk around town and learn our surroundings. We also need to find a place to stay, unless we're staying here the whole time?"

Martin had forgotten about his encounter with the man at the check-in desk the night before. That felt like five years ago, not twelve hours.

"For now, I think it's best if we move locations every few days. We can stay here a couple more days then move to another hotel. I don't think a permanent place of residence is a good idea anymore. Just in case there are Road Runners following us."

Sonya rolled her eyes. "You're so paranoid, but I still love you."

They had discussed buying property in downtown, and selling it when they returned to 2018 for ten times the price. Martin supposed they still could, but his bigger concern was dodging the Road Runners, not adding to the millions of dollars that awaited him in 2018.

"We still need clothes, toiletries, food," Sonya said. "There's a lot to get done."

"Then let me wash off and get ready."

Their dirty clothes piled on the ground at the foot of the bed, covered in dust and sweat from their prior day's journey. Yes, they definitely needed a new wardrobe, especially in a time where everyone left their home dressed up. The last thing they needed was to look like hobos as they explored the city. Although, wouldn't that be an even better disguise?

"I'll call down for some breakfast," Sonya said. "Or lunch. Whatever they're serving now. Go get in the shower."

Martin rose from the bed, undressed, and disappeared into the bathroom.

* * *

Two hours and two gourmet chicken sandwiches later they stood outside the hotel.

"It really doesn't look much different," Martin said of the area. "Just no tall buildings."

The Brown Palace was one of the taller buildings at the moment, a few years before skyscrapers would start to go up and take over every corner of the city.

Men in suits filled the sidewalks and crossed the streets. Cars motored by at a snail's pace. It was definitely the middle of a workday in Denver, and the sensation made Martin nostalgic for 1996 when he had worked downtown every day, right before life went down the shitter.

They crossed the street to the next block of buildings, passing everything from restaurants, butcher shops, clothing, and grocery stores. Everything they needed was within a one block radius.

The best part was how few people there were. Traffic was scarce compared to what they were used to, but the narrow roads and slow vehicles caused more jams. That and the lack of traffic lights. Every intersection had stop signs to control the flow of traffic.

"Well, I know my way around the area," Martin said with a proud grin. "Everything is the same, just smaller, or different businesses in the buildings."

"Alright, smart one, but we need to buy things and find where we're going to move next. What other hotels are around here?"

"The only other old hotels I can think of are on the other end of Sixteenth Street—maybe a 20-minute walk from here. There might be others closer that I don't know about."

"Is the Oxford around in this year?"

"Great idea, it should be."Martin led the way, heading south two blocks to reach Sixteenth Street—still decades away from becoming an outdoor shopping mall—and soaking in the area once they arrived. To the east stood the state capitol, appearing the exact same with the exception of its future golden dome appearing more bronze in the old century. To the west, the street ran a mile into the distance, lined with more shops and office buildings.

A man dressed in raggedy clothes hobbled toward them. Dirt and grime covered his skin and he revealed yellowing teeth as he grinned; only it wasn't a friendly grin.

"You people don't belong here," he barked. "Go back where you came from!"

Martin looked down to the hunchbacked man, and immediately clenched his fist, ready to swing if the hobo tried to make a move.

Sonya took a step back and grabbed Martin's arm.

"We're just out for the day. Carry on," Martin said, remaining frozen. He had encountered plenty of the homeless population when he had worked downtown. They always asked for money or food, or stared awkwardly as he passed by, but never did one approach him directly with their seemingly random blurting of words.

"If you knew what was good for you, you'd turn around and never come back," the man said, not breaking his intense stare toward Martin. He pivoted and limped down the sidewalk, mumbling to himself, "If I could leave I would. This idiot has no idea."

Martin and Sonya sighed in relief. "Looks like the bums haven't changed much," he said, getting a nervous chuckle from her.

"Shall we?" she asked, taking back her spot at his side, keeping her arm intertwined with his.

They walked down Sixteenth Street and Martin pointed out all of the buildings that he knew still existed in 2018. The 1919 version had a much homier feel with the classic setup of the business on the ground level, and living quarters on the second floor. The entire mile-long walk was filled with these small businesses. It felt more like a small town instead of the capital city of the Centennial State. All of the structures were built from bricks or stones, no hints of the glass skyscrapers that would become the norm in the next century.

After 20 minutes of walking and window shopping, they reached Wynkoop Street where the local Union Station welcomed floods of travelers. In 1919 traveling by train was still common enough to make the station a bustling area. It stood in all its glory with a couple stores across the street and dirt lots along its sides.

They turned north onto Wynkoop and walked one more block to the Oxford Hotel, Denver's other famous landmark hotel. It lacked the glamour of the Brown Palace with less golden decorations and virtually zero curb appeal, but when they entered, they found an upscale world of fine chandeliers, polished oak floors, and more suited men pacing around frantically on their day's mission.

"What do you think?" Martin asked.

"It looks nice," Sonya said, admiring the lobby.

He crossed the lobby that had a U-shape of couches facing a fireplace in the wall, and met a tall man at the check-in counter, again dressed in a three-piece suit and white gloves.

"How may I assist you, sir?" the man asked in a faint European accent.

"Just curious about your room rates for a stay of about a week. Possibly checking in tomorrow."

The man flipped open a notebook and ran a thin finger down the page.

"One night's stay is thirty dollars. We're currently having a special, though. You can get two nights free if you take a free tour of the hotel and recommend us as a place to stay to your friends and family."

"A tour?" Martin asked. "What exactly do we see on the tour?"

Martin had only toured the Stanley Hotel in Estes Park, but that place was infested with ghosts. He didn't realize regular hotels had special tours.

"We like to show you all of the hotel so you can speak of it with more detail. We meet here in the lobby at four o'clock, then go down to the basement and work our way up to the

Presidential Suite."

The man spoke in an uninterested voice, as if he had made this same pitch 54 times already today. Perhaps this was the past's version of sitting through a timeshare presentation. No one actually wanted to buy anything, just give us the free shit already!

"So if we come to the tour, do we have to book our free nights right away?" Martin asked.

"No. You can use them whenever you'd like within a month."

He turned to ask Sonya what she thought, but she was too busy studying the art that hung on the walls, likely suffering from an intense case of sensory overload from getting to live in the past.

"I'll have to check with my wife and get back with you," he said. "But we'll probably be here at four for the tour."

The man scoffed, likely at the suggestion that Martin had to run an idea by his wife. "Certainly."

Martin left the appalled man and joined Sonya across the room, now staring deep into the whipping flames in the fireplace.

"So are we staying here?" Sonya asked casually, still lost in the flames.

"I think so. They invited us to a hotel tour at four today for two nights free."

"Sounds riveting."

"Is everything okay?" Martin asked. "You've seemed out of it since we got here. Are you nervous about finding your grandparents?"

"Not so much. I think I'm just tired still. Yesterday took a lot out of me. I'm getting too old for this."

Martin understood, as did his sore joints. Maybe on this trip into the past he would focus on eating right and staying in shape. His trip into 1996 saw him give up drinking, at least by his standards, so why not try another self-improvement on this go round?

"We only have another 40 minutes until the tour starts," he said, checking his watch. "Anything you want to see around here? Union Station?"

"I just want to sit down, honestly. Want to grab a drink at the bar?"

"We might as well, before they take all the alcohol away," Martin said, still baffled that the government would soon make alcohol illegal. The law of the land, and a complete pile of horseshit. As if removing alcohol would somehow create world peace.

They found the bar on the other side of the fireplace and sat down for their final drink together.

18

Chapter 18

"Are we going or not?" Sonya asked, slurping down the last of her martini. The drink had brought her back to life, putting a smile on her face and the temptation in her eyes.

Martin downed two doubles of whiskey and felt ready to conquer the old century, only he dragged his feet for the upcoming tour.

The clock behind the bar read three minutes till four, and all he wanted was to stay at the bar and drink until midnight. The booze numbed his aches and he didn't want the sensation to fade. Sonya still wore the long dress she had brought, but he followed the outline of her legs underneath, having a sudden urge to run his hands along her bare skin. A quick romp under the sheets would have everyone feeling normal again.

"How about we go back to our hotel?" Martin proposed. "Forget about this place. We can come back any time."

Sonya giggled. "We're already here. Let's just get it over with. How long could it even be?"

"Okay, then, let's go before they start without us."

Martin slapped a five dollar bill down on the bar top and

helped Sonya out of her stool.

A small group of people gathered in the hotel lobby. There were four men and one woman huddled around the man who had worked behind the front desk. He met Martin's eyes and waved them over.

"Good evening, folks," the man said. "My name is David, and I'll be guiding you throughout the hotel. This tour should take us approximately 45 minutes. We'll start here in the lobby, then go down to the basement to work our way back up to the Presidential Suite. The suite is currently vacant so we'll be able to take a look around."

David's tone had completely changed from earlier when he was a grumpy check-in worker. A new wave of energy spewed from his mouth as he explained the hotel's brief history.

Martin felt an instant relief when seeing they wouldn't be alone on the tour. *We can all suffer together.*

"Where is everyone in town from?" David asked the group.

"New York," one man said.

"We're from Philadelphia," the other man said for himself and the woman.

"Chicago."

"Atlanta."

"We're from Texas," Martin said.

David nodded. "Welcome to Denver. We're not nearly as big as any of the places you're all from, but we hope to be one day. For now, we're a major destination for people traveling from the east coast to California. That's what caused this hotel and many others around town to open. There are currently more hotels than houses in downtown Denver, to give you an idea of the surrounding landscape. The Oxford Hotel is proud to be the first hotel that opened for business in Denver in 1890.

We opened here due to our close proximity to Union Station, where ninety percent of travelers arrive."

David continued with more history about the hotel, its founder, explanations of the artwork on the walls, and anything that could be used in a trivia game later.

File it right next to all the other useless knowledge in your head.

After five minutes of random facts, David led the group to the elevator. They shuffled into the small cage and David manually slid the cast iron gate closed. *Elevators sure have come a long way,* Martin thought. The ancient elevator hummed and clattered to life, the sounds of a million tiny mechanisms grinding in unison as they lowered to the basement level.

David pulled the gate open and led them into the gloomy basement. The luxury of the main lobby gave way to concrete walls, dim lighting, and pallets with boxes full of hotel equipment.

They stood in an open space, but a hallway stretched further into the distance to what appeared to be small offices.

"Here we are," David said excitedly. "The heart and soul of the hotel. Down here we have a furnace, power generators, freezers, and storage for everything from food to towels. The room we're in is obviously storage, as you can tell from all of the boxes. The basement is also home to all of the executive offices. There was simply no room in the main building for offices. If you'll follow me, we can take a quick stroll down the hallway to see the offices."

David led the group, Martin and Sonya directly behind him. For feeling like a dungeon when they entered the basement, the row of offices had a more normal appearance. They passed open doors that showed quick snap shots of hotel executives' lives: family portraits, calendars, inspirational posters. Their desks were wide, or maybe only appeared so from the lack of technology. There were no phones, keyboards, or any of the clutter common in 2018, simply stacks of paper where all work had to be manually completed.

"This is our main conference room," David said as they reached the end of the hall, stepping into the largest room of the underground. A chalkboard hung on the wall and overlooked an oval-shaped table with chairs around it.

"We try to use the hotel's conference room on the second floor whenever possible, but sometimes we'll have meetings down here. Please come in."

The tour group filled the room as David crossed to the chalkboard. Martin never heard the door close behind him, let alone the click of it being locked by one of the tour members.

Two of the men remained in front of the door like bouncers.

"That was too easy, Martin," David said with a grin. "Sonya, I thought you said he was smarter than this."

Martin stood at the table and looked from David to Sonya, clueless.

"He *is* smarter than this. Apparently hotel tours are his weakness," Sonya said, and the rest of the group erupted in laughter.

Martin spun around to find everyone looking at him, laughing as if there was an inside joke they all knew about.

"What is this? What's going on?" Martin asked, a waver in his voice. He saw the closed door and the two men guarding it. His gut wrenched and his heart beat a little faster.

"Please, have a seat, Martin, we're not here to hurt you," David said in a gentle voice.

"I demand you tell me what's going on. And open that door!"

David shook his head. "That door is staying closed until we

have a little talk. Will you please sit down?"

Martin locked eyes with Sonya, who immediately looked away.

"Sonya, what is this? What the *hell* is going on?"

Everyone had taken a step back and watched Martin, including Sonya.

"If you sit down, David will explain everything," she said.

Martin obliged, realizing whatever the hell was happening wouldn't proceed until he sat at the damn table.

"Thank you," David said. "Tell me, Martin, what do you know about the Road Runners?"

Holy fucking shit. This is it. We're dead. Did they already threaten her? Did she save herself by turning me in?

Martin's mouth hung open, his eyes bulging as he scanned the room and realized he had been ambushed by Road Runners. They were all in on the secret.

"Wait," Martin said. "How do you know about the Road Runners?"

Martin knew they were Road Runners, but needed to stall. For what, he didn't know. For an obvious death, he presumed. Death in the Oxford Hotel basement, where not a soul would hear his screams. In a few years he'd be a ghost haunting these same halls on a future tour.

He was too flustered to notice that everyone in the room, except for Sonya, had their bodies mostly covered. The men wore suits and gloves on their hands. The other woman wore a dress that ran from her neck to the floor. Martin wanted to see glowing skin, but they all hid it so well. If he could get up close to one of their faces he'd likely see the faintest hint of the golden glow.

"Martin, we *are* the Road Runners," David said. "Well, not

125

just us. There's thousands of us. But we are part of the team, and we wanted to talk with you about joining us."

Martin thought back to Chris warning him about this exact moment. *They'll do anything once they you have you in their possession. There's no getting out.* He would need to play along, maybe even agree to join, then run away in the middle of the night. Would they follow him if he returned to 2018? Would they find him if he constantly stayed on the run, jumping from year to year? Or would they let him go? Why go through the hassle to get someone who clearly wants no part of your club?

Martin's heart pounded ferociously in his throat as he fought to steady his trembling hands.

"Okay," he said, gulping. "What do you need to tell me?"

What kind of stupid question is that? Get your shit together if you wanna get out of here alive.

"I asked you first," David replied. "What do you know about the Road Runners?"

Martin looked around the room, all eyes staring back in anxious anticipation. Sonya still refused to make eye contact. *What did you get us into?*

"Okay," Martin said. He was outnumbered and could only talk his way out of this situation. "All I know is what I've been told by Chris. I assume you know who that is."

The whole room laughed, David nodding with a cheesy smile. "Oh, yeah, we know him. Let's hear what he told you about us."

"Well, he's always told me to be on the lookout. That you're dangerous and will go to any extremes to recruit someone to join the Road Runners."

How the fuck did I get into this mess already? Martin felt surprisingly calm once he started talking. Maybe they weren't as bad as Chris made them out. They had all shared a laugh twice already. Then again, psychotic people laugh, too.

"He told me to stay on the run, to avoid being captured. He told me there is a war between you and him. He also said you were all responsible for killing Calvin in 1996 by burning down his liquor store."

David smirked at this last part and nodded. "Well, it sounds like Chris has fed you a lot of bullshit. I expected as much. We're used to it. Who knows the last time he's told the truth?"

Martin watched Sonya nod to herself, and he could take no more. "Sonya, tell me what's going on. Right now."

All eyes in the room turned to Martin's girlfriend.

"I'm sorry, Martin," she said. "I know this is hard; I was just doing my job."

"Doing what job?" Martin demanded. The truth was knocking on his door, but he refused to answer it.

"My job was to get you here. I'm sorry." She spoke flatly and stared into space. "I'm a recruiter for the Road Runners."

Martin watched these words hang in the air as all eyes returned their focus to him. The room fell silent as he processed this disturbing truth. If the room wasn't full of strangers, he likely would have allowed himself to vomit all over the table. After a minute, he finally spoke. "So our entire time together has been one big lie? The night we met at the bar, you already knew what the next six months held?"

"All I knew was that you would be there and I needed you to fall in love with me. I didn't know how anything would turn out, especially your coma. We would have never let that happen if we knew about it."

"So the entire time I thought I was keeping this life and death secret about time travel, and you already knew."

127

Sonya shrugged and remained silent.

Falling in love with Sonya became the highlight of his trip to 1996, especially after he failed to save Izzy. Sonya, his first true love since Lela, turned out to be a hoax.

"So it was all a lie?" he asked. "The story about your grandparents. Us. All of it?"

Sonya nodded.

"Well, good for you. You must be quite the professional. You don't even seem bothered."

"Of course I'm bothered," she snapped. "This is a dirty job and this particular part is never easy. But we can always move past it."

"Wow, so I'm not even the first schmuck to fall for this trap. I'm honored. Thank you for toying with my life and ruining everything."

Martin wanted to leave these people behind and go home to 2018. Hopefully his bar was stocked, because long nights of drinking awaited.

David spoke. "Look, Martin, there's a lot to process here. And we fully intend on giving you time to decide, but there are some things you need to know before you leave here today."

Martin stared at the table, trying to listen to David as his mind pieced together the lies from his 1996 life.

"Chris is probably the stupidest person you'll ever meet," David continued. "He finds people at their weakest and talks them into trying his pills. At that point, it's too late to turn back. No one who gets a taste of time travel is simply going to walk away from the opportunity to right a wrong in the past. He's got that much figured out, I'll give him that. He really does feed on people's emotions. He loves sorrow and fear, and tries to create that when he exchanges the bottle of Juice."

"If Chris is so bad, then why doesn't he just keep the Juice for himself and leave people emotionally scarred?" Martin asked. "He has no reason to hand it over unless he was honest."

"It's all a big game to him," David said. "He loves destroying people and watching them try to fix everything. He's sick. But this is where he gets stupid, you see. He gives the Juice out to so many people and never questions their loyalty. They enter this realm of time travel thinking it's going to be some constant life adventure, not that they'll be forced to choose a side in this war. He doesn't see the big picture that continually ruining people's lives leads to them seeking revenge. That's where we come in since there are so many of us working to kill him."

"Why kill him?" Martin asked. "Why not strip him of his powers, take his pills and potions away?"

David sat down in the seat across Martin, the tension fading with each question.

"We need to kill him. He's trying to infiltrate each era of history, one country at a time. He takes his knowledge from both the past and future and uses it to manipulate the world."

Martin recalled when Chris had mentioned he was tending to a war in Africa. Had he caused the war?

"What about Calvin?" Martin asked.

David nodded. "We did kill him. He was working for Chris and plotting an attack on us."

"So you shot him and burned his store to the ground?"

David sighed. "This is a war, Martin. It's not pretty. Our people have died. Their people have died. We're fighting for a world of prosperity. Do you know how much good can be done with this gift we have?"

Martin wanted to trust these Road Runners, but they had

tricked and lured him into a fake hotel tour. Sonya manipulated him and played him like a fiddle. They might preach about all the good they do, but their tactics were simply off the mark.

"Who's to say Chris isn't doing good? Why are you so convinced you're the only ones doing good?" Martin asked, a hint of rage suppressed in his voice.

"Martin," David said sternly. "We've been following Chris for years. Hundreds of years, or even thousands. It's hard to tell time for sure when you're constantly jumping around. We have people in his inner circle, learning more and more. We know what he's planning. We know he's not human and can't be killed through traditional means. He's very complex, and all we want to do is overthrow him before we live in a world of darkness."

"Then why not capture him?" Martin asked. "If you already have your people surrounding him, tie him up and bring him here."

David shook his head. "It would never happen. He constantly has two dozen people watching him. It's impossible to get him. He rolls deep with security—has more protection than the president. Even if we did manage to capture him, all that does is put a target on our back. It would be a manhunt around the clock until they found him."

Martin understood and nodded. "Why do you need me? I don't have any special skills."

"We need everyone we can get. We're setting up eyes all around the world, all throughout time, watching, learning. The more coverage we get, the closer we get to cracking the code on how to take him down. Like I mentioned, we don't expect you to make a decision right now, but we do expect you to make the right one in due time. You can always find me here at this hotel if you decide to stick around. Should you choose to go back to 2018, you can find a gentleman named Adrian in this same hotel. He'll know who you are. How about you take a week to think matters over and get back to us?"

Martin sat silently, staring at his twiddling thumbs. The Road Runners were as good as advertised. They made a flawless sales pitch on why he should join them, but something whispered in the depths of his mind to hold off. Give it the full time to think over—his mind currently consumed with what the fuck had happened with Sonya.

"Okay, I'll get back to you guys by next week. Not sure if I plan on staying here or not, though." Martin spoke confidently and maintained relentless eye contact with David.

"We appreciate that, Martin. We'll see you upstairs and act like we're finishing the tour so you can leave here without any suspicion."

David slapped the table and stood, everyone in the room shifting toward the door. Martin rose and followed suit. One of the large men who had stood guard pulled open the door and stepped into the hallway.

A pistol fired and the man collapsed to the ground into a pool of his own blood. Everyone froze in place, still safe inside the conference room.

"Well, well, well," a familiar voice said from the hallway.

"It's *him*!" David whispered loud enough for everyone to hear. They all drew guns from their waists, cocking them in a harmonic unison, and pointing them at the door.

The fallen man twitched on the ground as the footsteps grew louder and Chris appeared in the doorway, grinning with his hands held high in the air.

"Oh no, please don't shoot me," he mocked.

"What do you want?" David demanded.

Chris ignored him, looking around the room and nodding his head to everyone who pointed a gun his way. "Sonya, my dear, always a pleasure to see you." He turned his attention to David, who had taken a step in front of the defenseless Martin. "I'm here for Martin. I'm no longer sitting back and watching as you gouge my people. Time to take action. You can hand him over and we leave peacefully, or I can have my crew of twenty men come in and take him by force, leaving you all here in an orgy of death. How does that sound?"

David held his ground, but didn't say anything, locked in a staredown with the old man.

"I'll go," Martin said. "No need for people to die because of me." He stepped around David and patted him on the back in a gesture of faith as he passed.

"How noble of you," Chris said. "I thought for sure they would have already brainwashed you about how evil I am."

"Chris, these people are full of shit," Martin said. Chris howled maniacally at this, grabbing his gut.

"That they are. Let's get out of here."

Chris turned and left the room. Martin looked back to David and nodded quickly before following. He looked to Sonya, who stared back with a blank expression.

It's over, Martin. She's gone. You've been conned. Just leave.

So he left without a word.

19

Chapter 19

Chris really did have twenty men in the hallway. Two of them had made a quick disposal of the dead body and rejoined the group by the time Chris and Martin stepped out of the conference room.

"Is everything ready?" Chris asked.

"Yes, sir," a short man squeaked from the group.

"Perfect, let's gather round," Chris said. The group huddled around the old man and Martin watched from two paces behind, unsure what to do. He glanced back and saw David peeking out of the door, but not stepping fully into the hallway as a handful of Chris's men still had their guns pointed in his direction.

"Martin, your Juice," Chris said, pulling Martin's flask from his inner coat pocket. Martin stared at it in amazement. "This is what I really went over for last night. Just wanted to see where you were hiding it so we could bring it to you today." Chris returned to the huddle and stepped aside to allow space for Martin. "Now, everyone, let's return to the main headquarters."

The men nodded and pulled their own flasks from their jackets, taking quick swigs of the Juice and promptly lying down on the ground.

Chris put his face in front of Martin's. "Go to the year 1981. Follow us outside and be ready to hop on the bus picking us up. We'll be going to a private jet to take us to our headquarters. Go to 1981 right now or I'll come back and slit your throat."

Martin had dozens of questions, but Chris quickly lay down, closed his eyes, and fell into an immediate sleep as his soul presumably traveled to 1981. He looked around, considered a trip back to 2018 instead, and immediately rejected it. Now was not the time to get cute with the old man.

Martin twisted the top off of his flask, took a sip, and lay down, thinking repeatedly of 1981. The familiar dizziness filled his head as he closed his eyes and slipped into unconsciousness.

1981, he thought a final time before falling asleep in 1919.

* * *

Martin promptly woke up in the same spot, as did the rest of the men who had fallen asleep in a big circle around him in the Oxford Hotel's basement. They were all on their feet by the time Martin arrived.

"Okay, we're all here," Chris said once Martin opened his eyes. "Let's head up to the bus."

Chris pulled Martin up by the arm as Martin shook his head to clear the fog that accompanied a heavy sleep.

The hallway they had arrived in appeared the exact same

as the one they had left, newer lights in the ceiling the only visible upgrade.

"Take the stairs," Chris demanded. "Quickly."

The men formed a single-file line and marched toward a door at the end of the hallway, past the conference room where the Road Runners had just held Martin hostage 60 years in the past, or two minutes ago, depending how you viewed it.

Martin, not knowing what the hell was going on, joined the back of the line, Chris rounding out the group behind him.

Boots clapped along the concrete ground, echoing throughout the hall as the line of men disappeared into the stairwell. Once in the stairwell, the sound reflected louder in the tighter space, like a marching band squeezed into a public bathroom.

They climbed one flight to reach the main level, just next to the main entrance, where they swiftly poured out of the hotel and back onto 18th Street. Martin followed and was relieved to see numerous skyscrapers in the city. They had certainly reached 1981 as Union Station also appeared in its more modernized version with neon lighting on its exterior.

"Around the corner!" a man from the group shouted as they slowed to a powerwalk.

The sidewalks were empty of foot traffic, suggesting it must have been the middle of a workday. It only became crowded during the lunch hour and after 3 P.M. when people started leaving for home.

They walked the direction opposite of Union Station and turned right at the next intersection where a small black bus waited. It reminded Martin of the kind that would eventually become commonly used as party buses, only this one lacked the flashing lights and built in ice chests full of beer bottles.

An older man with a white beard and a black fedora craned

his neck as the group filed onto the bus. He had a cranky expression, his face scrunched into years of fatigue.

"We're all here," Chris said as they filled the bus. "Let's move!"

He clapped his hands excitedly.

Martin sensed they were being followed based on the urgency with which Chris barked his orders. After learning firsthand what the Road Runners' main objective was, he didn't exactly feel safe sitting in a bus full of Chris and his men. What if they tried to bomb it? Surely they would sacrifice Martin's life if it meant wiping Chris and twenty of his goons off the planet.

He shook the violent images that filled his head and stared out the window as he plopped down in a seat near the front. Chris had sat directly behind the driver and they appeared to be catching up on the day's activities.

Martin watched as the city passed by his window. Everything had changed since 1919, both in the buildings and the few people he saw out for an afternoon stroll. Gone were the days of everyone dressed in suits and magnificent gowns. Now people wore jeans, mullets, and carried boom boxes over their shoulders. *We're definitely in the 80's.*

The bus rumbled through the city, reaching the freeway within five minutes and revving up to a much higher speed. The men remained silent, keeping to themselves and looking out their windows. Martin hadn't noticed earlier that they were all wearing sunglasses and long pea coats, looking like a group of mobsters on their way to a fancy dinner.

Chris leaned back in his seat and Martin took the chance to move up one row to speak with him, sliding in beside the old man.

"I know you have questions," Chris said. "You always do."

"Can you blame me?" Martin replied. "You like to leave all of the details out when we speak."

Chris smirked. "I literally warned you last night about the Road Runners, and you still managed to get captured within 24 hours. You're not the sharpest knife in the drawer, my friend. A hotel tour? Really?"

"They told me you're trying to rule the world. Is that true?"

Chris sighed. "These people will say anything to recruit and brainwash. I'm not trying to rule the world. I'm part of a coalition trying to make the world a better place. I have counterparts on each continent. I'm in charge of tying to gain control over North America, as my counterparts are trying to take control of their continents."

Sounds an awful lot like trying to rule the world, Martin thought.

Chris laughed. "We're not trying to rule the world."

Shit. Martin forgot that Chris could hear his thoughts.

"If we wanted to rule the world," Chris continued. "We would've done that already. It's as easy as manipulating some governments and running them from the inside. In a sense, that's what we're trying to do, but not in the evil ways it may sound."

"So you're glorified lobbyists?"

Chris nodded. "You could say that. We definitely have the funds to lobby for anything we desire."

The bus rattled as it slowed, turning off the highway. They had driven ten minutes east of downtown and arrived to Stapleton, a small neighborhood only known for its airport in 1981.

"We're here, gentlemen," Chris announced, standing and

facing the rest of the crew. "Remember to get on the plane quickly. Dinner will be served."

The bus turned into the airport grounds and drove around a small building to the back where private hangars awaited, each with private jets lined up neatly beside each other.

"You have your own jet?" Martin asked. "I thought you could go wherever you want – why waste your time flying?"

Chris chuckled. "Martin, please. I'm not Harry Potter. I can go to any *time* I want. If I need to go somewhere else in the world, I still have to physically travel there."

"Where are we going?" he asked.

"Our headquarters are in Alaska," Chris said.

"Alaska?"

"Yes. It's a perfect hideaway. And it's not just Alaska; it's northern Alaska, practically on a glacier. No one ever thinks of going there, or even *wants* to go there. I'm pretty sure your Road Runner friends know about it, though, and I believe they've set up a similar type of hideout nearby."

The bus came to a complete stop at the last hangar, and the doors swung open.

"Let's go, gentlemen!" Chris commanded, leading the way out.

Martin followed him into the hangar where they approached a luxurious private jet with glossy blue and red exterior, appearing freshly waxed. There were no words, logos, or anything that could identify the plane as belonging to anyone in particular.

Chris approached the stairs that led up to the jet and walked up without any hesitation. He looked over his shoulder and waved to his group of confidants below, still making their way across the hangar.

Martin followed, his legs trembling with each step, not sure what the hell he was getting into. *I don't belong with this group of people. They all carry guns and sit in silence, taking orders from Chris like he's the goddamn president. I just want to explore, not get caught in the middle of this stupid war.*

Martin entered the jet to find a world of luxury. It was clearly from the future, not 1981, as flat screen TVs hung on the walls, oak tables decorated the lounge, and wide, cushioned recliners were the only options for sitting. Laptops and tablets were piled neatly on the tables, and Martin longed for a return to 2018. It felt like a mere pit stop between the trips to 1996 and 1919, and now 1981.

Where is my true self? he wondered. When he left for 1919, his body was asleep in his bedroom in 2018. But when he jumped from 1919 to 1981, what happened then? Could he fall seven dimensions like that movie *Inception*?

And what the fuck happened with Sonya? *Is she really a Road Runner? Or is this all some big joke?*

His chest felt like it had taken a bullet in the heart, the blood of his pain spreading throughout his body. His mind waited in a state of shock for the truth to reveal itself, and he found himself unable to focus his thoughts on anything aside from his six months of life with Sonya in 1996.

You're stunned. That's what this is. Just like the morning you realized Izzy was gone, and just like the night you accepted that she was never coming back. Stunned.

If she really was a Road Runner, then all of their time spent together had to have been part of some epic plan to get him to join their team. What other explanation was there for them to all end up in a hotel basement together?

She played you. Your wife fucked your brother, and your new girlfriend only dragged you along to fight on her team. Now here you are, on an airplane with a madman, and your life no longer in your own hands.

Whatever was happening, he'd have to wait for answers. The rest of the crew piled into the jet, conversation a low murmur among them all. Chris grabbed a recliner in the main lounge and ordered a meal from a young waiter who had appeared out of nowhere.

Martin approached the old man.

"Chris, I'd like to know what's going on," he said calmly, even though he wanted to burst with a flood of questions.

Chris looked up to Martin and rolled his eyes. "My god, Marty, can you ever just sit down and relax? All you ever want to do is ask questions. I've told you we're going to our headquarters. We'll have a meeting when we get there to discuss our next steps. Now find a spot and shut up. You're on a fully equipped, private jet with anything you can imagine. Order dinner, have a drink, I don't care. Just leave me alone."

"Sorry."

Martin left Chris and found a lone recliner looking out a window. The old man had really snapped at him, making him feel like a disciplined child sitting in timeout. He didn't know if he should mingle with the men in pea coats and sunglasses, and decided to keep to himself.

Everyone had settled in their spots as the airplane rumbled to life. The lights dimmed, and many of the men removed their sunglasses and slid sleeping masks over their eyes. Martin wanted to sleep, exhausted from the day's events, but his mind wouldn't allow it.

Something had felt off since Chris and his gang arrived. Were they really there to rescue him from the Road Runners? He sensed that more was at stake. Why did both sides show such an interest in a middle-aged, out-of-shape man with no skills aside from chugging beer and whiskey? Martin only had to take a quick look around to see that he was the only one who didn't belong with the rest of the group.

All of the men seemed like programmed robots, rarely speaking to each other, obediently doing exactly as Chris demanded. Nothing about them seemed realistic except for the fact that they *looked* like humans.

Could Chris be trying to brainwash me and turn me into one of them?

Martin lay back in his recliner, his brain torn between sleep and a desire to keep his eyes open. The latter won, and he watched Chris for the entire duration of the six-hour flight. The old man eventually fell asleep after finishing his steak dinner.

What are you really *up to?*

20

Chapter 20

Six hours later the plane landed in the small town of Barrow, Alaska. The pilot announced their arrival, but Martin had no idea where to find the city on a map. Chris explained it was the northernmost tip of the state with a shore that touched the Arctic Ocean. The city had an airport with a small neighborhood practically on the landing strip.

The jet's door opened and they filed out, Martin gawking at the Arctic Ocean in his immediate view, glaciers floating like giant ice cubes. He had never seen a glacier, or iceberg, or whatever the hell they were called.

Giant chunks of ice.

He immediately shivered, as the town was known for high temperatures in the mid-30s. The heatwaves of summer might push the thermometer to 45 on a good day.

The airport was smaller than the one they had left in Stapleton, a lone office building standing at the end of the airstrip, with only one hangar that housed two other jets.

Another bus waited for them, and they wasted no time crossing the tarmac to enter it.

"Welcome home, gentlemen," Chris said proudly once everyone had settled into the bus. "We have some long days ahead of us, so tonight will be a relaxing night. If you didn't eat on the plane—which it didn't look like anyone did—get a good dinner tonight and sit back, watch a movie, read a book—whatever you do to unwind. Tonight we will all return to the current time in 2018. Tomorrow we'll start planning to get another of our own back, just like we rescued Martin today."

Chris looked down to Martin, who sat in the row behind him again, and winked.

One of our own? Martin thought, then immediately shut down his mind since he was close to Chris. He hadn't declared an allegiance to any side in this fight, and didn't intend to. He just wanted to go home, dump his bottle of Juice down the drain, and pretend none of this had ever happened. No 1996, no witnessing Izzy's death, no Sonya. None of it.

You can't do that now, remember? his mind cut back in. *Your mother now has dementia because of you, or did you forget already? Are you really going to leave her to rot away in her own mind? Let her talk to you like a complete stranger?*

The bus ride had only lasted ten minutes when they turned onto a dirt road for another mile and pulled up to a mansion that looked as large as the White House. The dirt road gave way to cobblestone and led them to a wide roundabout in front of the house. A thin layer of snow covered what would have been a lawn. The mansion was made of dark stone, reminding Martin of a medieval castle. Two rows of a dozen windows lined the front, all of equal size.

"What is this place?" Martin asked when the bus came to a complete stop.

Chris looked over his shoulder with his usual grin. "My house. Our headquarters. *Chateau de Chris.* Whatever you want to call it. It's where you'll be living for the next few weeks while we figure out what to do."

"Do with what?"

"With the Road Runners. We'll have plenty of time tomorrow to discuss. Tonight is all about relaxing. I know that's a difficult concept for you, but give it a try. You might even smile for once."

Martin couldn't take any more of Chris's snide remarks. No, he didn't want to relax. He had lost his daughter, his mother, his girlfriend, his life as he knew it. If things could go back to the way they were, drinking into oblivion every night, eating his pistol once a year, then he could relax. Routine brought him the calm he desired, not being kidnapped and flown to the fucking North Pole.

The bus door slid open, and the robotic men all stood and filled the aisle, waiting for Chris to lead the way. It became more apparent with each passing second that these men were incapable of thinking for themselves. They simply followed Chris around all day and did as they were told.

Chris rose, bones cracking and popping, and led the parade to the mansion.

The house had no exterior decorations, a plain fortress on a private lot, far from the town that was already off the map. They reached the entrance, a lone wooden door, and Chris pulled it open, leading the crew inside.

The interior was something out of a movie, and certainly didn't fit in this small town. They walked into an entryway with a spiral staircase that led up one level and down another. A kitchen was to the left, and a lounge area to the right. A crystal chandelier hung above them, illuminating the room with abstract paintings as decorations.

Martin stood frozen as the men all made their way up the stairs to the second floor. He looked up to the skylight windows that provided a glimpse of the gray sky.

"Shall we?" Chris asked once the men had cleared out, leaving them in silence, the only audible sound a fireplace crackling somewhere around the corner. "Quite the scare the Road Runners gave you back there."

Chris crossed his arms and waited for Martin to respond.

"Yeah. They didn't seem too evil. In fact, they were gonna let me walk out before you showed up."

"Oh, please. They only play nice to try and trick you into trusting them. How can you trust a group who sent Sonya to trap you?"

Martin had tried to push Sonya out of his mind, wanting to forget the fact that she had been playing him like a used piano since they first met. All of the lovemaking, late-night talks, and romantic dinners had been a lie to land him in a basement conference room with the Road Runners.

"I'd rather not talk about that," Martin said.

"Understood. Let me show you around." Chris raised his arms as if soaking in his surroundings. "This house is four levels. We're on the main level. Kitchen, lounge, laundry – pretty much any of your basic needs. Food is always stocked and nothing is off limits on this floor. Make yourself at home."

He shuffled to the stairwell. "Downstairs is the basement and somewhere you'll never need to go. We have an entire team down there conducting research throughout history and the future, creating databases and algorithms, and a bunch of other things I don't really understand until they summarize it in a weekly report for me."

Martin joined Chris at the stairwell and looked down to a pit of darkness. Chris pointed up.

"Upstairs has two more floors. The top floor is all bedrooms. The second floor has more bedrooms along with meeting spaces and my main office—well, more of an office and bedroom combo. It's where you'll usually find me."

"I take it I have one of these bedrooms?"

"Of course. You'll be on the second floor. I've already stocked your closet with winter clothes, or else you'll freeze to death in this city. The highs are usually in the 30s, but the nights get as low as 20 below. You'll want to stay inside, but don't worry, our lounge has a fully stocked bar."

"Sounds like quite the bachelor pad."

Chris cackled. "It certainly is. Any questions?"

Martin wasn't given much of a tour but more of an explanation of the layout. He'd have to explore on his own apparently, although it seemed there wasn't much to look at beyond the main level.

"Yes. Are your men okay? They seem a bit . . . out of it."

"Ahhh, yes. They're just fine. You see, traveling through time in rapid succession is very draining on the mind. Me and my men had just jumped around ten different decades looking for you. We have eyes all over. There were lots of false tips claiming to have seen you. The guys are just drained and need to sleep. That's why they slept on the flight and will probably sleep right through lunchtime tomorrow."

Martin nodded. "I'm pretty tired myself. I didn't get any sleep on the plane."

Chris grinned and started up the stairs. "Follow me, I'll show you to your room."

Martin followed up the spiral staircase, looking over the edge to the basement, nothing but a black pit of death. He felt the perfectly human urge to go where forbidden. What was really down there?

They reached the second floor landing and Martin looked both ways down a hallway that stretched far into the distance.

"This way is all the bedrooms," Chris said, pointing to the left. "The other side is my office and other meeting rooms. If the doors are open to a meeting room you're more than welcome to use the space. If closed, you need stay out. There can be highly confidential meetings taking place."

"Understood," Martin said, inching further into the hallway.

"Now, follow me." Chris turned left and led the way down the hall, stopping at a door only three from the end. The old man rummaged in his pocket and pulled out a small silver key. "This is for you. All bedrooms are complete with queen-sized beds, bathrooms, dining rooms, and satellite TV. If there's anything else you wish to have, just let me know and I'll see what we can do."

"Thanks." Martin didn't know what else to say, and now that the excitement of being kidnapped twice had worn off, his head spun in fatigue.

"I'll leave you to it. Come find me if you need anything today. I'll introduce you to our house assistant tomorrow. He'll be the one you can go to anytime for anything. Have a nice nap."

Chris nodded and turned, strolling down the hall and disappearing into a door on the opposite end.

Martin jiggled his key in the door and pushed it open to a breathtaking view. Past the bed and mounted flat screen TV was a window overlooking a blanket of whiteness. This mansion was hidden in the middle of an open field with the ground covered in at least two inches of snow as far as he could see. Having lived his entire life in Colorado, he couldn't recall ever seeing an area of land so flat. Snow-capped trees completed the landscape that looked like a Bob Ross painting.

He sat on the foot of his bed, wondering how Chris managed life this far from civilization. Within seconds, Martin's body and mind gave way as he sprawled across the bed, staring at the ceiling, falling in to a heavy slumber.

21

Chapter 21

"I think we need to send him to the basement," Chris said. He sat in his dim office, the curtains drawn, and his trusted confidant, Duane, across the desk. Chris kept a tight inner circle, but Duane was the only one he could tell anything.

Duane had been there since day one, always curious and willing to test new theories in the past or future, willing to do anything short of risking his life. It was the sort of loyalty that money couldn't buy, and Chris needed that. Everyone else closest to him had lucrative incomes, leaving him to wonder if they remained obedient because of the money or if they truly believed in their work.

Duane nodded, his wavy brown hair jiggling slightly. He snapped his round-framed glasses off his face and rubbed tired, brown eyes. "If you say so."

"Do you not agree?" Chris asked. Duane rarely disagreed with him, so when he did, he knew there was a good reason.

"We've reached an unfortunate point in this war, Chris," Duane said, standing up. He was of average height and build, and always wore a fine suit. "We're at a crossroads. Right now we have fifty Road Runners in our basement."

"There's room for fifty more," Chris added.

"No. Listen. We've reached a point where there's so many people traveling through time that they make friends and develop relationships. They bond. They become important to each other. When someone goes missing, they all know about it. They make plans to find their friends. We have reason to believe the Road Runners have increased their surveillance and are implanting location chips into their people. Just to find you."

"What are you getting at?" Chris had heard enough and wanted to get to the point.

"We can't keep taking people and stashing them in the basement. It's going to get us caught at some point."

"My soldiers are highly trained and won't make mistakes."

"It's not about mistakes. One day we're not gonna be fast enough when we take someone. You didn't know it, but someone had followed you out the hotel when you took Briar. They were on foot and couldn't follow once you got on the bus, but it's one step closer. Next time, there will be someone ready in a car to follow you. I wish you'd stop snatching people every time you get a hunch. But at this point, I think it's best for you to let Briar go. Put him on a flight back to Denver, and wish him the best. We can only hope he won't run off to the Road Runners, but we are getting crushed in that department anyway. They're 200,000 strong now."

"And we're 1,000,000. You worry too much."

"They were only 50,000 two years ago and we were at 600,000. You tell me if you like the direction of that trend."

Chris leaned back in his seat. Duane loved to discuss numbers and strategy like he was a general in charge of a war.

While he appreciated the information, Chris believed in bold approaches to problems.

"So then we should kill everyone in the basement. Briar, too."

Duane shook his head. "You're not understanding. That's not going to do anything but keep the search alive. We have two options: release them slowly back into the world, or kill them and publicly dispose of their bodies so the Road Runners know it's one their own."

Chris grinned. "Now you're talking my language."

"That doesn't mean it's the best option. That only leaves more clues behind. You know how advanced science becomes in the future; leaving a corpse behind puts us at a high risk of being caught."

"Fine. I'll think it over. But Briar needs to go. He slept with Sonya, and I can't forgive that."

"*You* need to let that go. Your daughter has slept with *numerous* people to trap them. She's gone, Chris. A full-blooded Road Runner, probably because you act so goddamn selfish all the time."

"Selfish?" Chris sat forward, hands in the air. "I give people my Gift. I let them share it with others and spread the joy. And you call me selfish?"

Chris knew Duane didn't have the energy to stay in arguments for too long, and rejoiced when his friend sat back down.

"You know what I mean, and I'll just leave it at that. You drove Sonya out of your life. No one else did."

"You know, Duane, you've told me that plenty of times before. I don't need a constant reminder of how things played out. If I need your opinion on my past, I'll ask you for it. Otherwise, I'd appreciate if you'd stick to business."

"What are you gonna do, Chris? Fire me? Kill me? Throw me in the basement? I don't like bringing these things up, but sometimes you go off the rails and I need to mention it."

Chris glared across the desk. "You've always been good to me, and I'd never do such a thing to you. You just need to stay in your lane. Now if you wouldn't mind leaving me be, I need a moment alone."

Duane sighed and let himself out of the office.

Chris crossed his hands on his desk and plopped his head down. He couldn't take any more arguing. He had lots of meetings lined up over the next few days, and even more difficult decisions to make.

He needed to interview Martin, see where he stood with matters before making the rash decision of sending him to the basement. A quick visit to the basement was in line as well. It had been a couple of months since Chris had stopped by to visit his enemies.

Chris rose from his seat and paced circles around the office, hoping he wouldn't have to send another lost cause to the basement. Martin didn't seem infected by the Road Runners; he did follow them this far, after all, without any protest, murder attempts, or acts of violence like others before him.

Martin was a perfect citizen, and Chris had no reason to suspect he was working with the Road Runners, but something felt off. The way Sonya had played him surely left him scarred and hurt. There are fewer things more frightening than a person with nothing to lose.

Chris left his office space and crossed to his bedroom at the opposite end. He sat on his bed and pulled open the nightstand drawer to retrieve a photo.

His fingers trembled with the picture of the young girl

smiling with her father. She was his world, and it showed in his eyes – youthful, sparkling, and excited for the future.

"Angelina," Chris said, brushing two fingers over the portrait. "Where did we go so wrong?"

He thought back to what felt like thousands of years ago when Angelina was a little girl, many years away from changing her name to Sonya. Time became jumbled when constantly traveling through it, so much that Chris often forgot where he came from. Seeing the picture always returned him to memory lane, and the perfect life he once had.

For now, he needed to stop by the basement and see his daughter's goons.

He placed the old portrait back in the nightstand and rose from the bed, crossing to a small door in the corner. Chris enjoyed having his own private elevator to get from floor to floor. At his age, the stairs took too much of a toll on his body. But he would take them in the presence of company, to show that he had no weakness.

He called the elevator with a quick push of the button on the wall and pulled open the door as it arrived. The car stood seven feet tall and was wide enough for two people to stand comfortably. Chris never let anyone besides Duane ride along with him, and even that was on rare occasions; he liked to have these stolen moments to himself.

He stepped into the elevator, pushed the *B* on the panel, and watched his office disappear from sight as he went down two levels to the dark basement. The elevator opened to a pitch-black corner of the basement; he liked to surprise his prisoners and never wanted them to know when he arrived.

He stepped out and turned the dark corner into the open space.

Everything he had told Martin about the basement was a lie. It wasn't some elaborate research center with dozens of men working toward a greater good. It was a prison for captured Road Runners.

The room stretched the length and width of a football field. Tape decorated the concrete ground, forming three by three foot squares, appearing like a life-sized chess board. Each prisoner was assigned a square, and only 50 of the 100 available spaces were occupied. Chris dreamed of filling the basement with desperate Road Runners.

Chris believed in killing only as a last resort. Road Runners held useful knowledge about their plot to overthrow him, and he wanted to gather all of the information possible. Perhaps the basement was a research center of sorts, after all.

Each square had a steel hook bolted into the ground and a shackle running from it to each prisoner's ankle. The shackles allowed them to reach the edge of their squares, nothing more, nothing less. Prisoners were given three meals a day, and had to relieve their bowels in whatever corner of their squares that they chose. One pillow and one blanket were provided after dinnertime.

The basement was usually silent, the forty plus men and handful of women all sitting in their squares, knowing they were hidden and wiped off the map.

"No one will ever find you where we are," Chris would tell them each upon arrival to the dark and dank room. "Ninety nine percent of the population can't even find this place on a map."

He loved teasing them with this line, watching all hope flee from their eyes.

The lighting in the basement was as bright as a movie theater.

The prisoners could all see each other, but not well enough to know who was who. With plenty of vacant spaces, Chris had the prisoners kept at least three squares apart to avoid any sort of plotting, not that there was a way to escape the shackles.

Road Runners were still a smart bunch—loyal, too—and he couldn't afford to have them brainstorming with each other.

When Chris emerged from the darkness all fifty prisoners stood up and started howling and screaming at him, making him feel like an infamous athlete stepping onto the field. He loved being hated by his enemies. Loved having them trapped as his prisoners. Sometimes when they screamed, he'd get an erection, about the only thing that aroused him any more at his ripe old age.

Not today, though. Today was a matter of business, not pleasure, in his visit to the basement.

I really should take away their ability to speak, he thought as the screaming grew louder.

Chris waved his hands in a shushing gesture. "Good evening, everybody," he shouted so the prisoners in the back could hear him. "Does anyone have information on Martin Briar?"

The prisoners looked around the room at each other, shrugging their shoulders.

"He is possibly one of you. I may grant a release for anyone who can provide information on Mr. Briar."

"I know some things," a voice shouted from the middle of the room. The voice came from square number 37, Terry Brooks, a short, thin man in his late 40's.

"Ah, Mr. Brooks. Perhaps today is your lucky day," Chris said with a grin. "I'll see to it that a guard brings you to a conference room so we can have a little talk about Mr. Briar. Our new arrival is sleeping, so plan to be moved in the next five minutes. As for the rest of you, have a pleasant night."

Chris bowed his head before turning back for the hidden elevator. The screams erupted again as he strolled away, and this time a slight amount of blood rushed to his crotch.

You're all mine. Forever.

He disappeared into the shadows to return to his office.

22

Chapter 22

Terry Brooks had lived a luxurious life as a Road Runner. He had millions in the bank and a huge Victorian house for him and his wife, settling comfortably in the year 2030. He had worked as a recruiter for the Road Runners before getting captured by Chris's people, and every day sitting in that shithole basement reminded him of the bad decision that had landed him there.

He knew better than to pursue new arrivals right away. They were always fresh arrivals from the University of Bullshit, taught exclusively by the crazy old man. The Road Runners may have passed the old man in terms of a long-term strategy, but Chris grew wiser by the day. They needed to be careful to not lose any of the valuable ground they had gained. This was still Chris's world, and they were only living in it until he one day croaked.

Terry had climbed high in the ranks, attending quarterly meetings with the Forerunners, the leadership group who overlooked the entirety of the Road Runners. He had received heavy pressure to increase recruits, and Terry promised to deliver. He had worked with Sonya on the plan to land Martin Briar, a prized target for the organization to acquire.

Martin still didn't know it, but he just might hold the key to taking down Chris. Terry wondered if Chris knew this, but if so, why have a discussion about the matter with another Road Runner? Why not just throw Martin in the basement and toss his key into the Arctic Ocean?

Yes, Terry knew where he was on the map, and yes, the Road Runners knew about the headquarters. Infiltrating the headquarters was another story. Guards covered the premises in a blanket of force and intimidation. Chris deserved credit for having an army of savage men ready to kill anything or anyone who posed a threat.

Bombing the mansion had been briefly discussed and promptly dismissed, no one wanting to take responsibility for the blood of 50 Road Runners, even if it was for the greater good.

"Brooks!" a voice barked from one of the mindless guards who hovered over the prisoners like a hawk. "On your knees, hands behind your head!"

Terry did as ordered, knowing any single disobeyed command could result in a bullet in the skull. He had seen a handful of friends go out this way, and it was never a pleasant sight.

A rifle jammed against his spine as he knelt with his trembling hands on the back of his head.

Just remember, you're more important than Briar. The Forerunners need you, not Briar.

"On your feet!" the voice shouted.

Terry couldn't see them, but knew at least two other guards hid in the shadows, guns pointed directly at his head. The shackles around his ankles jingled as someone worked their way around the ground with a set of keys clanging with every movement. Within seconds, the pressure around his ankles released, and he was free to walk outside of his tiny square.

"Try anything cute and you'll be dead," the deep voice said from behind.

"Understood," Terry responded in a wavering voice.

"Hopkins!" The voice returned to a shout. "Let's move!"

Hopkins must have been one of the guards hiding in the shadows. A tall, muscular man emerged from the darkness with a mean grin, and stepped in front of Terry who had to look up to meet the man's eyes.

All of these motherfuckers look the same. Giant cavemen with no mind of their own.

"Follow me and put these on," Hopkins said, clicking on a flashlight to illuminate the path ahead while handing over a pair of thick sunglasses.

"What are these for?"

"You've been sitting in the dark for months. If you don't wear those, you'll go blind the second you step out of the basement."

Terry marched at the same pace as Hopkins, still aware of the rifle directly behind him. He only knew the basement as darkness, nothing visible from the confines of his square, so seeing the rest of the room, albeit limited by a flashlight, was a rare treat.

If I get sent back here, I'll at least know a way out if I can ever break free of the shackles.

The freedom of his legs gliding across the floor reminded him of his old life, where such tasks didn't need to be taken for granted.

They reached a wall where Hopkins pushed forward, swinging open a door to a well-lit stairwell. Terry recognized it as the main spiral staircase from when he had arrived at this hellhole of a mansion over eight months ago.

Eight months, he reminisced. Eight months of eating slop, shitting where he slept, and praying for his fellow Road Runners to break him and his friends out.

"Up we go," Hopkins said with a glance over the shoulder. "No funny business on the stairs or we'll kill you."

I already know that, asshole.

They moved single-file up the stairs, the mystery rifleman trailing behind, patiently waiting for any sudden movement from Terry. They reached the main landing where he saw the house's front door before continuing up to the second floor. So far everything had looked the same from when Terry arrived. Now he approached new territory.

On the second floor, which equaled the basement in eerie silence, he saw a hallway that stretched from his left to his right. Hardwood floors with elongated throw rugs provided a path to dozens of doors on either side of the hallway. Pictures lined the gray walls further down the hall, but Terry couldn't make out their images from a distance.

The rifle nudged him in the back, bringing him back to reality.

"This way," Hopkins said, and turned to the right where there were fewer doors. He led them to the end of the hallway where the last door stood ajar. Hopkins entered the room where Chris sat behind a massive oak desk.

"Ah, Terry Brooks, how are you my old friend?" Chris asked with an evil grin.

Terry fought every urge to rant about their inhumane treatment in the basement, and to let him know that the Road

Runners would take great pleasure in slitting his throat. But, he remembered Chris could read his thoughts and likely didn't give a shit what Terry thought about the living conditions in the basement. This was war, after all.

"I'm doing just fine," Terry said with as much sternness as he could muster. He glanced around the room and admired the lavish lifestyle that Chris had lived. Flat screen TVs lined the walls, a grandfather clock stood in the corner, its pendulum swinging back and forth as each second passed. A canteen of scotch called out to Terry from a table behind Chris's desk.

"Care for a drink?" the old man asked.

As much as he wanted one, Terry didn't trust anything from Chris. He knew too much of the old man's history and how he always surrounded people with temptation.

"No thanks, I just want to leave this place," Terry said.

Chris snickered. "Have a seat, Terry, we have a lot to discuss." He gestured to the chair across the desk. Hopkins stood in the doorway, now equipped with a rifle of his own. Chris nodded to him and Hopkins closed the door, remaining on the outside.

"Now that we have some privacy, Terry, you know I can't just let you go. You're too important to the Road Runners and will just run back and tell them everything about this place."

"We already know about this place."

"Yes, of course, but no one knows what goes on inside this house. I've kept a tight lid, and observations can only be made from the outside. I doubt your people know about the basement."

"We do." Terry bluffed. "But you don't have to worry about me, Chris. I'll live my life in exile. Won't even be that hard if the Road Runners don't know I'm free. You can drop me anywhere in the world and I'll live out my life there. Just get me out of this house."

Chris smirked as he looked down to his crossed hands on the desk. "I'll see what we can arrange. But first, you need to tell me everything you know about Martin Briar. What's the Road Runners' angle in using him? I know him well and don't exactly see him as your typical type of foot soldier."

Terry nodded. "I agree. I actually fought against his recruitment, but our team insists he has a talent."

"A *talent*?"

"I honestly don't know the details. It's been kept under a tight lid. I think only Commander Strike and her inner-circle know about it. But they seem to think he has some special skill."

"Have you met this guy?" Chris asked, sitting up and chuckling. "There isn't much special about him. The guy is a dud, but I'm intrigued at knowing he holds some value for the Road Runners. You're sure you don't know what they love about him?"

"Afraid not, sir. I only know he's highly valued, and it's a secret."

Chris stood up and paced to his window, gazing out to the snowy landscape, stroking his chin. "This is interesting. I suppose I need to make him as comfortable as possible here, really sell him on this life with the Revolution." Terry didn't know if he should respond, so remained silent. "It would be a shame to see him pushed away where you dirty pigs would likely swoop him right up."

"That is probably what will happen, yes."

"Perfect. That's all I needed to know. You can go now."

Terry gulped down the spit that had formed in his mouth.

"What do you mean?"

Chris grinned. "I mean you can leave this house. You've provided me plenty of information and have revealed a new secret weapon. You just better do as promised and not return to the Road Runners. If you do, I'll kill you myself."

"I don't know what to say . . . thank you."

"I'm not as bad as you people think. I'll always be fair when possible, and I'm certainly a man of my word. Hopkins will see you outside."

As a reflex, Terry stuck out his hand to shake with Chris, instantly realizing he didn't owe an ounce of gratitude to the scheming old man who had held him hostage. But mercy was mercy, and all Terry could see in his near-sighted vision was freedom.

"Best of luck," Chris said as the men locked hands. "Hopkins!"

The door creaked open, and Terry's old friend from the basement showed himself with his usual stern, dead expression.

"Please see Mr. Brooks out of the house. He is free to go." Chris gave one final grin to Terry before Hopkins entered the room to lead him out.

"Follow me, Mr. Brooks," Hopkins said in a deep baritone.

Terry followed him back down the hallway, descended the spiral staircase to the main floor, and to the front door that had a half dozen locks for Hopkins to tinker with before pulling it open.

Terry saw the outdoors for the first time in months, and the sight sent an instant flutter to his chest.

Time to get the fuck out of here.

"Thank you," Terry said to Hopkins as he passed him in the doorway and took his first steps into freedom.

163

The crisp air filled his lungs as the orange sun fought to provide heat on a cold day. He'd need a jacket and some thicker clothes, but he'd have time. Besides, the Road Runners kept a secret hideout nearby. Surely they would have some extra clothes for him.

Not knowing which way to go, Terry started for the stand of trees 100 yards in front of him. He'd walk a straight line until he found a city or a road, or the Arctic Ocean. The snow crunched beneath each step as the pine trees ahead swayed in the breeze.

Wait till everyone hears about the basement, he thought, his pace increasing with each step.

Terry looked over his shoulder and stopped in his tracks. The house, now 100 yards behind him, had somewhat shrunk in his vision, but he could still see Hopkins standing on the front porch, a rifle cocked and aimed in his direction.

"No!" Terry shrieked in unison with the rifle's explosion on the otherwise silent day.

For that brief half of a second, Terry swore he saw the bullet fly out from the muzzle. Before he could blink, it struck him square in the forehead, and he collapsed to the ground.

23

Chapter 23

"Holy shit!" Martin panted under his breath. He watched the entire thing unfold, at least from the moment the man started walking across the open field toward the trees. From his window, he could barely make out the guard standing on the porch with the rifle now slung over his shoulder.

He couldn't take his eyes off the dead body, lying limp at the base of a pine tree, face down in the snow. *Who was that? Why was he walking out there? And why did they shoot him? Did he try to escape?*

Without having seen the rest of the mansion, Martin sensed something off about the place. The way the guards all worked together—and all looked the same—he couldn't help but feel a bit like a prisoner. If he wanted to go out for an evening walk, could he? If he asked to borrow a vehicle to drive into town, would they allow such a request?

Regardless of what they allowed him to do, Martin settled on one new priority: getting out of the mansion.

After having an afternoon to sleep and meditate on the last twelve hours of his life, he decided that anything involving

Chris led to no good. Sure, the old man and his army of clones had busted him out of the trap set by the Road Runners, but were the Road Runners really the bad ones in this war? How was Martin supposed to know?

The Road Runners had caused him no harm, and didn't so much as suggest they would. Hell, he had apparently lived with one for six months in 1996 with no sign of danger. So what exactly was their angle?

Something is going on behind the scenes much bigger than you, he told himself. *You're wanted by both sides in this conflict.*

"But why?" he said to his empty bedroom. Since arriving and taking a quick nap, Martin had studied the bedroom further to find it was set up like a hotel room: private bathroom, fridge, closet, ironing board, and the TV mounted to the wall. Landscape paintings hung on the beige walls, showing a glimpse into his Colorado life with a cabin in the snowy mountains.

Martin's internal alarm sounded off, demanding he leave the mansion. His door wasn't locked, and he could wander down the hallway, but he still felt a resistance. His gut told him to remain and wait. How hard could it be to walk out of the mansion? Even if he escaped, he had at least a mile to the main road that led back to town; he couldn't even spot it from his elevated bedroom window.

Stay, the voice in his head said.

A knock came from the door, startling him as he jumped away from the window. *Do they have cameras in here? How would they know I'm awake?*

Martin considered this, knowing Chris could have any sort of technology from the future implanted in his room. The paintings could have cameras in them the size of a needle

166

tip, and there could be microphones as small as ants propped anywhere in the room for listening. And there was still Chris's ability to hear his thoughts. Did he have the range to do such a thing simply by being in the same house?

Clear your mind right now.

Another knock echoed around the room, this time louder and harder.

"I'm coming!" Martin shouted, irritated, as he dragged his feet across the carpet.

He pulled open the door to find a grinning Chris. "May I come in?"

Martin stepped aside and allowed the old man into his room, keeping his mind clear of any thoughts.

"Did I wake you?" Chris asked as he crossed the room to study the portrait on the wall.

"No, I just woke up a few minutes ago."

"Very good. I wanted to see how you're holding up. Today was pure chaos, especially for you."

Martin nodded as Chris turned his attention to him, and closed the door to lean against it.

"I'm doing fine. Glad you got there when you did. I don't know what would have happened if you never showed up. How did you know?"

"When you arrived in 1919, you were being followed from the moment you made it downtown. We followed the Road Runners who were trailing you. This war has progressed to a point where they are becoming a viable threat. They've been poaching people I've given the Juice to by promising a lavish life. A life safe and free from me, like I'm some sort of monster. What these people don't realize is that they can get their dream lives all on their own. How much money did you have waiting in your bank account when you arrived home after your journey to 1996?"

"Millions."

"Exactly. That's because you're smart and a forward thinker. The Road Runners try to plant doubt about me and the success people can find while traveling through time, then they insert themselves as the only solution. It's gross, but I suppose all is fair in love and war, right?"

Martin nodded, continually fighting off the urge to think about his encounter with the Road Runners. "That is true."

Chris smiled as he crossed the room toward the window, and gazed into the landscape where Terry Brooks had just been shot dead like an elk in the woods. "How are you liking the place so far?"

Chris had his back to Martin, and this caused Martin to release the tension in his shoulders that he hadn't realized existed. "My room is nice, very modern, but that's all I've seen. Am I allowed into the rest of the house?" He asked this like a curious child.

Chris chuckled before turning back around to face Martin. "Of course. This can be your home for as long as you'd like, so get yourself acclimated. You're by no means obliged to stay here, but keep in mind the Road Runners are looking for you, so it's not exactly safe out there at the moment. In here, you'll have the highest level of security. No one gets into this house unless I say so."

"I thought you can't die by traditional means. You don't even eat food, right? So why have so much security?"

Chris locked eyes with Martin and sent chills up his spine. "The security isn't for me, old friend. I'll be just fine. It's for the secrets buried in the walls of the house. If the Road

Runners were ever to get ahold of the information that lies within this house, the war would be over in ten minutes."

These words hung in the air as Martin tried to process them. "The secrets of time?"

Chris nodded. "Among other things, yes. Now, I don't want you to get hung up on this. Everything is fine and safe in this house, including you. Feel free to wander around, it's really just the main floor. This floor is all bedrooms, and the basement is locked and off limits."

"What about outside? I can't stay cooped up in the house all day."

"Impressive, Martin. You wouldn't have said that a few months ago when you spent every day drunk in your apartment with no idea what time it was."

"Even then I would go out to my balcony for some air," Martin responded with obvious sass in his voice.

"You can go wherever you want, Marty. You're not a prisoner here. I just wanted to make sure you weren't kidnapped or killed. You're encouraged to stay for your own safety, but you can do as you please."

It was rare when Chris called him Marty, but he hated it the same every time. That was a nickname from his mother and for use by close family and friends only.

"I'll leave you to it," Chris said. "Let me know if there's anything at all you need. Consider this your home for the time being."

"Will do. Have a good night."

Chris crossed the room and left, closing the door gently behind him.

Martin sat on his bed and had an instant urge to plan a way off the property. Chris clearly had a lax approach for keeping him in the house, and he needed to take advantage of that before anything changed.

"Do I move tonight?" he whispered to himself. He grabbed the remote off the nightstand and turned on the TV, letting it play as background noise so he could continue to speak to himself. "There's something going on that no one is telling me. Why would Chris want to keep me safe? He just offered me everything he said the Road Runners offer to lure people: a lavish life and protection."

Martin's leg bounced wildly on the bed and he focused to make it stop. "Why am I nervous? He essentially invited me to leave. Maybe he's counting on me loving the mansion. I can't afford to explore it and fall into a trap of comfort. I need to move tonight."

A quick pep talk to himself was all it took for him to decide he would flee the mansion at night. He had no idea what kind of surveillance was on the property, but moving in the darkness was always an advantage. If any of the guards followed him, he'd lose them in the woods. Since Chris clearly wanted to keep him alive, he dismissed the possibility of being shot. If they had wanted him dead, it would be done by now.

Martin jumped off the bed and rummaged through the closet. There was one coat, a couple pairs of sweatpants, and three shirts. They all looked slightly small for him, but would manage as he needed all the layers possible for his escape in the North Pole.

"I need to move fast into the woods. The trees will give cover so I can run to the main road." His senses had been heightened during the drive over as he kept track of every move the van made.

His stomach growled when he checked the clock that read

4:03.

"Don't go into that kitchen. Everything in this house is designed to trap you into staying." Martin kept whispering to himself, pacing around the room. Once the adrenaline kicked in, he'd forget all about his hunger.

His curiosity throbbed, begging to see the rest of this luxurious mansion that made his new house look like a shack. He pulled open the door and stuck his head out.

The long hallway stretched into the distance, but no one was visible. All of the doors were closed, much like a hotel, and he realized that was exactly what this hideout was designed to feel like: half hotel, half home, with the kitchen and who knows what else on the main floor.

"Act casual, pretend you're exploring the house and see how far you can get without being seen."

He stepped into the hallway, slight creaking beneath his feet from the hardwood floor, and glided the door shut with steady hands.

"Just act normal."

Instead of tiptoeing down the hall like he wanted, he broke into his usual stride and walked toward the stairs. When he reached the steps that led to the main floor, he noticed an open door at the end of the hallway, light spilling out in a yellow sheet.

The incoherent mumble of voices came from the open door, and Martin took the softest steps he could manage toward the voices. He stopped within ten feet of the room once he could hear the voices clearly. One belonged to Chris, the other to a man he didn't recognize.

"Did you dispose of the body?" Chris asked.

"Yes, we moved it into the woods. Will let the animals have

some easy dinner."

Both men chuckled. They had to be talking about the person who he just watched get shot. Would Martin's fate end the same way if he tried leaving?

After the laughter faded, Martin heard the soft clink ice made in a glass when you took a drink.

"So what's the word on Briar?" the unidentified man asked.

Martin's adrenaline exploded at the mention of his name.

"I don't know what to think. Terry says the Road Runners have a secret about him—I think he was talking out of his ass to try and get out of here. Briar doesn't seem like anything special. Was there anything you noticed in your research?"

"Interesting. Nothing at all from my end." the man responded with an elevated pitch in his voice.

"I figured as much. I just want to create an environment so that he doesn't want to leave us—pretty much gave him free reign here around the property. I highly doubt he'll bother trying to find his way home, but we'll help him once he's ready. If anything, we'll just brainwash him and make him another soldier for us."

The men roared laughter one final time as Martin turned and shuffled down the hallway. "I'm getting the fuck out of here tonight," he whispered as he approached his door.

He returned to his room and slammed the door shut in a panic, collapsing to the ground, heart trying to burst through his rib cage. He gasped for air as adrenaline flowed through his veins.

His eavesdropping just confirmed two things: there was definitely something bigger at play that involved him, and he would be leaving the mansion as soon as the sun disappeared.

24

Chapter 24

Martin forgot the daylight situation was all fucked up in Alaska. He was also fortunate. Had he arrived two months earlier, they would've still been in their cycle of 24-hour sunlight. They were still a couple of months from around the clock darkness, so he had to settle for the sunset that arrived shortly after 8 P.M.

He wanted to kill time like a normal person, pacing circles, flipping through the TV channels, reading books that were tucked away in the nightstand drawers. He even spent a good half hour gazing out the window, trying to plot his exact path when he escaped the house.

None of it mattered.

A constant paranoia tickled his every thought, waiting for Chris to barge into the room with his guards to take him down to the basement. The basement had to be either a prison or a slave ring, he decided, and he had no plans on finding out which it was.

The adrenaline from his eavesdropping had given way to a twisting knot of stress in his gut. Every instinct in his body told him that if he didn't leave tonight, he never would.

When eight o'clock finally rolled around, the sun disappeared behind the horizon, leaving an orange glow to collide with the swarming deep blue sky. Waiting for the sun to set reminded him of that fateful night when he had gone back to rescue Izzy. He had stared out the window in the same manner, contemplating what happened next. The old Martin would have had a panic attack and drank every drop of alcohol in sight. But enough adventure had made him numb to the sensation of the unknown. Minus the bubble guts, he was ready to take on the next mission.

Martin slipped into the tight sweatpants and pulled the extra shirts over his current clothes. The jacket zipped up with no problem, despite him feeling that his body might burst through all the layers.

"Are these clothes for children?" he asked, and let out a nervous giggle. Within fifteen minutes the orange glow outside had vanished, leaving a purple splash that would soon melt into complete darkness. "It's time."

He checked himself in the mirror and found that he looked rather normal despite the three layers of clothing. Wearing the baggiest layer on the exterior made it rather simple to achieve. He certainly *looked* like he would be going out for an extended walk around town, but would tell anyone he might run into that he only wanted to explore the property.

Martin drew a deep inhale before crossing the room to exit. He left the light turned on, wanting to give the appearance that he was still in his room, and pulled open the door. The hallway remained empty.

Does anyone here ever leave their room?

He started down the hallway and took the stairs down to the

main level. The mansion's front door was the first thing to greet him. Voices carried from another room, presumably the kitchen from the sounds of silverware clashing with dishes. Laughter broke out, making Martin jump, but the voices carried on in their murmur of conversation.

Don't just stand there, get out of the house and run!

Martin studied the door before stepping up to it. There were four dead bolts and two chain locks scattered around the doorframe.

Clearly no one is supposed to get into this place.

"Or out of it," he whispered, and lunged for the door, twisting at the locks until the final one clicked. He grabbed the knob with a shaking hand and pulled open the door.

A cold rush of air burst through while one of the men stood guard on the front porch, pacing back and forth with a rifle slung over his shoulder. The man, who stood equal in height with Martin, swiveled around on his heels and met Martin's gaze.

"Good evening," Martin said, heart drumming wildly.

The man nodded. He was bundled up in a puffy red jacket so that only the tip of his nose showed, matching the shade of the jacket, and he studied Martin with curious blue eyes.

"Hello," the man said, robotically.

"I was hoping to do some hunting later this week, and wanted to look around the property. Don't mind me."

Martin took a confident step off the porch and had started toward the woods before the man stopped him. "Wait."

Martin froze, convinced a bullet was coming his way. *Please let it end quick.* He turned back to the goon and was relieved to see the rifle still perched on his shoulder and not pointed at him.

"The best spots for hunting are behind the house. You're going toward the main road, there's nothing there."

Martin almost burst into laughter. Not only did the guard not want to shoot him, he even gave directions during his escape.

"Oh, thank you," Martin said, and started toward the back of the house, the frozen snow crunching beneath each confident step. "Just around this way?"

The man nodded, and kept his gaze to the woods in the distance.

"Thank you. Have a great night."

Once Martin rounded the corner of the house and confirmed the guard was no longer in sight, he broke into a sprint toward the woods on the backside of the house. It hadn't felt cold until he started running, the falling temperatures biting at his bare face as his feet crunched the snow below. As long as he kept moving, the cold wouldn't get the best of him. Lacking gloves, he stuffed his hands into the jacket pockets for relief.

It only took him thirty seconds to arrive to the outer trees that housed the rest of the woods. Once the mansion was far enough, looking like a regular-sized house in the distance, he stopped and dropped to his knees, huffing and puffing, gasping for the cold air that felt like icicles filling his air pipe.

"Oh my God," he wheezed. "I'm too old for this shit."

After a couple minutes, he gathered himself and rose to his feet. The guard had confirmed the direction of the main road, and Martin started walking through the trees in that general direction. He had the cover of the trees, and no one from the mansion would be able to see him as he worked his way through the darkness.

He debated taking a swig of the Juice to return to 2018 right now, but had no clue how different the world would be at that precise time in Barrow, Alaska. He had to work with what he had and focus on getting out of the city. It would only be a matter of time until Chris realized he was missing, at which point he'd travel back a few minutes—or hours, hopefully—to track down Martin. He and his soldiers would be on his trail within a day, so he couldn't afford to waste a moment.

He had run a lot further than he thought. It took him five minutes to weave through the trees and get back into position on the front side of the house. The guard remained on the front porch, continuing the circular pacing in his best effort to stay warm. What a boring job. Who would ever find a hideout in the middle of nowhere?

With the guard to his back, Martin continued into the woods at a brisk pace. Stumps, logs, and sticks attempted to trip him, so he focused on each step to avoid falling.

Doubt remained stuck on his mind like a bug on a windshield. What if the guard had led him into a trap? They surely couldn't be too dumb if Chris had chosen them for protection. What if there was no world beyond the woods, and it was a ploy? Chris had mastered time travel, and creating an enclosed, fake world wouldn't be too difficult considering the access he had to future technology. Chris wouldn't agree to let him wander around the property if there really was a way out, would he?

As Martin progressed through the woods, he kept his hands in front, anticipating an invisible force field that would surely bounce him back to the mansion where Chris would howl laughter. Then he'd be off to the basement.

He continued for ten more minutes, the mansion completely out of sight, nothing but tall, skinny trees in every direction. The moonlight provided just enough of a glow for Martin to see the trees in front of him, but beyond that was pure blackness.

He hadn't realized how much light the mansion had provided when he first left, and now felt lost.

Maniacal laughter echoed throughout the woods, carried by the soft breeze that brushed the tops of the trees.

From the mansion? Martin wondered. At his pace he'd be close to a mile away from the house. *No way a laugh would carry that far.*

The laughing continued, swirling around Martin's head to the point he had to stop walking. *It's just the wind howling, keep going. You can't stop.*

He held his breath, planted his feet in the ground, and listened.

The sound continued, steady and uninterrupted.

That's not wind. It's a real laugh. Like a madman.

The thought sent chills down Martin's back that not even the stinging cold had accomplished. The trees continued to sway from fifty feet above, the leaves rustling as they provided Martin cover from the moonlight.

He remained frozen as the sound of sticks crunching on the ground grew louder behind.

Fuck, they're already on to me.

He peered through the trees, squinting to make out any shape in the darkness. The crunching approached him from directly behind and stopped.

Martin spun around and shouted, "AAAAHHHHHH!"

He swung fists into the air and collapsed to the ground when he saw nothing there. His heart pounded in his head as adrenaline tried to burst out of his eyeballs.

"What the fuck?" he panted as he pulled himself back up, brushing off the snow clung to his coat.

You've been in the woods for 20 whole minutes and are already losing your mind. Keep going.

Alone in nature, Martin continued toward where he believed the main road awaited. His mind kept returning to Izzy, now buried peacefully in the cemetery in 2018 Denver. Her disappearance led to this exact moment, and he felt her presence beside him, assuring him it would all be okay. The parent was supposed to console the child, but perhaps the roles switched when the child became an angel.

He closed his eyes and imagined her soft, gentle voice. "Go, Daddy. You can make it."

Her voice was no longer in his imagination; he *felt* her speaking in his head.

"Go, Daddy. Run!"

Martin obliged and pulled himself up, immediately breaking into a sprint despite his legs protesting and his tar-filled lungs begging for mercy.

The road was closer than he realized. After three minutes of running, leaping, and dodging through the trees, asphalt greeted Martin's feet, its unexpectedly even surface nearly causing him to tumble after his escape from the rocky terrain of the woods.

With the trees separated by the road, the moonlight provided a mystic glow. Martin looked both ways, each direction winding into more darkness, unsure which way to go. He ran to his left for no reason other than following his gut instinct that told him which way was north.

Martin didn't run for too long—his legs and chest grateful—when he stopped at the sight of approaching headlights a quarter mile up the road, but moving with rapid speed as they drove along the twisted street.

Hide.

Martin took two long lunges and dove off the road, tumbling into the woods where branches and rocks scraped his hands as he rolled to a stop. He momentarily lost his bearings as he brushed the debris and snow off his clothes, but found them again when the car's engine roared like a lion in the still night.

He hid behind a tree, hands on his knees, panting for breath, the freezing air stinging his lungs with each inhale while his vision blurred in and out of focus.

Relax, it could just be a car driving by.

He wanted to believe this, but knew better. With the events that had transpired in the last half hour, it surely wasn't a coincidence that some asshole was driving 70 miles per hour in the middle of nowhere.

Martin crouched, studying the headlights that grew closer with each passing millisecond. With the car roughly 100 yards away, he could make it out as a four-door sedan, a dark color, possibly black or navy.

The brakes slammed, splashing red light on the road and trees behind it. Smoke rose from the screeching tires, complemented by the stench of burnt rubber. The car had stopped directly in line with Martin, no more that thirty feet from where he hid behind a tree trunk, as if the driver knew exactly where he was.

It's gotta be Chris. Who else would know how to find you when you're lost?

The car's engine puttered, blowing gray clouds of exhaust. The world felt still. *Too* still. As much as his mind was stuck in a panic, Martin noticed the trees no longer swayed. Silence filled the air, thick enough to cut into with a plastic knife, his breathing and drumming heartbeat the only audible sounds within his conscience.

"Martin!" a voice whispered loudly from the car.

His blood froze as a new layer of goosebumps broke out on his back and legs.

They're certainly here for you. No mistaking that now, big guy.

Martin didn't recognize the voice, and because of that, stayed behind the tree, praying to God that the mystery car would drive off and mind their own business.

"Martin!" the voice called, louder. A man's voice.

It's not Chris. Sounds too young.

"Martin, I know you're there. Come get in the car. I'm with the Road Runners."

He had no way out of this. They called him out by name and were shouting directly to the tree he hid behind. He had two options: to get in the car on a blind leap of faith, or sprint back into the woods where he would further become lost, unequipped for an overnight stay in the blistering cold.

Could it be Chris's men posing as Road Runners? Why would they take that approach? Martin had never done so much as hinted that he trusted the Road Runners. He willingly fled their capture with no second thoughts.

But you've been thinking about them more. The Road Runners are the good guys in this war.

"Martin! Get in the fucking car or you're gonna freeze to death!" the man barked, impatience dripping from each word.

No more energy or willpower was coming. Running was off the table of options, leaving one obvious, but hesitant choice.

Martin stepped out from the tree, hands raised in the air like he was under arrest.

"Quit dicking around and get in the car!"

A young man hung out the passenger window, someone Martin had never seen before.

Martin crawled up the slope back to the road, thighs burning and demanding a rest as they wobbled beneath him.

"Hurry!" the man called, returning to his hushed tone.

Martin approached the car, doubt swirling, and pulled open the backseat door.

"Get in," the driver said. He appeared a similar age as Martin, suggested by the gray streaks in his goatee. Piercing blue eyes studied Martin as he lunged into the car.

The passenger who had been shouting rotated in his seat and craned his neck to look at Martin. He was as young as his voice had sounded, fresh out of college by Martin's guess.

"Out for an evening stroll, Martin?" the young one asked, blinking his brown eyes that surely charmed the ladies at the university.

"Who are you guys?" Martin asked, still catching his breath as the tension of the last thirty seconds started to wane. After all the urgency they had thrown his way, the men seemed content sitting in the middle of the road as they got to know each other.

"We're with the Road Runners," the older man said. "My name is Bill Jordan, and my partner here is Julian Caruso. We're sorry to meet you under such stressful circumstances."

"How did you know where I was? We're in the middle of nowhere."

"Yeah, this place is a fucking dump," Julian said, head still craned awkwardly. He gawked at Martin as if the two men had stumbled across Sasquatch sitting in their backseat. They had a calming presence, and Martin leaned back as if he had jumped into a car with friends.

"Seriously," Martin said. "How did you find me?"

Bill chuckled, his small double chin jiggling as his shoulders trembled with delight. "Finding you was the easy part. How the hell did you get out of that place? That's the question we've been dying to ask."

Martin furrowed his brow and scratched his cheek. *What's going on?*

His stomach dropped, not out of angst, but more out of frustration at the growing sense that he was some minor cog in the vast time travel world.

"I walked out," Martin said, unsure what sort of explanation the men wanted.

Both men threw their heads back and howled like lunatics.

Martin watched them and wished he could be anywhere else besides the backseat of this car. Were they here to rescue him or make fun of him?

"That's a good one, Martin," Bill said. "Tell us. Did you have to fight off Chris's bodyguards? Or were you just faster than them?"

"I told you. I walked out of the house, then ran through the woods."

Now it was Bill and Julian's turn to stare at each other, confused. "You mean you weren't locked away?" Julian asked.

"No. I was in my own private bedroom, kind of like a hotel."

"What a fucking moron," Julian murmured under his breath.

"Excuse me?" Martin demanded.

"Not you. Chris. He's a complete moron. I'll never understand how he rose to power, but I suppose we should be grateful he's calling the shots. He just handed you to us on a silver platter."

"I'm not on either side of this. I just wanna go home and dump my Juice down the drain."

Bill shook his head. "You're way beyond that point, my

friend. You're in this war whether you like it or not. And I think you already know what side the good guys are on."

Martin still hadn't had any true exposure to the happenings of this supposed war, but it was obvious that the Road Runners had a much less aggressive approach, at least in terms of dealing with him.

"What if I refuse?" Martin asked nonchalantly.

Bill and Julian exchanged glances again, speaking to each other through mere eye twitches. They may have been different in age, but it was impossible to know how long someone had actually existed in this time travelling ordeal.

"We'll let you speak with the Commander about that," Julian said.

"The Commander? Who is that? And when will that be?"

"Right now, and she's the leader of the Road Runners in North America," Julian said. "She flew up here as soon as we told her you were captured."

"She's waiting," Bill said before turning his attention back to the steering wheel. "It's time to go."

Bill made a U-turn and drove along the dark road. Martin slouched, trying to relax, but remained ready for what would come next.

There's definitely something they want from me.

25

Chapter 25

The drive lasted ten minutes, and all three men remained silent for the duration. The small chat ended, and Martin sensed the tension weighing down on the car.

"We're here," Bill said, but Martin only saw darkness through the windows. They had pulled off the road half a mile ago and were still in the middle of nothingness.

Martin's heartbeat had calmed since the two Road Runners picked him up. He didn't sense any danger, just unease of the unknown.

Bill killed the engine and stepped out of the car, prompting Julian and Martin to follow suit. Sticks and rocks greeted their feet as they trudged along a small path that had been cleared of snow toward a small structure, no bigger than an outhouse.

The leader of the Road Runners hangs out in a shitter all day?

Bill led the way and pulled open the creaky wooden door. There was no toilet, just a four by four slab of concrete. "We all fit, let's go." He stepped in, Julian and Martin following into the cramped, dark space.

Julian rummaged his fingers along the blacked out wall, the

clicking sound of buttons being pushed as the only audible noise over the three men's hoarse breathing.

"The Commander is excited to meet you," Bill said, this time with a chipper voice.

Julian pulled the door shut as a loud humming sound filled the outhouse, the ground rumbling beneath them.

"Nothing to worry about," Julian said after seeing Martin's bulging eyes. "Just a different kind of elevator."

The ground lightened as the concrete descended at a snail's pace into the earth. The darkness concealed everything until they reached their destination where two dozen people were scattered across a room that stretched back at least two hundred feet.

They all sat at desks in the open space, computer monitors glowing, keyboards clattering, attention focused on their tasks at hand. A bell let out one shrill ring as the elevator came to a complete stop, and all heads turned to Martin.

He stood behind Bill and Julian, but felt the stares burn right through them. A blanket of silence fell over the room as the three men stepped off the elevator.

"Commander Strike, he's here!" a giddy voice from the back called. "He's here!" The squeaky man was near hysterics, running across the back of the room like he had just remembered a meeting he was late for.

"Everyone back to work," Bill barked with authority. "Nothing to see here. Move along."

The two dozen heads held their ground for a couple more seconds before ducking back into their computers.

"This way," Julian instructed, leading them to the left.

Bill's and Julian's boots clapped and echoed along the concrete ground as they passed the area of desks that formed a large rectangle across the room. Above the desks hung 100-inch TV screens that lined the length of the room. Some showed images of people and places, others showed maps with different colored dots splayed about. Every section of the office had at least one person with a close eye on the screens.

"This is our headquarters," Julian said.

"*One* of our headquarters," Bill corrected.

"Just because it's not as glamorous as some of our other locations, doesn't mean it's not our *main* headquarters. We have other places around the world, but since this is where all of our studies on Chris are conducted, it's considered the most important headquarters."

Julian explained this as if he had built the place himself, and Bill grunted as they reached the middle part of the room. Martin hadn't noticed the offices that lined the perimeter.

All of the private offices appeared roughly the same size, big enough for a desk, a corner plant, and two chairs for visitors to sit. Only one office stood out as special, and that was the door they stood outside of. It was also the only door that had frosted glass, keeping any wandering eyes from seeing inside.

Bill rapped on the door with a balled fist.

"Come in," a woman's voice called.

Bill pushed open the door and stepped in first, keeping Julian and Martin at a distance.

"Good evening, Commander Strike," Bill said. "Glad to see you made it in so soon."

"I hopped on the jet right away. Is everything okay with Mr. Briar? Were you followed?"

"Yes, and no," Bill said proudly. "I have him right here, and he has loads of questions."

"Thank you, Bill. I owe you and Julian. Have Mr. Briar come

in and leave us in private, please."

"Absolutely." Bill bowed out of the room and held up an arm to welcome Martin. "Commander Strike is ready to see you."

Martin stepped into the doorway and locked eyes with a blue-eyed, light-skinned woman who greeted him with a warm smile. Her red hair was pulled back into a ponytail, revealing early wrinkles that had formed on her temples. Martin judged her to be in her mid-forties as her face lit up with a flash of youth.

"Mr. Briar," she said, standing and crossing the room with an extended hand. "It's such an honor to meet you. I'm Commander Strike."

He shook her hand and admired its smooth texture. She was dressed casually for someone who was called Commander—jeans and a sweater—but she apparently just got off a plane. And they were in Alaska.

"Nice to meet you," Martin responded, unsure of a certain protocol for greeting the leader of the Road Runners.

"Please have a seat. We have lots to discuss." She was tall, almost six feet, and walked with her shoulders held high and a swagger that dared someone to mess with her.

Martin obliged and stepped all the way into the office. Strike had the same set up of a desk and two chairs, but also had a sofa along the front wall with portraits of men and women covering every inch of space, monitors in every ceiling corner, and another side door that led to either a bathroom or closet. There was also a table along the back wall, and Martin couldn't help but notice the bottle of scotch standing unattended with two glasses at its side. The days of heavy drinking were long gone, but he still drooled at the sight of scotch. Who was this lady, anyway? Tall, strong, in charge, and a scotch drinker.

Maybe his next love interest?

Fuck that. No more time-traveling women.

The wounds still hadn't closed from Sonya, mainly because he hadn't had any time to grieve, let alone process what the hell happened. He'd been running for his life ever since the Road Runners dropped the bomb that Sonya had been a ploy to lure him into their possession. Maybe Strike would have some answers.

She situated herself in her wide, cushioned chair that was clearly out of place for a typical office setting, appearing more like a black throne. "I can't tell you how excited I am to meet you."

"Thank you?" Martin responded.

"I know you have plenty of questions. It's been brought to my attention that you don't even know the extent of your abilities. You won't leave this office with any more questions; I can guarantee you that much."

"I just want to know what's going on."

Commander Strike chuckled. "You're invaluable." Martin stared into Commander Strike's eyes, as if the truth would magically jump out. "You have a rare gift, Martin. Something even more rare than the capability to travel through time."

She paused, looking for a reaction, but Martin gave none.

"You're what we call a Warm Soul. Beyond time travel, there are others with different abilities. There are some who can freeze time. And on the flip side of that, there are others who can *resist* the freezing of time."

Martin's eyebrows elevated to his hairline. "What do you mean by freezing time?"

"When time is frozen, everything comes to a complete standstill. You can be in the middle of a run through the park, and be frozen mid-stride. We could freeze in the middle of this conversation, and the thing is, we would never know it—well, *I* would never know it. *You* would."

If Martin scrunched his face any more it would fall off his skull. "Are you saying I'm immune to this?"

Commander Strike nodded, her ponytail bobbing joyfully.

"Wouldn't I have noticed that everyone around me was frozen?" Martin asked.

"Not necessarily. This isn't something that happens often. There are only a handful of people in the world who can freeze time, and even less who can resist."

"Why me? What did I do?"

"That's one question I wish I could answer. We don't have any knowledge on how this actually works. As far as we know, it's all random. We've conducted studies on those who can resist frozen time, and have found no similarities across subjects."

Martin squirmed in his seat, uncomfortable that he had such a unique ability. His dreams of going home to a normal life were shot. Although, maybe he could leverage this situation for his personal gain. Strike hadn't said it yet, but he had something they wanted. He stared blankly across the table. "So what is it exactly you want from me?"

"We want you to be a Road Runner. To fight on the right side of history."

She let her words hang in the air, pressuring Martin to speak next after a few awkward seconds of silence.

"How do I know you're on the right side?"

Commander Strike stood from her desk and paced along the back wall, rubbing the bottle of scotch as if debating to pour a glass or drink straight from the bottle.

"Tell me everything Chris has told you about his plans." She tossed her hands in the air. "Go ahead."

"Well, he never tells me much. He told me some of the rules for time—"

"I don't care about that. Tell me about *his* plans for the future."

"I can't say he's told me anything. He's mentioned that he has counterparts on every continent. . .but that might have been the Road Runners who told me that before Chris came and busted me out of the hotel. Today has been an absolute blur."

"That's exactly my point. I can tell you everything about our plans as the Road Runners, where we've been and where we're going."

"I'm listening."

"Our main reason for existence is to keep Chris and his friends from ruling the world. It is true that he has counter-parts on every continent, even Antarctica. And they're all as equally bought in to their mission of taking over the world. It's why they're on each continent. They're slowly manipulating every country's government to the point where they have rule over those countries by planting their own people in positions of power."

"So, they're like the New World Order?"

"You could say that, except this is real. Their movement is called The Future Revolution, and they call themselves the Revolters. They're real, and they're powerful. They travel throughout time to learn what can make each government fall, and how to manipulate people into believing what they're selling."

"Which is?"

"No different than anyone else who makes empty promises: a better world, a better future. Every action they make, every word that is spoken, has a direct purpose behind it with a specific goal at the end. Their end goal is to rule a world where there are no people who can think for themselves, and it's frightening. They're succeeding, in fact. But that's the beauty of there *not* being linear time—we can always inflict change in any era and save the future from itself."

"Is there a point in time where you see an end to this war?"

She crossed her arms and frowned. "There's not necessarily a time where the war ends, but there's a time where it becomes obvious that The Future Revolution rules a majority of the world. What year is it in your current time? 1995?"

"No, *1996* is what I traveled back to, to save my daughter. I'm from 2018."

She nodded as if she should've known this. "The takeover has already begun by 2018. The world is going mad by then. It's one of our main eras of focus."

"And you want me to help stop it from happening?"

"Yes. We're just not sure how yet. We have so much to learn about time freezing that we won't put you in a situation that we don't understand ourselves. One thing I can promise you is that every decision is made methodically and we never put a Road Runner's life at risk. Unlike Chris, who rotates through his soldiers like it's World War One all over again."

Martin processed this information with care. Aside from their encounter in his mansion bedroom, Chris had never discussed plans of any sort, and left many answers vague. Martin had always sensed the old man was hiding something, even back when they had first met.

"Be honest with yourself, and with me," Strike continued.

"What has Chris done for you? Did he deceive you into a better life by granting you time travel? Hurt your family? Try to lure you into comfort with a luxurious life?"

Martin looked to the floor and nodded. "He's done all of that."

"That's what he's done to all of us, one by one. Every Road Runner received their Juice through Chris—there's no other way, although we're getting closer to reverse engineering it. The point is, you're not alone, and it's why we believe so strongly in our mission of taking him down. There are people who will fall for anything and get sucked into Chris's tricks. The rest of us become Road Runners." Martin smiled at that last line, the ultimate sales pitch. "I'm not going to stand here and make you empty promises for agreeing to join us. We're not going to deposit $100 million dollars into your bank account in exchange for your soul. Any dipshit with the Juice can find a way to make easy money. We believe in helping each other build a life that you can be proud of—whatever that means to you."

"I like everything you've said, but I really need to think things over. I didn't ask to be sucked into this, and I'm honestly not interested in joining a war that never ends. I have a sick mom at home—thanks to Chris—and I just want to be with her."

"I'm not going to argue with that. We can get you on a plane back to Denver in 2018 within the next hour. All I ask is that you give this serious consideration. And keep one thing in mind: you're never going to be able to watch from the sidelines. Without us, Chris will come after you and make you his prisoner. And if you reject us, we don't really have the resources to protect you. As much as you hate to hear it, you're going to need to pick a side, or one will be picked for you, and it will never be us who force the matter."

Martin's heart beat a little faster. He didn't know for sure if the Road Runners truly would leave him in peace, but he had no problem believing that Chris wouldn't.

"I'll consider this. You have my word. But I really do want to get home to my mom."

Commander Strike nodded and smiled. "Alright, then. I'll have Bill and Julian take you to our private jet. Do you know where the Chop House is in Denver?"

"The restaurant? Yeah."

"When you make your decision, go to the parking garage behind the restaurant. Go to the stairwell and go as low as you can and wait. I'll have someone meet you there so we can discuss your decision."

Chills broke out down Martin's back. *How big is this underground network? It's like an entire society living in another world.*

"Okay. I can do that."

"Perfect. I look forward to seeing you again. I'll grab Bill and Julian and let them know the plan. We'll be in touch."

Commander Strike left Martin alone in the office, leaving him in silence to ponder what the rest of his life would now look like.

26

Chapter 26

Commander Strike followed her word. She left Martin alone in her office for ten minutes before Bill came knocking to retrieve him.

"Jet's being fueled and will be ready when we get there. Any last questions for the Commander before we leave?"

Martin shook his head.

"Alright then, let's head out." Bill gestured for him to stand.

When Martin stepped out of the office, a few of the Road Runners tried to sneak a peek at him. They made it less obvious than when he had arrived, but they all eventually caught a glimpse of their secret weapon.

Julian waited in front of the elevator, pacing back and forth like a guard.

"Let's get Mr. Briar back home," Bill said.

The three stepped into the elevator, and stood in the same positions as when they had arrived. "Pretty cool place, huh?" Julian asked as the elevator door cut off the view of the underground headquarters.

"Yeah. It's crazy to know this is all going on."

"You should see some of our other locations: swimming pools, racquetball courts, all kinds of amenities. It's hard to get those kind of things all the way up here in Santa's land. Besides, the Commander doesn't think we should be playing when we're so close to Chris. That's really the only reason for this location, to follow his every move."

"Was his mansion on one of those screens?"

Bill laughed. "One of those screens? Try half of those screens. We watch that house like a hawk."

"Have you ever seen the inside?"

"No. We're hoping you'll tell us about it later. Whether you join us or not." Bill said this last line in a *how-dare-you-consider-rejecting-us* tone.

"How many Road Runners are trapped in that house?" Martin asked.

"At least fifty. We want to know about the basement..."

"I didn't get to see it—wasn't exactly exploring the place—but I think that's where they're all being kept."

"We sent in some people, undercover, to try and learn about the inside of the place. They were all volunteers, but Chris snuffed them out as liars and we've never seen them again. We just assumed they were dead. We've recently implanted tracker devices into Road Runners—for reasons like this."

"But no one volunteers to go into that house any more," Julian cut in. "If we could get just one person to go, we could know for sure if our people are being kept prisoner or being killed. But it sounds like you may have the answer to that question."

Martin shook his head as the elevator door opened back into the outhouse on ground level. "But I don't. I just know about the existence of the basement. All he told me was that the basement is where they conduct research that spans all eras of time. No idea what that actually means."

The men stepped back into the freezing Alaskan air where the car they had arrived in waited. Bill returned to his position behind the wheel as they all filed into the car.

"We'd love to sit down with you sometime and draw all of this out. If we even had a rough sketch of what the inside of the house looks like, it might be a game changer."

"If you guys have such intense surveillance on the house, why don't you just shoot Chris when he steps outside?"

Julian giggled. "If it was that easy, we would. He's not mortal. All of us *are*, even all of those who work for him are, too. But he's not. We've shot him, square in the head. He just plucks the bullet out of his skull like it was an annoying hair and laughs."

"And this is why we have so many eyes on him. There has to be a way to kill him, we just don't know it yet."

Martin slouched in the backseat. As open and honest as the Road Runners had been, it sounded as if they were still light-years behind Chris. There were too many questions unanswered. How would they ever win a war that way? The sales pitch back in Commander Strike's office suddenly felt unstable, a cheap attempt to get Martin to join their circus of the unknown. Their entire operation was built around killing a man who, quite possibly, couldn't be killed.

They drove in silence for the next ten minutes, Julian occasionally whistling a tune.

"We're here," Bill announced as they turned into the hangar. Most were empty as they drove to the far end where a small blue jet waited.

"Are you guys coming with me?" Martin asked.

"Afraid not. We have lots to do here. You're going to have a relaxing flight back to Denver. Be sure to take your Juice *after* you land to get back to 2018."

"We'll leave you here, but go check in with the pilot. I believe Wendell will be flying you tonight. He's a great guy."

"We'll see you at another time hopefully," Julian said.

Both men reached a hand over the center console and Martin shook each. "It was great meeting you guys, thanks for rescuing me."

"The pleasure is all ours," Bill said. "Best of luck with your decision."

Martin left the car and strode to the jet where a portable staircase welcomed him, much like it had on Chris's plane.

I could get used to this life.

A young African-American man stood at the top of the steps and waved. "Come on up."

Martin climbed the steps, feeling he should have luggage, but remembering his suitcase and belongings were in 2018, and somewhere in 1919 was a briefcase in an abandoned room at the Brown Palace.

Sonya, Goddamnit.

After checking in with his mom when he arrived home, his next priority would be an intense crying session. Or maybe a fit of rage. He could visit the shooting range to blow off some steam. He couldn't fault Sonya for what she had done, but he didn't have to accept it, either.

"Good evening, Mr. Briar, how are you today?" the man asked, sticking out a hand. "My name is Wendell and I'll be flying you to Denver."

"I've had better days, Wendell, but I'm doing well."

Wendell patted Martin on the back as he stepped into the

plane. "Well, we can certainly help make things better. I have a full bar, and a decent-sized menu."

The plane was half the size as Chris's, but still housed plenty of luxury. It wasn't built to carry two dozen Revolters, but rather a half dozen Road Runners as six reclining chairs graced the sides along the windows. Toward the back was the bathroom next to the aforementioned bar, sleek trim lighting around its edges.

"Get comfortable. It's a five-hour flight." Wendell checked his watch. He dressed like any other pilot Martin had encountered. "We should be landing in Denver at 5:30 A.M. local time."

"What time is it now?"

Martin had left his watch at the Brown Palace and his cell phone in 2018. It could have been 3 A.M. for all he knew.

"It's 10:30 here in Alaska, and I get the sense they're going to have a late night at the headquarters. Commander Strike sounded excited and flustered. No one gets any sleep when that happens. Anyway, we'll get going shortly. It's just me, you, and Leanna. She'll be tending to you if you need anything. She's also a certified pilot, so can take over if I have a heart attack."

Wendell howled at this, too young to worry about a heart attack. The pilot pushed a button on the wall that closed the plane's door, and worked his way into the cockpit.

Just one drink before bed. Lots to do tomorrow.

Martin crossed the open space and sat in the front row seat furthest from the door. Within minutes they rumbled along the jet way, and elevated into the night sky. He never meet Leanna, as he fell asleep three minutes after take-off.

27

Chapter 27

Martin didn't wake when the plane landed, and if Wendell hadn't poked him back into consciousness, he might have slept for the next ten hours. His nap in the mansion felt like decades ago as his body demanded every second of shuteye.

But he was now back in Denver, and somewhat back to reality—whatever that meant anymore.

Wendell had opened the plane's door where a new flight of stairs waited.

"Thanks for the flight," Martin said, groggy and bleary-eyed.

"The pleasure is all mine, sir," Wendell said as he stood by the door waiting for Martin to deplane. "Happy to fly a friend of the Commander any time."

Martin wished Wendell a good night and descended the stairs. They were in the middle of nowhere, creating a brief spark of panic that vanished as soon as he remembered it was still 1981.

Downtown Denver glowed in the distance. "Home sweet home."

Martin was back on his own. No one waiting for him. No Sonya. No Izzy. Judging by the distance to downtown, he was maybe a ten-minute drive west of town, putting him somewhere in or near the city of Lakewood.

He remembered he was originally asleep in 2018, having bounced all around the world and throughout time. When he sipped his Juice to return to 2018, he would wake up in his bed in his brand new house where he and Sonya had lain next to each other to take what was supposed to be an adventure into the past.

She was probably already gone. Or never left with him to begin with.

Bed. Your *bed. That does sound lovely.*

Martin sat on the concrete ground, a lone landing strip in the middle of an open field, and pulled the flask from his back pocket. One rule he had learned on this journey was to never let his Juice out of sight.

He twisted off the cap, and held up the flask to toast the Road Runners' jet.

"Off we go," he said, taking a small sip, and thinking about his present time in 2018.

He lay on his back and stared at the stars, crickets chirping all around him as he dozed.

* * *

From his recollection, they had left 2018 shortly after lunch, but when he woke, it was five in the evening.

I returned and stayed asleep. That's how tired I am.

His brain finally felt refreshed, however, and the sensation made him ready to tackle the world.

Sonya was gone, the outline of her body sunk into the comforter where she had lain.

At least you know she was real, and that you haven't truly lost your mind.

"Lost my mind? No. Lost my life again? Yes."

Martin rolled off the bed and looked around his room as if it were a foreign place. Everything reeked of Sonya. She had decorated the house. From the stupid throw pillows, to the porcelain figurines that stood on the wall shelves. She had done it, not him. Martin would have a blank, empty room with a nightstand and bed if he had his way.

How long until the Road Runners come knocking on the front door? Maybe another hour? How long until Chris shows up? That desperate lunatic.

Even without knowing an exact timeline for the next day of his life, Martin sensed the urgency in his upcoming actions. He decided to do what should have been done in the first place when Chris made the initial proposal of time travel: ask his mom for advice.

He had been too afraid of how she might judge him for bringing up such a bizarre topic, but he was well beyond that point now. He'd seen too much shit for anyone to even try arguing with him about his sanity. You can stare out the window to the world, but do you really know what's happening behind each closed door?

His mom might resist at first, but she had no proof. No grounds to call him crazy. And the best part is that she would still offer him advice whether or not she believed his story.

"I only have a few more months to save her mind." Martin

needed to say this out loud to remind himself where he was and what he was doing. The Alzheimer's still gnawed at his mom's brain like ants on fallen crumbs. If the Road Runners expected him to join their team, they better damn well understand that saving her mind was his number one priority over anything else. Anyone else with an agenda for what he should do with his gift could go right ahead and fuck themselves.

He studied himself in the mirror above his dresser. Dark bags hung below his bloodshot eyes. More gray hair had filled in since he last checked. *Nothing like aging five years in ten minutes.* Apparently, the reward of not aging in the past didn't apply to the common side effects of stress. At this rate, he'd be sixty going on ninety if they thrust him into the middle of a war.

Nothing lasts forever, especially your brown hair, his mother once told him shortly after Izzy's disappearance brought his first gray hairs at the age of 32.

Martin left the bedroom, refusing to waste another second, and went downstairs to the main level where his mother stood in the kitchen, stirring something in a pot on the stove.

She turned and smiled, the wrinkles on her face seeming to have multiplied over the past few days. She brushed her silver hair behind an ear and said, "Sleepy much?"

"You could say that. What are you making?"

"I *was* going to make some pasta, but we don't have any. I could've sworn I saw some in the pantry the other day."

"Don't worry about it, we can order some takeout."

Marilyn scoffed at this. "Restaurants can't make dinner as good as me. Besides, there'll be a day where you can't enjoy my cooking anymore."

"Mom, you don't have to say things like that."

She raised a hand. "It's fine. I've prayed on this and accept my fate. I still have at least five years until things get horrible. I'll be out of your way by then. You don't have to care for me as this reaches its peak."

A tear rolled down Martin's cheek. The last day had been emotional enough without his mother talking about her dementia plans.

"Mom, that's not happening. I need to talk to you about something important."

"Okay, what's on your mind?"

"I think we should sit down—this may take a while."

"Where's Sonya?"

"That's part of this."

Her bony hands shot to her mouth as she shook her head. "Oh, Marty, please don't tell me she left."

"It's not what you think. Please. Let's sit at the table."

Marilyn hobbled to the table where Martin had already pulled out a chair.

"I think this will be best if you just let me talk. Don't ask any questions until I'm done, or else we'll be here for eight hours."

Marilyn obliged, and Martin began.

He started from the beginning when they had first met Chris at the Wealth of Time store in Larkwood. He told her how he went back the next day to buy the ring she had sworn was her grandmother's—a ring he never ended up taking due to the distraction that followed. From that point on, life had been nothing but adventure with Sonya, Izzy, Road Runners, and now the people known as Revolters. Martin explained every detail from the night Izzy was killed, all the way up to the last few hours when he had met Commander Strike.

His mother nodded throughout the one way conversation, eyes bulging at some parts, mouth frowning at others. When Martin finished, she stared at him blankly, like Jesus Christ himself had just told her his entire life story.

"Do you think I'm crazy?" Martin asked.

Marilyn scratched her head and scrunched her face. "I don't know. It's one hell of a story, that's for sure. You were never one for creative endeavors, so I don't know what would compel you to make this all up. I suppose being dumped by a beautiful girl is a good excuse, but there are far too many details."

"Everything I said is true. Believe me, I know it's absurd. There are still times where I don't think it's real. I can leave to a different time whenever I please, and that's what I really wanted to talk to you about first. But I need to know that you actually believe this is all real."

"I'm not ready to call it real, but I'm even further from calling it fake."

"I'll take it."

"Well then, what exactly is it that you want to discuss?"

"Two things. First, I plan to travel into the future to get medicine for you."

"Impossible."

"None of this is possible, but it is. And the best part is I can go into the future to find your medicine and be back here in the next ten minutes, even if I have to spend 20 years in the future looking for it. It doesn't change what happens here in our current time."

Martin leaned back and studied his mother. She looked at the kitchen table as if expecting it to speak to her, growing disappointed that it didn't.

"How do you know a medicine from the future can cure what

I already have?"

"Why wouldn't it? It's medicine for Alzheimer's. Even still, why wouldn't you want to at least find out?"

"What's the other thing you wanted to discuss?" Marilyn asked, dismissing the medicine topic.

The sudden change caught Martin off guard and he hesitated with his mouth hung open.

"This war," he said. "I've all but been told that I'm going to be forced to be a part of it. With this gift I have, they consider me too valuable to let me live my life like a normal person."

"Why not just hide in another country?"

"These people are all over the world. And they can find me even when I don't know where I am. It's like they have eyes on every corner of the globe."

"What side would you join in this war?"

"The Road Runners. I've experienced both sides and it seems they're the good guys. Chris is a lunatic con man who will say anything to get his way."

"It sounds like a unique opportunity. I think you should seize it and run with it."

Martin bolted upright, planting his elbows on the table. "Wh-what do you mean? There's a good chance I could die."

"No shit, son. Guess what? There's a hundred percent chance you're going to die one day. No one gets out of this thing alive."

"Where is this coming from?" Martin never knew his mother to have such a careless attitude on life. Caution had always been her forte, anything to avoid a bad situation.

"I've spent my whole life being held back by myself. Always afraid to take a chance at anything, playing it safe so I could make it to the finish line. But these last couple of months have taught me that was a huge mistake. They say you shouldn't die with regret, but I think everyone who plays it safe will die with regret. There were so many things I wanted to do—even had the chance to do—but never did."

"Like what?"

"I could sit here all day and tell you, but that's not the point. The point is you have an opportunity to change the world. To actually make this shitty place better, and all you can think about is me. Why bring this cure back just for me? Why not bring it back for everyone?"

"Mom, I'm not worried about everyone."

"And that's why the world has changed so much. We all get so caught up in our own lives that we forget the stranger on the bus is probably going through a similar hell as us. I'm not asking you to save the world, but I'm urging you to consider it—whatever it may mean to you."

Martin leaned back again, and now he studied the table. When he had run through this conversation in his mind, he thought he and his mother would be packing a bag to go live in an exotic place where no one could find them. Instead, she was talking him into not only joining the Road Runners, but to enjoy it and make a difference.

A couple more tears rolled down his cheek. "Mom, I can't leave you to go fight bad guys that I just learned about."

"Yes you can. Don't make an excuse. Once you let go of excuses, you open your heart to a whole new world. Besides, you said you'll only be gone for ten minutes no matter how long you spend in the other world."

Martin had never heard it referred to as the "other world," but that's exactly what it was: another existence that was taking place without anyone's knowledge from the present time. He looked up to the ceiling, hoping a reasonable response would fall from the sky.

"You can look for all the excuses you want up there," she said. "But just know this. No matter what you decide, you're going to look back to this exact moment as the one that shaped the rest of your life. You just need to decide if you want this moment to look glorious or regrettable."

Martin nodded. "I love you, Mom. Your energy and courage after all that has happened is so admirable. I'm gonna fight this war so we can kill Chris, *and* I'm coming back with the cure for Alzheimer's. I want you to stop talking about death; you're going to live another thirty years, and we can stay in this house for all of it."

Tears streamed down both of their faces as they stared at each other with glossy eyes.

"And I'm proud of you, Marty. I know your life has been pure darkness since Izzy died, but you still found a way to turn it around after all these years. Do this in her honor, let her know her daddy's a hero."

"I do everything for her."

"Good. So what are we ordering for takeout?"

They both wiped their eyes and laughed into the empty house.

28

Chapter 28

Martin's excitement grew the more he thought about joining the Road Runners. His mother was right—this was a once-in-a-lifetime opportunity at a new life. Izzy was gone, Sonya was gone, and his mother gave her blessing to pursue this. He had no reason to say no, and couldn't stop his legs from bouncing while they sat through dinner at a local Italian restaurant.

He warned her that if he died in the past or future, he would die in his sleep in 2018. She could sit by his side for a mere ten minutes, and wait for him to either wake up or stop breathing.

His gut churned at the thought of driving downtown to meet with the 2018 Road Runners. Would the Commander be there? Did they already know what he was thinking, like Chris? They could have had eyes on his house and heard the entire conversation with his mother, already making arrangements for his arrival.

Regardless of what the Road Runners had planned, Martin rode the energy of his personal renaissance. He imagined killing Chris, not knowing exactly how since the old man was immune to bullets and blades. He closed his eyes and pictured himself hoisted in the air by other Road Runners, hundreds of them chanting his name, because dammit, he was the secret weapon. And the hero.

Martin grew nauseous while he drove his mom home after dinner. "I don't know what's going to happen, but I'll make sure they let me come home before sending me anywhere else."

"Not necessary. Let this be our goodbye. And if I never see you again, just know that I love you."

Neither had any more tears to shed, but Martin had every intent on returning home before officially jumping into a war.

"I love you, Mom. Do you want me to help you inside?"

"No. I can see it in your eyes. You're ready. Don't waste another minute. Go wherever you're going, and start your new life. I'll be here."

She leaned over the center console and kissed him on the forehead before pushing open the car door.

"I love you, too," she said before she closed the door. She looked over her shoulder, eyes wet.

Martin watched her wobble to the front door and had a brief flash of memories from his childhood, his mother prominent in every one. She had always been there to guide him through life, and he would be forever grateful for the final lesson she had given, pushing him into a whole new world.

He pulled out of the driveway, the sun starting its descent. Darkness would swallow the city by the time he arrived downtown, so he flicked on his headlights and drove out of his neighborhood, passing the other large houses, imagining the lives that carried on as normal inside their walls, oblivious to the thousands of people battling across the spectrum of time for the betterment of the world.

Carry on, everyone. I'll be back. I promise.

* * *

The drive downtown took Martin just under thirty minutes. He paused when he reached the Chop House, a two-level steakhouse where Denver's finest gathered to dine. The building hid behind Coors Field, but glowed elegantly in the night, its red neon letters sure to draw the attention of any passersby.

He passed two valet workers, and drove to the back where a separate, public garage awaited.

The garage's bright lights splashed across the road in front of him. He pulled in, took a ticket, and drove toward the corner stairwell. It was a quiet evening, so he had no issue finding a spot.

Martin parked with the stairwell door in his rear view and waited a moment in his car. He wondered if they were already watching him from underground, then cracked his knuckles and stepped out of the car.

The garage remained deserted as he strode toward the stairwell, eyes bouncing from corner to corner. He pulled open the door to the stinging stench of urine soaked into the metal steps where numerous homeless spent their nights off the streets. He briefly reminisced on kicking the bums out of his parking garage way back when he had managed one in 1993.

Those good 'ol days when you had a family and life seemed perfect.

Martin immediately shook the nostalgia from his mind as

211

he descended the stairs, his footsteps thudding and echoing. The garage was a small one, only two levels into the earth, so Martin reached the bottom landing within a minute.

He stood at the door that entered back into the garage and found it abandoned. Surely no one would drive so low when there were dozens of spots on the ground level, and probably a hundred more on the level above.

These Road Runners sure do find the best hiding spots.

"You also never thought this was real," he said aloud, no longer worried about eavesdroppers.

Five minutes passed as he waited at the bottom of the stairs. The dim lighting proved why a homeless person would choose this location as their overnight hotel. It was just warm enough for comfort, and just dim enough for a good sleep. Not to mention the privacy provided when the garage was barely in use.

Did they tell me the right spot?

As if his thoughts could be heard, footsteps came from the top of the stairwell, thudding with each heavy step, vibrating the entire building with it. Martin's heart thumped harder, anticipating the encounter that would change his life.

What if it's just a bum ready for bed?

But it wasn't.

It was Bill.

"How did you get here so fast?" Martin asked, trying to do quick math in his head that ruled Bill's appearance as an impossibility.

"We have more than one jet."

"Why didn't you just ride with me?"

"Commander Strike wanted you to have a moment alone to gather your thoughts. We all had a good laugh when you fell asleep right away." Bill chuckled to himself.

"I wouldn't have minded. If she would've just asked, I'd have told her I planned on sleeping."

Bill raised a hand. "It's no worries, we have jets all over the world and can refuel them for incredibly cheap in the past. She wanted a familiar face when you arrived, and asked for me to come right away in case you made a quick decision, which it appears you have."

Bill's old face cracked into a warm grin.

"Yes. I had a long talk with my mother, and spent time reflecting on what I want. I'm ready to discuss terms."

"Glad to hear. Let's go meet the Lead Runner here in Denver-—he's been anxious since the Commander got on the phone with him after you left Alaska. You drove, right?"

"Yeah."

"Good, you can drive us over."

"I thought this is where we're supposed to be."

Bill looked up and around, examining his dim surroundings. "This is a parking garage."

He slapped Martin on the back and cackled. "This is just our meeting place—we don't actually conduct our business in a parking garage."

But you do out of an outhouse basement?

"We have some office space about ten minutes away, walking. But I'm tired. So you can drive us there in 2 minutes. Let's go."

Martin noticed the droop in Bill's eyes. The old man was probably ready to relax for the evening after having found the Road Runner's most prized person. Then Commander Strike sent him on a five-hour flight across the country to meet with that same man. He led the way to his car and drove to the office building that really was two minutes away. On the exterior, a sign hung on the brick building to welcome them to Centennial Marketing. The windows provided a view into the office where unattended computer monitors glowed in the darkness.

"There's a parking space up front just for this building. Take it."

Martin obliged and wiggled into the tight space.

"You conduct all of this business out in the open like this? Anyone could just walk in."

"Oh, Martin, we're not dumb like Chris and his obnoxious storefronts. This really is a marketing company, operated by us. There's a staircase in the far back of the building, behind the manager's office, where no one from the public would even be able to get to."

Martin nodded. "Another basement hideout?"

"*Always* a basement hideout. Being underground doesn't allow things like our cell phones or other electronics to be detected. It's the safest way to conceal what we do, and it's worked forever." Bill opened his door and stepped out, prompting Martin to do the same.

Martin gathered his surroundings, and found they were only three blocks south of the Chop House, and one away from the Oxford Hotel that seemed to live three hundred years in the past.

Bill climbed up the three short steps to the office building, wiggled a key in the lock, and pushed open the door with a steady *swoosh.*

Martin joined him inside and let the door close, the lock clicking shut immediately. Bill had already worked his way through most of the office and was toward the end of the long hallway. "Let's go, Martin, lots to do."

Martin walked faster to keep up and joined Bill outside of a door that had *MANAGER* written in big letters.

"Right through here."

Bill pushed open the door to a standard office: desk, computer, filing cabinets with papers bursting out. He crossed the messy room and tapped on a cabinet along the back wall. A vibration rattled the ground as the sound of a humming motor filled the silence. The cabinet slid aside, revealing a dark hole that led into the ground.

"This way," Bill said, dropping a foot into the darkness. As he did, a light flickered to life, illuminating the path below. The steps and walls were all made of stone, lined with modern fluorescent lights that appeared out of place.

Bill started down the stairs, boots clapping and echoing just as they had in the parking garage moments ago.

Martin followed, taking careful steps, expecting the ancient stone to suddenly crumble beneath his shoes. No such thing happened, and he reached the bottom landing to find a whole other world.

The layout was similar to the one he had seen in Alaska, with desks spread across the middle of the floor as TVs hung on the walls. This location had an aquarium in the ground, a billiards table in the back, glowing glass refrigerators, and sofas in an area that appeared to be a lounge.

"Whoa," Martin said, glancing around the room. No one froze to gawk at him like he was a rare species. At least forty men and women kept their focus on their computer screens, some appearing more relaxed than others as they watched movies instead of tracking down Revolters.

"Welcome to our Denver office," Bill said, looking around the room in search of someone. "I've only been here a couple of times—I go where the Commander goes, usually. Tarik runs Denver. I just don't see him anywhere."

On cue, a man no older than 40 raised his hand in the furthest corner of the room and started jogging toward them. Bill waved back and they waited.

"Good evening, gentlemen," he said, sticking out a hand. "Martin, I'm Tarik. We'll be working closely together since I oversee our Denver operations. I understand you're a native of the city?"

"I am."

"Fantastic. Beautiful city. I'm originally from Egypt, but moved here ten years ago on assignment from the Commander."

Martin couldn't help but examine Tarik. His new Egyptian ally had brown skin, buzzed black hair, and muscles that would rip his t-shirt apart if he did so much as sneeze. He had all the appearances of a military man, even down to the cargo pants that hung loosely around his waist.

"Shall we step into my office?" Tarik asked.

Bill nodded and they followed Tarik around the corner into an office that looked no different than the Commander's, only this one had no bottle of scotch. Hard to justify alcohol when you had to maintain muscles strong enough to rip a head off a body.

Tarik guided them in as he closed the door behind. "Commander Strike gave me her blessing to accept your response and negotiate on her behalf." He crossed the office and sat down in his well-cushioned chair across from Bill and Martin. "Let's get right to it. We want you, Martin, and are willing to work with you to ensure you'll join the Road Runners."

Martin nodded and folded his hands on his lap. "I'm

interested in joining. But I do have a condition."

"Let's hear it." Tarik watched Martin with studious, brown eyes.

"My mom has Alzheimer's disease, recently diagnosed. It's my understanding that there's a cure for it in the future. No matter what I get tasked to do with the Road Runners, I want it known that my main priority is to get this medicine to my mom as soon as possible."

"Did Chris tell you there's a cure?"

"Yes," he lied, relying on faith that there would be such thing.

"Hmmm. I'm not sure that there is, but I'm happy to look into it for you. I caution against traveling to the future alone—it's a truly dangerous time."

Martin's stomach sunk at this news. "Well, what can I do? This is kind of a deal breaker. I *need* that medicine."

"Look, I don't know how far in the future we may need to go to find this. Just because I don't know off the top of my head if it exists or not, doesn't make it definitive. I can look. I'll even look tonight. If it's real, it's yours."

"Thank you. I'd like to know soon. Tonight preferably."

"Consider it done. And what do you plan to do if the medicine isn't real? Surely, you can't just go home and forget all about this."

"I can, and I will. That's all I care about. Your war has gone on for years; I highly doubt I'm the secret ingredient."

"You'd be surprised. But before I get into that, I want to make sure there's nothing else you want to discuss."

"Sonya—I want to see her."

"What for exactly?"

"I never got closure. I just want to leave her knowing nothing was held back."

Tarik squirmed in his seat. "I'm afraid we can't accommo-date that request."

"Why not? She's a Road Runner. It should be pretty straightforward to arrange a meeting with all of your fancy jets."

"It's not the logistics we can't handle. You see, Sonya is actually a part of your mission should you join us. And we can't have you seeing her before we give the green light."

"Part of my mission? How?"

"You're going to kill her."

29

Chapter 29

Martin sat in silence for the next three minutes, staring from Tarik, to the ceiling, to the floor. Tarik let his words sink in while Martin fidgeted in his chair like a student in detention. Bill remained quiet, as he had throughout the entire exchange, staring at the walls, likely praying someone would let him out of the office.

"I'm sorry," Martin finally said. "Did you say you want me to *kill* Sonya?"

Tarik nodded with his hands folded beneath his chin.

"Absolutely not. Are you crazy?"

Martin fought his urge to jump across the desk and choke this meathead. It wouldn't end well going up against such a strong man, but one should never underestimate the power of a fit of rage.

Tarik raised a finger. "Trust me when I tell you this was not *why* we wanted to bring you on board, but a unique opportunity has arisen because of it. We've also never killed any of our own, but some new and critical intel has shown this as a likely way of killing Chris."

"So killing Sonya is a way to kill Chris? Do you know how stupid that sounds?"

"I know how stupid it sounds to someone who doesn't know how this all works, yes. But there is evidence – overwhelming evidence – that this will work. Killing Chris will end the war in North America."

Martin shook his head, his lips pursed.

"You're right, Martin," Tarik continued. "This war has gone on for too long. We've exhausted thousands of options, tried hundreds of tactics, all to no avail. This option has been debated dozens of times in the last two weeks, and both sides feel strongly."

"What side are you on?"

"I'm against it." Tarik paused and looked down.

"But...?"

"But it should work. Is taking one life worth the millions that can be saved? I used to say no, but having been to the future and seeing what becomes of this world, it's hard to argue against trying anything to prevent it."

"It can't be that bad."

"Oh, it's not bad. It's fucking *horrifying.* It's not a world you want to live in, or have anyone live in. It's hell on Earth."

"Why does Sonya have to die?"

"Sonya is Chris's daughter."

Martin opened his mouth and closed it, and then scrunched his face into pure confusion. "I'm sorry, did you say his *daughter*?"

"I'm afraid so. We'll have plenty of time to go into the history, but Chris tied his soul to her. As long as she lives, he remains invincible."

"There's no such thing as tying your soul to something,"

Martin said flatly, frustration bubbling beneath every word.

"Right, just like there's no such thing as time travel, or freezing time. Open your mind, Martin, this is all real."

"What does it mean?"

"It means that if Sonya is alive, Chris is immortal. If she's dead, he becomes a regular human being just like you and me. Bullets can actually puncture his lungs, his skull can explode. None of that is possible as long as Sonya's still breathing."

"Does she know that his soul is tied to her?"

"Yes. He told her when she was a teenager. The funny part is she pretends to not know about it anymore, probably for good reason."

"So that you won't kill her to end the war."

"Exactly. She doesn't know that we've had teams putting in heavy research on Chris's earlier days before he became a Revolter and master of time. It's been grueling espionage, especially with the amount of eyes Chris keeps on him and his property—he always has. We've got to a point, though, where we found this to be true. We overheard the conversation between him and Sonya when he admitted what he had done. The planting of his soul has no bearing on her, other than making her a prime target for anyone wanting to take down Chris."

"So if I kill her, you guys kill Chris?"

"At the very next moment we get, yes."

"Why do I have to do it?"

"We think she's on to us. There have been some half-hearted attempts at a quiet execution—we don't want the community to know that we're willing to kill our own. It goes against our values."

"Then why do it?"

"I'm not going over this again. We need to save the world from itself, and this has become the main option. Believe me, we love Sonya. She's been a factor in every major decision for the Road Runners. And now she still is. The ultimate sacrifice."

"Again, why me?" Martin was growing sick of Tarik beating around the bush. Bill continued staring into space.

"She has never spoken of anyone like she does about you." This statement sent an instant flutter to Martin's chest. "We believe she'll let you close enough to actually pull this off. She'll let her guard down. We think she has feelings for you. We tried to get her to admit it, but she refuses every time. But we sense it."

"You want to use her love for me to kill her." Martin said this more for himself to process, his guts twisting like a rung out dishrag. *She loves me and they want me to kill her. I love her, too.* "I can't do that. It's absurd, and I'm not a killer."

"We thought you'd say that. We really need you to look at the big picture. If you want to join me on a trip to the future to see how bad it will get, I'm happy to do that. Again, this is our last resort. Even the people who voted in favor of this are against the thought of having to kill Sonya. But we have no choice."

"I'm not killing the only person I've loved in the last 20 years. Even if it was all a lie."

Tarik stood up. "Let's take a break. Commander Strike is on her way and should be here in the next hour. We can reconvene at that time and you can discuss any further concerns with her. How does that sound?"

"That's fine with me. I'm still interested in being a Road Runner—I just can't go through with this specifically."

"Understood. Feel free to relax in our lounge, and we'll have someone come grab you when Commander Strike gets here."

Tarik pulled open the office door and gestured for Bill and Martin to leave.

* * *

Bill parted ways with Martin when they stepped out, telling him to take time alone to think. One thing had become clear about the Road Runners: they truly didn't believe in forcing the issue. In their eyes, they had the most prized possession of the war in Martin, and yet no one had done more than try to persuade him into joining the cause. Chris hadn't even had a direct conversation with Martin and already had plans to make him a robotic soldier if he didn't oblige.

Martin crossed the main floor, where the mood was relaxed compared to the tension inside Tarik's office. Still, no one so much as looked up at him. Everyone remained deep into their computer screens, and some had even pulled out beds from under their desks and prepared for a night's sleep.

Do these people live here? he wondered, and would ask the Commander when she arrived.

Martin went to the lounge and plopped down on a sofa. Refrigerators hummed in the background as the soft murmur of voices faded into distant whispers from the office floor. He wanted to lie down, but decided it wouldn't look good for their savior to take a nap while everyone else worked diligently.

He thought back to his talk with his mom, wondering if she would have given the same advice if she knew killing was part of the job.

How am I even supposed to kill Sonya? This is barbaric. If they want to do it so badly, they should do it themselves. They can hide out so well around the world, surely they can cover up a simple murder.

Martin buried his face into his palms, clammy with sweat, and prayed for a way out of this situation. Maybe the calling for a new life was reserved for those with ambition. He would still be content running off to an exotic country and spending his money and life there until the end. He wouldn't live into this supposedly scary future, and no longer had a child who would, either. None of this was his problem.

I can give them some of my blood so they can run tests on what makes me so special, but I don't need to be a part of this. I'm not going to get a desk in this office and sleep under it for a war that has no end. This is all a sucker's bet. They claim that leaving isn't an option, but it always is.

He thought about how Chris had randomly shown up at the cabin when he and Sonya had left town for a few days after the coma. Chris had been the furthest thing from his mind, yet he still showed up, uninvited and in the middle of the mountains.

You know he'll find you. He probably already knows where you are. The Road Runners aren't the only ones in this war. He has ways of finding people, too.

Martin felt queasy and fought off nervous belches that tried to make their way up. He suffered a mild out-of-body experience when everyone in the room stood up and faced the entrance.

"Good evening, everyone," a woman's voice called, prompting Martin to stand and see the Commander across the room. "I want to thank you all for the hard work you've been putting in. We're getting closer. Believe in what you're doing every day, because every small step that each of you make leads to one huge leap for the Road Runners."

The room broke into brief applause as Commander Strike bowed her head and worked her way across the room to Tarik's office where she closed the door behind her.

Everyone settled back into their places and Martin sat back down on the sofa, debating if he should rummage through the cupboards for a snack.

He had no time, as Bill started toward him from one of the side offices. He waved a hand and grinned. "They're ready for you."

"Already? She just got here."

"Tarik briefed her over the phone on her way. Things move quickly in this organization; don't be surprised if you're already thrown into the middle of things tomorrow, should you still agree to join us."

"What should I do, Bill? Am I crazy for not wanting to kill Sonya to end the war?"

"Not at all. This has been a polarizing topic for us. The topic was put up to a vote for all Road Runners in a position of leadership, minus those who work directly with Sonya. Across the world, we had 600 total votes cast. 301 came back in favor of killing Sonya, 299 against. I don't think Commander Strike has slept in four days. She's a huge fan of Sonya—once had talks with her about moving into a higher position in her office. But, she's a bigger fan of ending this war. This decision has been eating away at her. I don't think anything can happen that will change her mind at this point."

"You're not helping me."

"I'm not trying to sway you one way or another. This is a heavy decision and I'm glad I'm not in your shoes. You have to decide what's best for you. But I suggest you get in that room before the Commander gets impatient."

Martin nodded and shook hands with Bill. "Thanks for everything."

Bill bowed his head in appreciation and Martin pivoted to return to Tarik's office. The door was cracked and he pushed it open to find Tarik standing in the corner of the room while Commander Strike sat behind the desk, hands folded beneath her chin.

"Hello again, Martin. How are you doing?" she asked with a gentle smile. Now that Bill had mentioned it, he noticed slight bags under her eyes.

"I've had better days, that's for sure."

"I know this has been a lot thrown your way, and I hope we can still reach an agreement on you joining us."

Martin nodded as he sat down in the seat across the desk. "I can't kill Sonya."

"I know. But we need you to. Hear me out. We believe Sonya is on to us. We tried poisoning her drink, and she conveniently knocked it off the table to look like an accident. She has stopped contacting some of her closest friends within the organization. All of her trust has vanished, and that's on me. We have someone slipping her information; there's no way she could have figured this out on her own. We've kept her duties the same as always, kept her security detail consistent, but she still knows."

"Not surprising. It sounds like there are some strong opinions on the matter."

Commander Strike nodded. "I know. I must have changed my mind at least a hundred times. But it's what needs to be done. It's one life against millions; it's really a no-brainer."

"It's not. Because Road Runners aren't monsters—I've gathered that much in the last day. You are good-hearted, well-intentioned people. You're the complete opposite of Chris. He would've had Sonya dead within five minutes of learning this information, if the roles were reversed."

Bill had said she wouldn't change her mind, but Martin felt obliged to at least try. He watched the wrenching decision swim behind her exhausted eyes.

"I appreciate the input. It means a lot coming from someone who is still technically an outsider, but the decision is made and we want to discuss it with you."

"I've already talked about it with Tarik."

Tarik nodded from the corner, arms crossed with a foot planted on the wall for support.

"We haven't discussed *how* you would go about this. We've considered multiple ways of carrying this out. We don't want anything vicious done to Sonya. It needs to be a painless death. We're not asking you to shoot her in the head or anything like that. We have three options prepared: more poison for a drink, an injection, and a letter."

"A letter?"

"It's covered in a poisonous powder—from the future. Our plan is to equip you with all three options when you go to meet Sonya. Each one will affect her in the same way. These poisons are designed to make the receiver fall asleep, and eventually slow down the heart rate until it stops. She won't feel anything painful this way."

It's like putting an animal down.

"Why the three options?"

"We want to give you flexibility. The plan is to have you meet with Sonya, spend some time with her and catch up."

"Catch up? It's only been a few hours since she even left me."

"Yes, but she left you with a laundry list of questions. I heard about the meeting in the Oxford Hotel basement. They said you were completely stunned, and I don't blame you."

"Do you guys always trick people like this?"

"Not always, but it's Sonya's role with us. She's even passed up promotions to continue doing it. She loves being in the field."

Martin thought back to that day at the cabin again. Sonya was upstairs when Chris had stopped by for his visit. They were that close to each other and she didn't even know it. What would she have done if she came downstairs and saw her father chatting with Martin on the balcony?

"It just feels like I'm being used at this point. All this effort to get me to join so I can kill Sonya. If I do, then the war ends. Then what?"

"Then you're a hero, and the world is saved. There will be a recovery effort that takes place. A lot of damage has been done at certain points in time that we'll need to evaluate how to fix. But we'll have the ease of knowing there will be no more attacks."

"Just because Chris dies, you think the Revolters will give up?"

"The Revolters are a lost cause without him. If Chris dies, so does their vision. He recruits weak-willed people who require guidance. Sure, there'll be a few who give it a try and attack us, but the majority will go into hiding. Because if Chris doesn't survive, how can they expect to?"

Martin looked in the Commander's direction, but not at her. He looked *through* her, into a future where he was considered a hero. A secret hero that the whole world wouldn't know about, just the Road Runners and Revolters. A hero in a second world that existed not by imagination, but underground, working every day to keep the world safe.

"It's not everyday someone gets an opportunity like this," Strike said. "We have a unique opportunity to give our-selves—humanity—a second chance at life by fixing things. One thing I've learned is that none of that matters. What happens in your current life is what will forever shape you. Even if you had managed to save your daughter, your soul remains forever scarred by her disappearance. That alone dictated the next twenty years of your life." Martin nodded. She was good. "Now you're here at the ultimate crossroads. You can go back to your life and spend the rest of your days on the run from Chris. Or you can be the one who ends him once and for all, so no one ever has to be running again."

"I want to know something. If I kill Sonya and Chris never steps foot outside of his house, will you blow up that mansion knowing there are at least fifty Road Runners being held captive underneath it?" Martin drew on his knowledge from the brief conversations he had with Julian and Bill.

"You're a forward thinker, and that's how I know you'll do big things for us, even after the war. To answer your question, no, we would not put those 50 lives at risk. There are ways to get to him even if he hides in the house."

Martin nodded, imagining himself slipping poison into Sonya's drink while she cooked dinner for him. He longed for his old life with her and wished it could've been real. He'd happily spend the rest of his life on the run if she was by his side.

He leaned back in his seat, relaxed for the first time in hours, and grinned at the Commander who watched him with anxious eyes.

"I'm in."

30

Chapter 30

Martin had no plans to kill Sonya, but the Road Runners didn't need to know that. All they cared about was that he *agreed* to go through with it. Who was to say he couldn't have a change of heart at the last minute?

Just get me in with the Road Runners and I can explore other options from there.

He had no clue the magnitude of their resources. There had to be a different option. Road Runners only murdered Revolters, not other Road Runners.

"I don't have to sleep in this office, do I?" Martin asked after Tarik had pulled a bottle of whiskey from his desk drawer. Turns out the Commander and her trusted leaders weren't so different after all.

Commander Strike threw her head back and laughed, an obvious wave of relaxation spreading over her like a wildfire. "Of course not. The folks in this office are researchers and watchers. We have eyes all over the world in offices just like this. They know that living here is part of the job when they accept it. A lot of these people come from lives destroyed by Chris. They feel they have no other purpose than to eat, breathe, and sleep Chris until he's pronounced dead."

"So what will I be doing?"

"You're on a special assignment in the field. We have even more people in the field than in offices, physically following Revolters in an effort to find their hideouts, among other tasks, of course."

Like killing your own?

"So what happens now?" Martin asked.

"Well, something new that we've been doing: injecting a tracking device into your body."

Martin's grin turned into an immediate frown.

"It's not so we can keep an eye on you, it's more to know if you're still alive and well. And if you're in danger, where you are exactly."

"Why is this new?"

"We decided once people started getting taken into Chris's house that we needed a way to check on them. We had no way of knowing if they were alive or not, making a decision difficult about what to do with the house. We still don't know, actually, as the only one who had a tracker was shot the same day you escaped."

"I watched that from my window." Martin remembered that moment, thinking he'd never make it out of the house.

"Yeah, we had to watch it, too. Had a car on the way to pick him up, but Chris never really meant to let him go. You know, you're not the first person to escape from his mansion."

"Is that so?"

"We've watched five of our own make a run from that house, all who were shot. We don't know if Chris just let them out to a hopeless escape, or if they actually broke out and were caught.

That's another reason we want everyone to have tracking devices—it just helps us gain more information. "

"Makes sense. After I get my tracker, then what?"

Commander Strike was beating around the information he wanted.

"We're all gonna rest tonight. Tomorrow morning we'll implant your tracking device, provide you with the poisons and the information about Sonya, and you'll be on your way. We'd like to see her dead tomorrow night, if possible. We already have heavily-armed crews surrounding Chris from a distance. Sonya has a tracking device already, so we'll know the moment she dies. Their deaths will nearly be in sync."

"That's pretty aggressive. Won't I need time to regain trust with her before trying to slip anything to her?"

Martin's plan was to stall once he was with Sonya, maybe find a way to warn her. It sounded as if the entire Road Runner community would be watching this play out like the Super Bowl. A death party. Can Martin pull off the impossible and save the world? Bring your chips and dips and find out, this Wednesday at six!

The thought sent a shiver down his back.

"We've been complacent enough, especially under past leadership. I don't believe in waiting things out. We have a mission, and it's time to complete it."

The smile left her face as she spoke sternly. Commander Strike was this close to achieving their biggest goal and wouldn't risk it so Martin could have small talk with Sonya.

"Now let's all get some sleep. I know I'm running on fumes and you probably are too, Tarik."

Tarik nodded, tipping his glass to finish the last of his whiskey.

"We have extra beds here, or you can go home and come back in the morning. It doesn't matter to me, just know you'll need to be here by seven."

Martin pulled out his cellphone (oh, how he had missed it) and saw the time as 12:30. It was already Wednesday morning.

"I'll just stay here." There was no point in driving home to toss and turn in his bed for five hours when he could just do that here. His mom wouldn't even be awake, and he had said his final goodbyes, just in case.

"Perfect. We'll get you a private room. Welcome to the team."

Commander Strike rose and stuck out a hand that Martin grabbed firmly.

This is really happening. I'm a Road Runner.

The nightcap in Tarik's office must have helped Martin fall into a deep sleep, because his mind still raced despite his body falling into a limp pile of flesh on the mattress. It turns out all of the offices doubled as bedrooms where beds pulled out of the wall, and the temperature adjusted to a perfect 70 degrees on the thermostat.

Martin fell asleep thinking about Sonya and the life they had made in 1996. It was perfect, and he wished he could've stayed. With his new knowledge of her, he knew that was impossible. No matter how long they would've carried out their lives together, it still would end with him joining the Road Runners. That was her job, and she was damn good at it.

He remembered when they played house—cooking dinner, doing dishes, and making love multiple times a week. It was a glimpse into the life that could have been if Izzy never died. Izzy always thought her dad was a hero, and now she could look down from heaven and see for herself.

I'm here because of you, and I need to see it through.

The thought of joining the Road Runners and taking on a mission of killing Sonya didn't worry him. Not knowing what his life would look like, say, in the next 48 hours, terrified him. He could wind up a hero just as well as dead. He was officially in a war now, and all is fair in love and war, right?

Except for when you use your love to kill someone for the war. Martin reflected—something he had lacked the time to do—on what he had accomplished during his first trip into the past.

Nothing. Not a goddamn thing. Izzy is still dead. Columbine ended up worse. I almost died. And I fell in love with a girl who was only trying to recruit me to this shit show.

Martin cried in his dark room, tears streaming from his face and soaking into his pillow. The fear of failing again, on such a grand stage, made him sick just thinking about it. Izzy, Sonya, and his mother all spun around in his head. His old life was gone, and forward was the only direction to go.

31

Chapter 31

Martin had set the alarm on his cell phone for 6:30 A.M. His brain itched with fatigue as his bleary eyes opened. He had made a point to not look at the clock while he tossed and rolled all night—that only made it worse. By his mental calculation, he had slept a total of two sporadic hours throughout the night.

He told himself that he could go through with whatever the Road Runners asked of him, but the thought of killing anyone kept him awake.

The next 24 hours would be spent on autopilot, and he preferred it that way. The excitement had worn off, the determination vanished, leaving him a sulking pool of regret.

I never asked for any of this.

Martin pulled himself up from the bed on wobbly legs. His mind protested having to do anything as a long day awaited. *They expect me to have this mission done tonight? I'm gonna need a nap. Maybe I'll take some of this poison and enjoy the ride. They said it doesn't hurt.*

He shook his head clear of the thoughts, knowing that was just the exhaustion speaking.

"Get off your ass and be the hero. For Izzy. She led you here."

Martin's pep talks to himself usually worked, but they fell on deaf ears this time. He crossed the room to examine himself in a mirror on the wall. His hair flew in every direction, eyes bloodshot and puffy. *I look how I feel.*

A knock banged on the door, startling him, and he crossed the room to open it.

"Good morning, Sunshine," Bill said, chipper with a cup of coffee in his hand. "I heard you're officially part of the gang now. Welcome."

"Thanks, Bill."

"Rough night? You look like a pile of shit that got run over by a semi-truck."

Martin chuckled. "You know, I've been hit by a semi before, and I'd have to agree with you."

Bill laughed and slapped Martin on the shoulder. "I know this has been a lot, but hopefully today goes quickly and smoothly for you."

Martin nodded, unsure what to say. Quick and smooth was the last thing on his mind. He preferred it to be dragged out and avoidable.

"I came to make sure you were awake and ready. Commander Strike is expecting you in Tarik's office at seven sharp."

"Yeah, I'm just about ready. I'll be there."

"Great, have fun. I won't be in there, have a couple matters to tend to, but wanted to wish you good luck."

"Thanks again for everything. Maybe we can grab a drink after this is all done."

"I'll hold you to it."

Bill patted Martin on the shoulder one final time before

turning toward another office down the hall.

Martin closed the door and returned to the mirror, patting his hair down with a quick spit on his fingers.

"You can do this—whatever *this* is."

He felt more alert, but couldn't ignore the tingling in his head that demanded sleep. It would have to wait. His cell phone chimed to let him know it was now 6:55.

He took one last look at the man who had overcome so much since 1996. Bouts of depression, alcoholism, and numerous suicide attempts weren't enough to bring him down. *And neither will this.* He smiled to himself before leaving his room to meet Tarik and Commander Strike.

Walking down the hallway felt like an eternity as he passed each door with increasing stress. When he reached Tarik's door he paused, knowing a new life waited on the other side.

"Come in!" the Commander called without him knocking.

She's good.

Martin pushed the door open and found Commander Strike with Tarik in their same positions as the night before. She had her hands folded on the desk, and Tarik fidgeted in the corner with a small syringe.

"Good morning, Martin," she greeted. "We had a team prepare a plan for you overnight. I reviewed it earlier this morning and have signed off on it. All we need to do is get you set up with your tracking device and you'll be ready to head back to 1996."

"I'm going back to 1996?" Martin asked, a sudden tremble taking control of his arms.

"Yes, that's where Sonya lives."

She played you, Marty. Played you good. All that talk about leaving her life behind. It was all an act.

"She's still in her same house?"

Commander Strike nodded.

The house he thought they had turned into a home together. How many other men had she laid a similar trap for throughout history?

"Here's the report." She slid a file across the desk with a sturdy finger. "It's only two pages. You can read it here, but you can't take it with you—can't have any trace of this mission when you go."

Martin grabbed the file and flipped it open. It contained instructions on the proper way to dispense of the poisons along with random information about Sonya's house and neighborhood, should he have to get involved in a foot chase. It had a clipped picture of her, not smiling and staring blankly at the camera.

"This is pretty standard stuff, especially since you lived in that house. The poisons are pretty straightforward," Strike explained, glaring across the desk

"I don't see my condition listed in here."

"What condition?"

"About getting a cure for Alzheimer's in the future, to bring back to my mom."

"This isn't a contract of any sorts, it's just a mission report."

"I want it in writing somewhere."

Martin spoke sharply and returned a hard gaze into Commander Strike's eyes.

She nodded and held out an open palm. "Okay, pass it here."

Martin handed it over and watched her flip a page and start scribbling notes. She passed it back.

"An effort to find a cure?" he asked. "I *need* the cure."

"Martin, we don't know if there's such thing. As soon as

this mission is done, we'll get people on it right away. I'm not going to put it into writing that there's a cure because I don't know that for sure."

Martin rubbed his eyes, the puffiness starting to shrink.

"I need this. Just as badly as you want Chris dead."

"You need this *because* of Chris. Don't forget that."

Martin nodded. "Fair enough."

Commander Strike turned to Tarik, who stepped to the middle of the room with the syringe held out. It looked like a regular shot you'd get at the doctor's office.

"I have your tracking device right here," Tarik said. "I'll inject this into your arm, and within 15 minutes the device will cling to a muscle and expand to the size of a dime. You won't feel a thing."

"That's what everyone says around here."

"Are you ready?"

"Let's get it over with." Martin rolled up his sleeve and held out his pasty arm.

Tarik stepped up and pulled the cap off the syringe, swiftly inserting it into Martin's flesh and pushing down on the lever.

"All done," he said with a grin as he pulled the needle out. "Not a drop of blood."

Martin checked his arm and saw nothing.

"Now we can officially say, welcome to the Road Runners." Commander Strike had a stupid grin on her face that wouldn't leave for the next hour. "You'll be leaving shortly. The poison is being prepared as we speak."

Martin thought he felt a bubble burst within his arm, but chalked it up to his imagination.

There's no hiding now. These people can find you wherever you are.

The thought was comforting and terrifying at the same time.

A knock banged on the door.

"Come in," Tarik barked.

A weaselly man with glasses poked his head in. "The project is ready."

Martin looked from the weasel to Commander Strike.

"Thank you," she said.

The weasel left as quickly as he had arrived.

"That's the poison," she said to Martin. "You're all set."

His gut dropped to his knees. He thought he'd have more time to stall, but clearly the universe wanted to get this over with as well.

"Are you ready?" she asked.

Martin nodded, avoiding eye contact.

Fuck no, I'm not ready to kill Sonya.

He'd been a Road Runner for less than a minute and was already thrust into the war. *She did say they move fast.*

"Where do you want to lie down before you drink your Juice?"

"Shouldn't I go to Larkwood?"

"You can go wherever. We'll give you a ride in 1996 if you need it."

Martin crossed his arms. "I'll just do it here. Can I do that?"

"Of course. This was still a hub back then, so someone will be here to take you to Sonya's house. We'll make sure the arrangements are made."

She nodded to Tarik, who promptly left the office.

"I want to wish you luck, and thank you in advance for the service you're doing." Commander Strike stood and crossed the desk to meet Martin. He rose and grabbed her hand to shake. "I know this is hard, but it should be rather straightforward. I don't foresee any complications if you act normal and keep your poisons hidden."

"Where is the poison?"

"Your driver will have it for you." She checked her watch. "You should get going. We'll be watching both of your tracking devices from here. As soon as we see Sonya has died, we'll move on Chris immediately. We already have five snipers surrounding his mansion."

Martin nodded and left the office, pulling his flask from his back pocket. He looked over his shoulder and saw Commander Strike still standing in Tarik's office, her arms crossed and her face scrunched into heavy anticipation.

He strode down the hall, and this time people stared at him. Those he made eye contact with gave quick nods as he passed. *They have my back. I wonder how much they know.* Martin returned the nods and even some smiles until he reached the office that had doubled as his bedroom the night before.

He took a sip of the Juice and started thinking about 1996 as he lay down on the bed. Within minutes, his mind drifted out of 2018 and started its journey to another world.

32

Chapter 32

Martin jolted awake on the floor and sat up, finding the room to be nothing but a storage closet as boxes lined the walls.

He stood and pulled open the door to find the office set up in the same manner, only with less people.

"Mr. Briar!" a man shouted from the desk in front of Martin. "Welcome to 1996. My name is Brett McBath." The man rounded his desk and met Martin in the aisle. "I'll be driving you to Larkwood."

"Thank you, Brett, nice to meet you."

"The honor is all mine, sir. It's not every day you get to meet a real-life hero. When they asked for someone to drive you, I couldn't resist the opportunity."

Brett spoke in jittery phrases and fidgeted with his fingers. Something about his eyes looked familiar to Martin, and after another glance, he recognized him as the weasel man from 2018. He would be 22 years younger in this current encounter.

"Thank you." Martin didn't know what else to say. He'd never experienced any sort of popularity throughout his life, and being called a hero certainly pushed him out of his comfort zone.

"Shall we get going then?" Brett gazed at Martin with blue eyes, and Martin saw the shock and awe swimming behind that stare.

"Yes." Brett's excitement rubbed off on Martin, making him determined to carry out this mission.

See, there are other people who are behind this. It'll be fine.

"Follow me." Brett walked away and took Martin down the familiar path to the stairwell that led to the marketing office above. The flat screen computer monitors had been replaced by boxy tanks that hummed and buzzed.

"No one gets into this office until 10 A.M." Brett checked his watch. "It's only 8:30."

He led them outside the building where a black sports car waited for them.

"You drive a Mustang?" Martin asked.

"Yeah." Brett laughed nervously. "I figured why not. I can drive any car in the world and I've always loved Mustangs."

"Nice. I like them, too."

They sat down in the car and Brett roared the engine to life, the vibrations rocking both of them.

"We shouldn't have any traffic right now, can get you to Sonya's house in a little more than ten minutes."

Ten minutes. The thought drained all the blood from Martin's stomach and chest. Ten minutes stood between him and a difficult decision. The more he weighed it, the more he considered actually going through with it. The glimpse into life as a hero appealed, but did he really want that for the rest of his time on Earth?

You couldn't save Izzy, but you can save others. Don't let her death go in vain.

"Are you nervous?" Brett asked. "I know I'd be nervous—actually I think I *am* nervous. For you. I have that feeling like there's a boiling pot of water in my stomach. You ever get that?"

"All the time."

"Oh, before I forget." Brett reached into the backseat and pulled a duffel bag that he dropped on Martin's lap. "This is your stuff. It's meant to look like you packed for this trip. There's some clothes, toiletries, and books. The special letter is tucked inside a book in an envelope, and the small jar and syringe with the poison are in the middle of the toiletries bag. It's all stored safely for you to touch, so don't worry about hurting yourself. Which one do you think you're gonna use?" Brett asked like an excited child asking to go out for ice cream.

"I don't know yet, I'll need to get a feel for the situation."

They drove off, weaving north through downtown toward Larkwood, where destiny awaited.

"I can't believe I'm driving the man who will end the war."

Brett kept his eyes fixed on the road, but Martin could still sense the emotion about to burst beneath his driver's surface.

"I appreciate your excitement, but if you don't mind, I'd like a few moments of silence to myself."

"Gotta get in the zone? I can dig it. Pretend I'm not here."

Brett hummed to himself, perhaps trying to make himself disappear. Anything for Martin, right?

Martin leaned back in his seat and closed his eyes.

What the hell am I going to say to her?

He tried to imagine how this would all play out. She would either send him away, refusing to explain herself, or she could invite him in, tell him why things played out the way they did. He assumed the latter, at least based on the person he thought

245

she was.

His emotions would try to reveal themselves, and he'd need to hide them. Sonya had always shown an ability to read him, and if he seemed distraught at the thought of having to kill her, she would definitely sniff it out.

"We're here," Brett said.

Martin opened his eyes to the familiar neighborhood. The houses all looked the same on the quiet block. Brett had pulled to the side as they faced Sonya's house at the opposite end of the road.

"I was instructed to leave you here and let you walk the rest of the way. They don't want Sonya seeing any car she might recognize."

"Thank you, I appreciate the ride."

"No. Thank *you*, Mr. Briar. Can you feel it in the air? The world is about to change forever."

Martin felt nothing in the air aside from the typical smog. "Glad I can help."

"Help? You're a living legend."

"Thank you." Martin shook Brett's hand and wondered how long it would be until his new friend washed it. It wasn't everyday you got to shake hands with a living legend. He stepped out the car, anxious to get away from his groupie, and slung the duffel bag over his shoulder.

He may have not sensed a shift in the air, but there was a definite change in his stomach. The urge to vomit had risen to his throat as his fingers turned slick with sweat. He started walking down the sidewalk on weak legs, trying to clear his mind and relieve the stress that throbbed on every inch of his being.

Brett had left—surprisingly—making Martin the only person standing outside on this pleasant Friday morning. His arms trembled and his vision blurred in and out of focus while his heart thumped like a rabbit's foot. When he was three houses away, he collapsed to the ground and vomited on the sidewalk, looking around as he wiped his mouth clear of any remnants. He could hear Chris laughing all the way from Alaska, daring him to carry this out.

Get your ass up and go.

Martin wondered if the past would push back on this mission. They hadn't mentioned anything in his brief preparation. Wasn't he about to embark on not only changing the past, but also completely alter the fabric of time? Perhaps killing Sonya wasn't the big event that the past was waiting for, but rather Chris's death. That is what would officially throw the world into a chaotic limbo.

Martin pulled himself back to his feet, convinced the world wasn't stopping him, only himself. He dragged his legs to Sonya's house, its green lawn welcoming him to his past memories. He stood at the driveway and remembered all of the good times they had together.

He remembered the long drive home from the hospital after he woke from his coma. They had sat in the driveway as Martin debated revealing the truth to Sonya—a truth she had known all along. He shook his head and walked up to the door, a sliver of confidence finally working its way into his psyche. He knew she was inside, waiting for him.

When he approached the door, it swung open and Sonya stood there, eyes bulging.

"I've been expecting you," she said. "Come in."

33

Chapter 33

Sonya was as beautiful as ever. Even though he had just seen her two days ago, it felt more like five years.

"Are you just gonna stand there, or do you want to come in?" she asked with a grin.

He stepped into the doorway and let the screen door fall shut behind him as he entered the kitchen. The house was immaculate as always, and the smell of bacon and sausage oozed from the stove. He looked around the house for any sign of another man living there.

"Sit down, relax." She left him in the doorway to turn off the stove. "So, what are you doing here?"

She leaned against the counter and watched Martin with a careful eye as he sat at the kitchen table.

"These last two days have been hell," he said. His stomach bubbled with anxiety; he could feel her studying him, waiting for him to make a move. *She has to know.*

"You could say that. We went through all of this trouble to get you in private, and that piece of shit had to barge in and take you. How did you get here?"

"I escaped from Chris's house. I ran until I found civilization, and took the next flight out of that place."

"I see." She crossed her arms, all but saying that she didn't believe a word coming out of his mouth.

"Look, Sonya. I came here because I need closure. I thought we were about to start the rest of our lives together, then all of this shit happened."

His nerves settled; speaking the truth had that effect.

"I was just doing my job. I don't enjoy the disappointment that comes at the end of my missions, but it's part of it. There's not really a way around it."

"I don't care what anyone says. I know what I felt. We had something real. You wouldn't have dragged me along for six months if you didn't feel the same. You could've lured me into a trap at any time."

"You wouldn't leave without Izzy. I wasn't going to bother."

"Did you know Izzy's outcome all along?"

Sonya bowed and let her blond hair hang over her face.

"Jesus Christ, Sonya. Are you fucking kidding me? You sat with me through all that planning knowing how it was going to end. Is that why you stayed parked across the street that night?"

She looked up and brushed her hair back, nodding. "I'm sorry, Martin. You shouldn't have come here. You're not supposed to know these things."

"So both you and Chris knew the outcome and let me wander around, pretending to be a superhero. You really are your father's daughter."

"Don't call him my father!"

"Is he not?"

"Yes, he's my father, but that's not the point. He ruined my life."

"Is that why you ruin other people's lives now? Needed a way to get revenge on the system?"

"It's not like that."

"How does it feel to be living a lie?"

"I don't live a lie. *You're* the one living a lie. You were gonna just jump into a new life and pretend that your past never happened. I have to live with my past every day, so don't feed me your bullshit."

They sat in silence for a minute, both looking to the ground and avoiding eye contact. Martin's legs bounced uncontrollably under the table.

"I saw the look in your eyes at the hospital," Martin said. "There was a genuine care and concern, and I saw the woman I loved."

"I was just doing my job, checking on you. We needed you alive."

"I'll always love you. I don't care what you say. I know it was real, and if you want to keep lying to yourself that it wasn't, then that's on your conscience."

"Martin, if I could love you I would. Being with me will keep you in the line of danger for the rest of your life. If you escaped from Chris already, he'll kill you the next chance he gets."

"I don't think he will. I can take this chance with you—I have nothing to lose."

"He will. I've seen it plenty of times to know. He has zero heart, especially once he considers you a traitor."

"I'm a traitor because I didn't want to stay a prisoner in his house?"

"Yep. That's how he thinks."

"Regardless, I'll do anything. If it means risking my life,

then so be it."

"Drop the act, Martin. I know why you're really here."

"What do you mean?"

"Don't play dumb with me." Sonya turned to the counter, pulled open a drawer, and retrieved a black pistol. She cocked it before aiming at Martin.

"Whoa, take it easy, Sonya. I don't know what you think, but it isn't this." Martin slowly raised his hands in the air.

"I'm not surprised about this grand scheme. I *am* surprised that you actually agreed to it. What's in that duffel bag over there?" Sonya nodded to the bag Martin had dropped on the ground by the front door. "Gonna spike my drink? Were you gonna propose a toast to us and watch me die?"

"Sonya, it's not what you think."

"It's exactly what I think. Did you know I've been with the Road Runners for more than 30 years? I joined them the day after I graduated high school and ran away from my dad's house. There's a lot you don't know, but you just barge in here thinking you can kill me. I've been to hell and back, and I'm not leaving this world on anyone's terms but my own."

"Sonya, I have no intention of killing you."

"I can't believe you. I hope you understand." The pistol wavered in her hand and Martin watched her debate pulling the trigger. "I've been waiting for this day. As soon as Chris took you from the hotel and they sent me home, told me to not worry about it. I knew something was going on. They *never* take anyone off of a mission until it's complete."

"How did you know?"

"I have many friends. I've been here forever—there are people more loyal to me than to the Road Runners, even in the highest of positions."

Martin wondered if Bill might have slipped Sonya the secret. He had said he was against it, and seemed to have also been a lifelong Road Runner. Commander Strike shouldn't have told a soul about this plan, but the burden of such a secret could crush even the strongest-minded person.

"I don't know what you want me to say," Martin said. "I came here to talk, honestly. Yes, I have poisons in my bag that they asked me to slip you, but I'd never be able to."

"I know you're probably telling the truth, but I can't take any chances. I hope you understand."

"Sonya—"

The pistol fired, its explosion echoing throughout the house. She had lowered it from his face to his legs.

A piercing, burning sensation immediately filled his left thigh, the warmth of blood soaking into his pants.

"Motherfucker!" he screamed, grimacing and squeezing his leg.

"I'm sorry, Martin," she said, and pulled the trigger again.

His right knee exploded, blood splattering across the tile floor like an abstract painting. Martin collapsed from the chair, sliding to the ground in his own pool of blood.

She had shot each leg, and he couldn't so much as wiggle his toes.

"If one day we can put all of this behind us, then I'd be open to giving life with you another chance. But odds are you'll never see me again. None of you will."

"Sonya," Martin gasped. The adrenaline rush had numbed his legs, but he still couldn't move them, let alone stand up.

"Don't follow me. Just let me go."

She tucked the pistol into the back of her pants and hurried out of the kitchen. Martin lay face-down and dragged himself with a half-assed army crawl, dark red smearing behind him in a messy trail.

Sonya had gone into her bedroom as Martin crawled through the living room. "Sonya!" he shouted. "Sonya, help me!" His entire bottom half had turned numb, and his arms became Jell-O as they trembled with each forced movement.

When he finally reached the bedroom doorway two minutes later, he found the room deserted.

"Sonya?"

A glass bottle of green liquid lay on the ground, a puddle forming around it. Next to the puddle was another pool of blood with what looked to be a chunk of flesh and a dime-sized microchip floating on the surface.

"Nooooooo!" Martin cried, rolling to his back.

She's gone. Forever.

She had drunk her Juice and vanished. Even though he hadn't seen one, Martin knew the chip was her tracking device that she would've cut out of her arm.

You've seen her for the last time. She has no way back. Wherever she went, she's staying there forever.

Martin kept his gaze to the ceiling, the same one he had looked at so many mornings, waking up next to Sonya, and wondering if life could get any better. Those memories were from another lifetime and he'd never get them back. A lone tear rolled down his cheek and splashed on the ground, mixing in with the stream of blood that had followed him from the kitchen.

I'm never going to be a hero, he thought, and then fainted.

34

Chapter 34

Across the spectrum of time, Commander Strike watched from the Denver office with the rest of the Road Runners gathered around in the bullpen. The technology of the tracking devices allowed the host person to be watched regardless of what year they were in. All attention was focused on the screen showing the devices for both Martin and Sonya.

Martin had arrived five minutes ago to Sonya's house, and Commander Strike announced to the entire room what was going on.

"Attention all. Today is the day. Our very own Martin Briar is currently in Sonya's house in 1996. There has been a plan in the making to assassinate Sonya Griffiths. Her death will open the opportunity for us to make a final, fatal move on Chris. We currently have snipers hiding in the woods around his property in Alaska, and have received confirmation that he's inside the house."

People gasped while others shouted in protest.

Commander Strike raised her hands and waited for the bickering to settle down.

"I need you all to keep a tight lid on this information. I'm trusting you with this secret since we'll be watching the outcome from here."

She nodded to a young woman who sat behind a control panel.

The master screen, a 120-inch wide monitor, flickered to life and showed a map of Larkwood. The young woman clicked around until the screen zoomed in on a satellite image of Sonya's house where they saw the roof and her car parked in the driveway.

Two green dots flashed within the image of the roof, one labeled as S. Griffiths and the other as M. Briar.

"I want you all to know this decision was not easy. We debated heavily on how to approach this, but ultimately decided to move forward with sacrificing Sonya to end this war."

Murmurs spread across the room like wildfire as people turned to each other. Mention of ending the war was rare and never taken lightly. Everyone had fallen into such a daily groove that they sometimes forgot there was a possibility for an end to it all—it just never felt like it would actually arrive.

"You heard me correctly. To make a long story short, if Sonya dies, Chris becomes mortal and we can kill him through regular means."

"Are you saying the war can end today?" someone shouted from the back.

"Yes, it can, and it will."

The murmur grew into a nervous chatter as people broke into conversation about the news.

"This is a day that will live forever in history. On this screen we'll be watching Sonya. When her sensor turns from green

255

to red, Chris will officially be a mortal human being. I have my phone ready to make the call to Alaska where the snipers will be instructed to shoot him at first sight."

More chatter.

"This might take some time—I honestly don't know. I hope Mr. Briar can carry out this mission within the next few hours, but I suspect he'll take his time. They do have a past together, so we're unsure how exactly that will factor in to their current encounter."

Everyone had abandoned their desks and gathered in the center of the room to watch the main screen that hung high on the wall. Commander Strike crossed the aisle and joined the rest of the team, excitement and anticipation in the air like a thick fog.

Rarely nervous, Commander Strike's stomach spun in wild cartwheels. Tarik and Bill joined her among the crowd of Road Runners anxiously waiting to see if their years of hard work would finally yield the result that had become a Holy Grail.

The screen zoomed in further, showing only the outline of the house, cutting off the front and back yards along with the surrounding neighbors. All eyes were drawn to the two flashing green lights that stood inches apart on the screen, not moving.

"They're obviously talking," Tarik said to the room. "This is good. We were somewhat worried that Sonya would run off as soon as she saw Martin, but that doesn't appear to be the case."

The Commander nodded, also pleased with this information.

Ten minutes passed and neither of the green dots moved from their place on the screen.

"Are we sure it's working?" someone asked from the crowd

of two dozen people.

The woman behind the control panel clicked a few buttons and said, "Everything is working just fine."

"They're in her kitchen," Tarik commented. "I've been to her house before."

"Give it a moment," Strike said. "They certainly have some catching up to do, and it appears Sonya is agreeing to it."

What if he's telling her to make a run for it? Commander Strike wondered. It was possible, but made no sense. They both had tracking devices and couldn't actually hide anywhere. *He wouldn't do that. He has no reason to be disloyal after a day. What could she be saying to him, though?*

Those watching the screen started to squirm as they stood and watched absolutely nothing happen. It reminded Commander Strike of watching TV coverage of election night in the United States. There was always great stress and impatience as to how the night would end, but getting to that point was flat-out boring.

Please don't converse all day.

Most wars didn't end with some dramatic climax, but rather quietly through negotiation behind closed doors. When she was elected as the new Commander, she avoided any sort of promise to ending the war, and leaned on guarantees to take another step closer. The Road Runners had grown tone-deaf to repeated promises from leaders who vowed to end the war under their watch, so she built a platform on community and teamwork to advance the team's knowledge on the Revolters that would ideally lead to knowledge on how to kill Chris. She had achieved this, though by accident. Then again, she believed if you remained diligent and put in the hard work, your chances of getting lucky increased.

The tension faded by the second, and the green dots remained frozen in place. She looked down and rubbed her eyes, frustrated at the prospect of waiting an entire day to find out if she would place the phone call to change the world.

"She's moving!" someone shouted, sarcastically. Whispers spread through the crowd as they watched Sonya's green dot move across the screen, leaving Martin in the same place in the kitchen.

The Commander's eyes darted back to the screen and waited in anticipation. *It could be nothing, she could just be going to the bathroom.* She considered this likely since Martin had stayed in place. It clearly wasn't a heated argument or both dots would show as flailing across the screen.

"She's in her bedroom," Tarik said, calm and stern.

"He's moving, too!" someone shouted from the back.

"No he's not," responded another.

Everyone squinted in unison as they tried to figure out what was happening on the screen. Sonya's green dot flashed in her bedroom, while Martin's moved like a sloth toward her.

"Whatever he's doing he's approaching her slowly," Tarik said, eyes bulging. "Is he sneaking up on her?"

The commotion had Commander Strike's heart ready to leap out of her throat. *This is it, he's going in for the kill.*

As Martin's greet dot continued to inch closer to the bedroom, Sonya's green dot remained still.

An eternity of five whole seconds passed before Sonya's dot turned into a pulsing red on the screen.

He did it. It's done. He must have handed her the letter and she took it to her room to read.

He still wasn't quite within proximity to have injected her with a syringe, and never was close enough to have slipped anything into her drink.

What should have been an eruption of applause was met with deadly silence. Sonya had just been killed, and all eyes in the room turned to Commander Strike in eerie unity.

She pulled her phone from her pocket, fingers trembling as she dialed the number to the Alaska headquarters. While the phone rang, she wondered what her legacy would look like after her term ended. She had over a year left, plenty of time to conclude the war and let it snowball into a legacy as the greatest Commander in the history of the Road Runners. Office buildings would be named after her where a new generation of Road Runners could work on something besides cracking the code of how to defeat Chris.

"Hello, Commander," Julian answered 3,000 miles away.

"It's time."

Chapter 35

Andrei Morozov sat on the top of a tree, a thick and sturdy branch nestled between his legs, and his rifle perched to aim at Chris's mansion that glowed in the dawn of a new day in Alaska.

Andrei had gained fame within the Road Runners as their best soldier. Killing 319 Revolters earned that sort of respect. At least 300 of his kills had been achieved in his native Russia, but as word spread from the United States that an opportunity was on the horizon to take down Chris, he couldn't reject the offer to board the next plane to Alaska.

No one took their job as a sniper more seriously than Andrei. He committed to a rigorous workout routine, diet, and hundreds of hours educating himself on the Revolters. When he woke up in the morning, he imagined shooting Revolters. Same thing when he went to sleep at night, and likely during his dreams that he never remembered.

It was easy for Andrei to dedicate his life in such a dramatic manner. When the Revolters blew up a village in 2008 that took the lives of his mother, grandmother, and two sisters, he had no choice but to seek refuge with the Road Runners.

Now he was here, ten years after the fact and loving every moment of life as a Road Runner. They supported him in anything he needed, which wasn't much. All he asked for was a house to be built on the same land that had been destroyed. The village remained deserted, so he lived alone on the northern coast of Russia, hunting animals and fishing. And immersing himself in shooting practice, 300 rounds a day, delivered fresh at the beginning of every week from the Road Runners.

The leaders of the European branch of Road Runners knew how to get ahold of him: a quick helicopter ride from Moscow. He would never be anywhere else unless they had authorized him to go hunting for Revolters.

When word arrived that he was requested in Alaska, he had his bag packed and was on the return helicopter ride to Moscow within thirty minutes. From there he boarded a jet and arrived at the Alaskan headquarters in five hours.

He spent three weeks getting familiar with the area. The climate was no different from where he lived, but he needed to know the grounds surrounding Chris's mansion like the back of his hand.

It all led to him on this specific tree that he had picked out last week as the prime location to land a clean shot on Chris the moment he stepped onto his front porch.

He led a squad of five other snipers, all surrounding different corners of the property in case Chris tried to run from a different exit.

"When the time comes, he shouldn't actually know that he's mortal. We're gambling on an eight-hour window until he learns he's mortal again. He'll feel things like physical hunger and fatigue." Commander Strike had informed him of the plan when he arrived, and by all accounts it made sense. When it came down to it, all Andrei cared about was if his slug would indeed kill the main leader of the Revolters. And there was only one way to find out.

None of these past events stuck in his mind as he currently sat in the tree. His senses heightened, and his eyes focused on the house through his scope. Andrei drew long, heavy breaths, an exercise he had learned to keep his heart rate down when sniping enemies from hiding spots.

He had watched the grounds since his arrival in hopes of learning a daily routine Chris might have, but nothing was an exact science. Between six and eight in the morning, Chris would step outside to get into his van and leave. Andrei didn't care where he went. He wasn't in this business to follow people, but rather learn their schedules and execute them when the time came.

Chris would then return between ten and noon, typically having been gone for two hours each time. Beyond that knowledge was a crapshoot. Some days Chris would leave again in the afternoon or night, other times he'd never come back outside until the following morning.

It was 6:15 in the morning when Andrei had last checked his watch, and he waited for the voice in his ear to buzz through and give the order. If they could authorize it within the next fifteen minutes, Andrei knew Chris would be dead within the next 90 minutes.

You can take that to the bank. After the morgue, of course.

All week, the other Road Runners who were assigned to this mission had discussed it like middle school children excited for summer break. They were happy just to be a part of history, and didn't take the necessary preparations as seriously as Andrei expected for such a delicate mission.

None of it mattered—he was assigned the prime shooting location. The only reason Chris would go out a different door was if he knew something was going on. Andrei knew the cameras on the mansion didn't reach this far into the woods, so no one had a reason to alert Chris of any foul play taking place outside.

Carry on as normal, my friend.

Now was the waiting game. Andrei had an earpiece as a direct line of communication to Julian back at the headquarters. He didn't like Julian, thought he was too book smart for such a high position of power as the Commander's number two.

The earpiece finally crackled to life and Julian's squeaky voice echoed in his head.

"Andrei, it's time. I repeat, it's time. You have the green light."

The voice left his ear, leaving the silence and steady breeze as the only audible sounds. Somewhere under his three layers of jackets was a small microphone that the other snipers could hear him through.

"Gentlemen, we're all set. Fire on first sight, and kill anything that tries to get in the way."

Andrei grinned as he lowered his head down to look through the scope.

* * *

Forty minutes passed before there was any movement from the house, but when it came, Andrei sat ready with his finger on the trigger and his scope focused on the mansion's front door.

Come to Daddy, he thought, still keeping his breathing under control despite the sudden realization that he was about to become an international hero among the Road Runners. They would ask him to speak at events, to offer his training services to the others who trained for combat. He would decline all of this, jumping right back into his daily routine of exercising, eating, and sleeping until the war was officially declared over.

Until then, there was no point in resting on his laurels; that was a surefire way to get killed.

These thoughts briefly rushed through his mind before the front door opened and the familiar white hair of Chris appeared. He was surrounded by his usual posse of four guards. They all checked the surroundings in search of anything out of the ordinary.

Andrei wondered why they did this if Chris was supposedly immortal. Perhaps it was for their own good and not necessarily for their leader.

He drew one final deep breath and held it in his lungs, a ritual he had done every time before lining up a long distance shot. From the tree to the front door was just under 600 yards, a range he was comfortable shooting within, but still required more concentration than most shots. He had to factor the wind, altitude, temperature, and weight of the slug to project the perfect shot. Fortunately, for him and the rest of the world watching, the altitude, temperature, and ammunition were nearly identical to his set up in Russia. The only difference, as it could change any given day, was the wind.

The breeze had been steady, no more than ten miles per hour, but there had been instances where it stopped altogether. He had maybe ten seconds to calculate all of this data as Chris strolled from the front steps to his van.

Under five miles per hour, he thought as he zeroed on Chris's head. *Almost no breeze, but not quite nothing.*

He still hadn't exhaled, now with the perfect shot aligned.

Pull, he thought, squeezing the trigger and exhaling in unison.

Chris's guards whipped their guns out at the crack of the sniper rifle, but it was too late. Chris had been struck in the head and his body fell to the ground four steps shy of the van.

The Revolters started shooting blindly into the trees, clearly unsure of where the kill shot came from. They were shouting, but the sounds were nothing but gibberish by the time they reached Andrei.

He lowered his jaw back into his jacket and spoke into his microphone. "Take them all out."

Andrei had a clear shot and took down one of the guards. Four other shots fired within the next ten seconds, and each Revolter had fallen face down onto the cold ground.

"Nice work, men," Andrei said.

Somewhere underground, all around the world, Road Runners were screaming and shouting at the TVs. If they could riot in the streets to celebrate, they would. But no one else in society would know what was going on.

Andrei sat up and looked outside of his scope for the first time in thirty minutes. The dead bodies splayed across the front of the house were the ultimate badge of honor as he admired their stillness in the cold day.

He squinted at the sight of something his brain wouldn't allow him to believe.

Chris's frosty head sat up in the middle of the dead bodies, prompting Andrei to lower his eye back into the scope.

"Don't celebrate quite yet, men. He's back."

Through the scope, Andrei watched Chris sit up, take a quick look around, then turn his head directly in his direction with a wide grin. The old man raised a stiff hand and waved to Andrei as he stood. He reached for his head with his scrawny fingers, worked around the side, and plucked the slug out as if it were an annoying hair. Chris examined it between two fingers before flicking it aside and returning another grin and wave to Andrei more than 1,500 feet away.

Andrei felt something he couldn't recall having ever experienced: goose flesh. Chris locked eyes with him through the scope, freezing him from pulling the trigger again. The others on his team apparently didn't have the same problem as they all fired their rifles in near unison.

Five bullets tore through Chris's head and chest, prompting a maniacal laugh from the crazy old man in the otherwise silent morning.

"What the fuck?" Andrei whispered, still trying to gain control back of his own mind. He'd never imagined such a thing to be possible, but he had once thought the same thing about time travel.

Chris plucked the rest of the slugs out of his body and head, flicking them aside like pocket lint, and turned back into the mansion. Heavy steel walls rose from the ground and swallowed the mansion, securing the house in a virtual bulletproof fort.

"What's going on out there?" Julian crackled from Andrei's earpiece.

"I have no idea. We just shot him six times and he walked back into the house."

Silence filled the airwaves as he assumed Julian was in a panic, on the phone with Commander Strike. Any celebrations that might have begun would've already ceased. Chris lived on, and the Road Runners now had a new list of questions as to why.

36

Chapter 36

"What do you mean he's *not dead*?" Commander Strike asked into the phone. She had slipped back into Tarik's office after watching the previous moments unfold.

She had watched the live feed that had cut out moments after Chris had risen from the ground, but hearing the confirmation from Alaska made it real.

"He's in his house and has barricaded himself," Julian explained. He had been the one to cut the live feed that was showing around the world.

"How is this possible?" Commander Strike demanded.

"There are two possibilities," Julian replied calmly. "Either our theory was wrong, which I don't believe is likely, or Sonya isn't actually dead."

"She's dead. She's still flashing red and hasn't moved in 20 minutes. Are you suggesting our tracking device technology is faulty?"

"The equipment is fine. We need to get someone to Sonya's house right away. Something's not right. Briar hasn't moved either and is still next to Sonya. He wouldn't just be lying next to her dead body."

"He might. He was deeply in love with her."

"I'm just suggesting someone goes there to see what exactly happened. Something's not right, and we need to have an answer ready for the people. They all saw Chris rise before I cut the feed. Although, many might have missed it due to celebrating. I know I almost did."

"I'll go myself. Me and Tarik. I'll call you when we get there."

"Be careful, Commander. Sonya is very wise and knows her neighborhood better than anyone. It could be a trap."

"I'll be fine."

Commander Strike hung up and rubbed her temples. "How the fuck is this happening?"

This was supposed to be a day of celebration, a future holiday for all Road Runners. As of now, it was nothing but another botched assassination attempt. Chris was alive and hiding in his house now, with dozens of Road Runners trapped in his basement. He might never come out, or maybe was already jumping to another era in time to plan his next move.

Strike slammed her fist on Tarik's desk, sending pens and paper clips out of place as they hopped around the oak. "Fuck!"

Tarik knocked and entered. "Commander, it's a dark mood out here. I think you should say something."

"I have nothing to say. You and I are going to Sonya's house. Now."

Strike crossed the office and forced Tarik aside, stepping into the bullpen where two dozen pairs of eyes all locked on her. She froze, and debated storming out of the building or addressing the crowd. She had never shown her frustrated side, and even though this was a justifiable moment, decided to keep her cool facade.

"Hello, everyone. As you saw, our mission has failed. We're not sure why, but I'm going out right now with Tarik to get to the bottom of this. Please save your questions, as I honestly don't have an answer. We hope to know more when we return."

The silence that hung in the room could have been cut with a plastic spoon. The hype had vanished, leaving behind a world of terrified and confused Road Runners. For nearly all of them, taking down Chris was their life's work. To have the illusion of having worked so hard, and come this far, only to see it all fail before their eyes was a gut check none had been prepared for.

Killing Chris had always seemed as likely as winning the lottery, and they understood that. But when Commander Strike informed them that it was finally a real possibility, a sense of fate settled across the room, and hope came out in full force.

I failed these people. I should've never said anything, and carried on like it was a normal day.

The thought was pure fantasy. People would have known something was going on the moment she arrived at the Denver office unannounced. It wasn't every day that the leader came down from Alaska to meet a new recruit. The rumors would've swirled and prompted her to address them anyway.

No one asked questions as she walked to the exit with Tarik chasing behind. She felt all of them watch her as she fought to bury the stress beneath her confident countenance.

She stormed up the stairs without a plan, hoping and assuming Tarik had a way to get them to Larkwood.

"I'll drive," Tarik said from behind as he joined her outside. Somewhere in 1996 Brett McBath would be returning to the same parking space after dropping off Martin Briar at Sonya's house. But on this cool day in 2018, an all-black Tesla sat in the spot, ready for their trip across town.

Commander Strike didn't hesitate as she walked straight to the passenger door and let herself in. If Tarik couldn't sense the urgency right now, then maybe she needed to find a new leader for the Denver headquarters.

He must have sensed it as he ran down the steps from the building and threw himself behind the wheel, clicking the remote to start the engine that quietly hummed to life.

"You know what's funny," Tarik said, buckling his seat belt. "They call these the cars of the future. You and I have seen the future, and the cars are nothing like this."

He chuckled as he put the car in gear and pulled onto the road. Commander Strike didn't laugh, although she did find the comment ironic. It also reminded her of how grim the future was, thanks to Chris. *Why didn't he just* die?

She clenched her jaw and shook her head. Everyone had executed their part to perfection. Even Martin, who she had half expected to back out at the last minute.

"How long to get there?" she asked.

"Should be ten minutes, assuming there's no traffic."

There was none, they had that much going for them, at least. She didn't even look out the window as they drove to Larkwood in silence, keeping her stare to the ground, sulking in confusion.

When they pulled in to Sonya's neighborhood, she asked Tarik, "Do you have a gun?"

"I keep one in the trunk. Why? Are you thinking we'll need it?"

"I don't think so. But Julian was warning me, like I should be ready for something to happen. Do we know if Martin has moved yet?"

"He hadn't when we left. I don't know if he has since then."

"Whatever happens inside that house, we need to leave with an answer, and we need to get back to work. Chris will be killing our people by tomorrow, and we need to have something prepared to tell the community."

"You mean to tell the world. The whole world was watching. People woke up in the middle of the night on the other side of the globe just to see history."

"Well, they saw it alright."

Tarik parked the car at the curb, blocking the driveway. He killed the engine and they both stared at the house as if it were a rare bird. Commander Strike noted the homey feeling from the front yard, with its green lawn, big tree, and front porch with two rocking chairs. A long time ago she had a life just like this, but hadn't been back since becoming Commander and constantly traveling the world to kill bad guys.

Those memories would have to stay buried in the past with her dead husband.

"Let's jump back to 1996 and go in. Is someone watching us?" she asked, referring to someone within the organization keeping an eye on their tracking devices.

"Commander, someone is *always* watching you. Even on the rare days you sleep."

"Very funny."

"It's true. So yes, you're being watched. I have no idea about me."

"As long as one of us is being watched then we'll be okay. Let's go."

Strike pushed open her door and went to the trunk where Tarik opened the door for her to get the pistol he kept concealed. Tarik joined her as she sat down on the sidewalk, unscrewing the lid off of her flask. They both took a quick swig of their Juice. After having taken thousands of trips through time, the process became as seamless as tying shoelaces. They briefly fell asleep and woke up in 1996 within one minute.

Without a word, Strike stood, dusted herself off, and walked up the driveway to knock on the door with a balled fist.

"Sonya, are you home?" she called. *Of course she's not home, because she's dead, remember?*

She knocked again, hoping for Martin to come answer, but didn't want to call out his name just in case Sonya was alive and hiding. She couldn't have her know that Martin was sent by the Road Runners.

They waited a minute, knocking a couple more times, before Commander Strike turned to Tarik and shrugged.

"Try the door," he whispered, creating a stealthy mood.

Strike nodded before turning the knob and pushing the door open with ease.

"Sonya?" she called again as she took her first step inside the house and froze.

The house appeared empty, but the splatters of blood on the kitchen floor and walls made her stop. She cocked the pistol and held it out in front of her body.

"Sonya, is everything okay?"

This wasn't supposed to be a bloody mess.

Her eyes followed the trail of blood that started at the kitchen table and smeared its way across the house, to the bedroom where the door stood wide open, and she watched the blood turn into it and out of sight.

"Is any one here?" she barked, thinking Martin better damn well respond.

Silence filled the house, the only sound being the hardwood floor creaking beneath her feet. Tarik had stepped into the doorway and couldn't take his eyes off the apparent massacre in the kitchen.

A thousand thoughts rushed Strike's mind as she now accepted the possibility of Sonya being alive. She could've killed Martin. Maybe the system was glitching because they were so close to each other. Sonya could be hiding in the bedroom over Martin's dead body, waiting for the next Road Runner to show up and try to end her life.

"If anyone is in this house, speak now, or consider yourself at risk of being shot."

Strike's voiced echoed and returned to her with no response. She turned to Tarik, his eyes bulging from their sockets as the realization sunk in that something terrible had happened just minutes ago. The terrifying part was not knowing what awaited in the bedroom.

"Commander," Tarik whispered urgently. "Shouldn't I go in first?"

Strike almost laughed. Only Tarik would pull out an official procedure in a time like this. Yes, it was written that if a dangerous situation should arise, the Commander is last to act, sending in others to the potential danger first. This was obviously done for the sake of keeping leadership in tact, but now wasn't the time to pull out the rule book.

"This is my mess," she spoke in her normal voice, not believing there was any living person in the house. "I'm going in first. I don't sense any danger."

Tarik glared to the blood splatters to say *are you shitting me?* with his eyes.

Commander Strike turned back to the bedroom and took

gentle steps toward it, pistol as far out as her arms would stretch.

When she was within two steps of the bedroom, she leapt across the doorway and into the room, pistol jerking from left to right as if she had expected someone to jump out and attack her.

"Martin," she said, seeing their newest member flat on his back, eyes closed, blood seeping from his legs. "Martin!"

Holy shit, he's dead. She killed him. But where is she?

She lowered the pistol, deciding Sonya wasn't in the house. Why would she hide when she could be in the 1400's already? "Tarik, get in here."

He had watched from the living room and let out a long sigh when the Commander called him in. He joined her, and immediately dropped to a knee to examine Martin.

"He's still alive," he said. "His breathing is fine."

Tarik poked Martin on the face, and snapped his fingers right next to his ears. "He's unconscious. If all of this blood belongs to him, he's suffered a pretty heavy loss. I see a bullet wound on both legs. One in the kneecap—that could've hurt enough to make him faint."

At first glance, Commander Strike thought the liquid on the other side of Martin was more blood, but with her nerves settling down, she recognized the green liquid for what it was after seeing it next to the spilled, empty bottle.

"Tarik, is that what I think it is?"

He was still hunkered over Martin and pivoted on his knee to examine the mess behind him.

"Oh, my God," he said, clapping a hand to his mouth. "She cut it out."

"Cut what out?"

275

"Her tracking device."

Tarik reached into the pool of liquid and plucked a small item that Commander Strike had originally thought was the bottle cap.

"Do you know how bad this would hurt?" he cried. "Never mind the cutting open of your own arm, but these devices *attach* to the muscle—it's how they stay in place. It wouldn't have just plucked out like a hair; she would've experienced excruciating pain."

"I don't care about her pain. Where the hell is she?"

Strike paced around the room, looking for the ultimate truth in this mystery. Every time traveler, whether a Road Runner or a Revolter, was guaranteed to have two things: a bottle of their Juice, and a small flask to carry that same Juice when traveling. There was no other way.

Sonya's bottle was on the floor, its liquid mixed with blood and no longer useful. Finding the flask—or not—would decide everything from this point forward.

Commander Strike rummaged through Sonya's dresser before moving to her night stand. Tarik watched her bounce around the room like an alcoholic searching for the private stash they hid from themselves.

"Fuck!" she barked from the nightstand, and sat down on the bed with a silver and blue flask clenched in her grip. She shook her head, looking at the flask like it was fake.

"What does this mean?" Tarik asked, knowing very well what it meant, but not sure what else to say in the spur of the moment.

"She's gone and not coming back. She has no way back." The life had left her voice as she debated lying all the way down on Sonya's bed and crying. How could they have been so close to ending this war, to only end up even further from a solution?

"Commander, if she drank one final drink of her Juice and left, where is her body? Shouldn't her body be lying here on the ground while she traveled to wherever she went?"

"She doesn't go by the same rules as us. Only her and Chris have the ability to travel without leaving their bodies behind. Their bodies travel *through* the dimensions of time. I guess it's a perk of being related to Chris."

"She can run, Commander, but we have eyes all over. We can alert everyone we have. At this point, we have to treat Sonya as an outlaw. She needs to be arrested on sight, and if she tries to run, then she needs to be shot."

This much was true, but it was the last thing Commander Strike wanted to authorize. *So fucking close. Sonya was expecting Martin.*

There was no other explanation as to why she would've shot Martin in both of his legs before fleeing to another time with no return trip home.

"Tarik, we can't tell anyone about what happened or what our next move is. I think someone has been leaking information to Sonya from the inside."

Chapter 37

Martin woke up in what looked like a hospital room; only it had no windows, no TV, and no beeping machines. There was a closed door with frosted glass, and he assumed he was back in the Road Runners' office, hopefully still in Denver, and hopefully back in 2018.

His bleary vision came in and out of focus as he looked down at his own body. White bandages were wrapped around both of his legs like a mummy. He tried to move his legs, but an instant blast of pain ruptured from his knee at the slightest movement.

Then he remembered what happened, which he was thankful for after once having woken up in a hospital and *not* remembering how he had arrived.

"Sonya," he croaked. *Did she really shoot me in both legs to escape? Did she actually consider me* that *dangerous that she felt she had to flee? If she would've just asked, I'd have just turned around and pretended to not notice.*

The door swung open and Bill appeared in the doorway. "Good morning, Sunshine." He turned back into the hall and shouted, "Let the Commander know Martin is awake."

Bill trudged into the room and approached Martin's bedside. "That's quite the beating your legs took. The doctor said it'll be six weeks until you can get out of those casts. I've never had a mummy friend before, so I'm not sure what to expect."

Bill let out a hoarse chuckle as he slapped a hand on Martin's chest. Martin couldn't help but grin in response.

"What happened? What year am I in? Did we find Sonya?"

Bill shook his head, his eyes drooping. "You're back in 2018, and I'm afraid not. She's as good as dead, the way I see it. She took off to some other time and has no way of returning; she left her Juice. For all we know, she's hiding out a million years ago with a group of triceratops. I'm sure we'll come across her eventually, but something tells me she's had this escape plan brewing for a while. She'll be hidden really good."

"Bill, I wasn't even doing anything. I wasn't even going to try and kill her, but she came out of nowhere and shot me before she left."

"Yeah, I understand. She has no idea who to trust right now. Can you blame her?"

"It just seemed drastic. We were literally talking in her kitchen, about our past, when she pulled a gun out of the drawer and started shooting."

"Well, at least you're fine. She spared your life, don't forget that. She could've shot you anywhere, but chose your legs. She's no dummy; that was intentional."

"I suppose. So what happens next?"

"Commander Strike will be in to get you up to speed. You have a long road to recovery ahead, my friend."

"There's not some magic medicine from the future that heals my legs in 24 hours?"

Bill laughed. "What exactly do you think the future is like? There's no magic."

Says one time traveler to another.

A rapid knock came from the door as Commander Strike entered, dressed in a sweater and jeans. The bags under her eyes had darkened to a deeper shade.

"Haven't you two become the best of friends," she commented.

"Martin here is the brother I never had," Bill said.

"Very good. Do you mind giving us a moment in private?"

"Sure thing, Commander." Bill patted Martin on the shoulder before leaving the room. Strike took slow strides to the foot of the bed.

"How are you feeling?" she asked.

"Well, it appears I can't walk, so I've had better days."

"Your legs are going to be fine. You'll have about a month in those casts, then will be walking within a couple weeks of that. You might have a limp, but we won't know until you actually start walking."

"Lovely, hobbling gets all the ladies."

Commander Strike giggled. "So what happened in there?"

"A paranoid woman shot me in the legs and vanished into dust."

"We know that much. How did it play out?"

Martin recounted the story from the moment he entered Sonya's house up until he crawled into her bedroom and fainted.

"Did it seem like she knew what you were up to?"

"She knew everything. She called it out, even told me where the poison was in the duffel bag."

"I was afraid so. We've already begun investigating to see

who was leaking information to Sonya. We're starting with everyone in this office since she had the closest relationships with people here."

"What's the word on Chris?"

The Commander pursed her lips at the mention of his name. "We don't know. His house is still barricaded. No one has gone in or out in the last 16 hours. We're worried he might have a secret way out, an underground tunnel of sorts. We have eyes on that place and all around Alaska, waiting for him to make a move."

"That's kind of scary."

"Don't mention it. We've had to tell the people that everything is under control, that we know exactly where Chris is."

"So what happens next? I know I'm not of much help at the moment..."

"We're officially back to the drawing board. We need a plan for finding Sonya, but that's more like the needle in a haystack. I guess we're just hoping to get lucky and stumble across her."

"One thing she made clear is that no one was going to end her life on their terms."

"Well, now that the secret's officially out, we can't exactly back off. We don't know if she'll go into hiding or possible retaliate. It's not to our benefit to assume one way or the other. If we can at least locate her and know where she is, we can figure it out from there."

"Exactly how far in time can you travel?"

"As far as you can think. If the year actually exists in the past, you can go to it. Same for the future. If you can't go to the year, then you'll just wake back up in your present day."

"Are you saying you know when the world ends?"

"It's not for a long time, but we can discuss that another

time. I need to know that you're still with us."

"Of course."

"I hoped so. Some would go running for the hills after going through what just happened to you. "

"I'm committed to this cause, maybe even more now. I still want what we agreed upon. I have to save my mom."

Commander Strike sighed. "I've been expecting you to bring that up. I have looked into the matter. The cure exists in the future, but it's not easy to obtain."

"I'll get it. Whatever it takes."

Commander Strike shook her head, causing some hair to fall over her face. "It's not what you think. The medicine is being held in secret by the government."

"Why would they keep it a secret?"

"You'll understand when you see this government—there's no interest in caring for people. It's all about money. Only the richest citizens have access to the medical secrets."

"Aren't we all rich? Can't we just buy some?"

"It's not a matter of only money. Every person who receives this medicine has to be vetted by the government. They hook you up to a lie detector—and this is an advanced one—and ask you about your loyalty to the Revolution. If they find you're loyal, they'll let you buy it. If not, they send you off, or might even execute you depending on your answers to their questions."

"The Revolters take control of the country?"

"Yes, that's why we have an urgency to end the war. We've seen the future with them in charge, and it's not a world anyone should have to live in."

"I've already lived through hell way before I met Chris. I'm not scared of a little danger."

"I knew I wouldn't be able to talk you out of this. We'll make arrangements for you to go as soon your legs are healed. As you'll need to be mobile. There aren't any more accommodations for handicapped people in the future."

"Why aren't you pushing back harder on this?"

"We owe you—I owe you," she said, crossing her arms. "I didn't think the situation we were sending you into would have any danger. You're not even trained to be in the field as a Road Runner, and clearly you should have been. I rushed into this decision and it almost got you killed. I have to live with that."

"There was no time to waste."

"There was plenty of time. We had eyes on Sonya. She wasn't going to move until we approached. She was waiting for us to make her escape."

"One thing I've learned since time traveling is to not dwell on past decisions. It's over, and I'm alive. You're not doing anyone any good by looking back. It's time to plan for what's next."

She nodded, appreciative of the comment. "Oh, I've been thinking about what comes next. Now that I know you're committed to the Road Runners, what do you think about taking a position in the field—after we get your mom's medicine, of course?"

"What kind of position?"

"I don't know yet. You would have to go through field training; it's a boot camp of sorts. From there, we'll have a better assessment of your strengths and weaknesses. But there are all kinds of roles you can take on, and we still haven't figured out how to use your special gift to our advantage."

Martin had forgotten all about being "warm." Perhaps he'd get to trail blaze a whole new role. "As long as I don't have to sit in there all day, I'll take anything." He nodded to the door where the dozens of desk workers waited on the other side.

"Don't worry, the office workers also go through a rigorous education program. Two years, seven days a week, if that interests you?"

"Nope."

Commander Strike laughed. "We'll get you a ride home so you can recover from the comfort of your own house. We'll come check in with you in a few weeks and see about your rehab schedule. Then we can plan from there."

They wrapped up their conversation with some small talk, and Martin couldn't stop grinning, despite the pain and drama he had just endured. He felt part of something bigger than himself for the first time in his life. The stress that Chris had created by leaving so many questions unaddressed had washed away. The Road Runners would support him in anything he needed going forward, and they proved that by staying true to their word on helping him obtain the cure for Marilyn's disease.

The future, which sounded like a dystopian nightmare by everyone who had traveled there, awaited Martin and his next adventure. He already knew the road ahead would bring more unforeseen twists, but he finally had control over his life, knowing what he wanted. And as he lay down, staring at the ceiling and pondering what his life would look like in the next six months, one thought played over and over that kept his spirits high.

I'm a Road Runner.

Bad Faith (Wealth of Time #3)

If you enjoyed Warm Souls, the story continues in Bad Faith.

Fulfill your destiny.

Heartbroken and on the mend, Martin is forced into his new life as the only Warm Soul on the continent. His freedom has vanished—his life now fully devoted to the Road Runners.

Martin's first official mission: traveling to the far future to obtain a special cure. He is warned against going to this era engulfed in corruption and chaos.

Determined to retrieve the medicine, Martin throws caution to the wind, only to encounter a darker world than anticipated.

Meanwhile, an underground war escalates as betrayal runs rampant. With the fabric of good stretched to its limits, Martin will soon realize the plan intended for him all along.

Bad Faith is the third novel in the Wealth of Time Series. If you enjoy fast-paced thrillers, twists and turns, and a cunning villain, then you'll love this high-octane series from international bestselling author Andre Gonzalez!

Buy Bad Faith today to join Martin as he encounters his inner greatness!

Get Bad Faith on Amazon today!

Now, enjoy a sneak peek of chapter one!

Martin Briar sprawled in the mud, a generous gash oozing blood over his exhausted legs, his arms screaming in protest, sweat rolling down his mud-caked face, his entire body numb with pain.

"Pain is weakness leaving your body!" Staff Master Collins had barked at least 200 times over the past two months in his sharp, intimidating growl. Martin particularly enjoyed when the belligerent staff master would drop to the ground as he completed his 150th push-up, shouting that same line in his face while demanding fifty more.

Martin had put on a few pounds during his twelve-week recovery and rehab from Sonya blasting his legs into uselessness, but the Road Runner Training Program was simply a nice way of phrasing "boot camp." With the calendar flipping to 2019, Martin shed all of the extra weight, and for the first time since his twenties, sported actual muscles.

"I'm too old for this shit," he had muttered under his breath on the first day, wondering how the hell he'd make it to the finish line. Staff Master Collins had promised to destroy the body and psyche of all those in attendance, a group of Martin and six others recently recruited to join the Road Runners. Only one had dropped out after the first week, leaving the rest to form a bond and push each other through the ten-week program.

"You people don't know true hell," Staff Master Collins had calmly explained one day after training ended. He stood exactly six feet tall, with muscles bulging from every centimeter of his dark-skinned body, a heavy brow line keeping his face in a constant frown. *Even his muscles have muscles,* Martin noted before the first day of training.

Collins liked to give his version of motivational speeches at the end of each day, always while the group panted for breath, hands on knees as they listened. "I've been to hell and fought the demons. You need to be strong, mentally and physically, because they will try to break you."

Part of the program was learning to survive. Each trainee was given a specific amount of water to drink each day, decided by their weight and age to determine the bare minimum needed to not faint during the rigorous workout.

"What happens if you travel into the future and get captured by the Revolters? Do you think they're going to give you a bottle of water? Maybe order a pizza and fix a soft bed for you? Hell *no!*" Whenever Collins shouted, spit flew from his mouth in messy droplets.

"These people will leave you to starve, leave you to thirst, and leave you to die. If they don't kill you right away, they'll take you hostage, wait until you can barely stand up, then beat you to death because you're defenseless and can't even lift your hand to wipe your ass! Do you understand, Briar?"

Martin nodded at the crazy bald man two inches from his face, bulging brown eyes burning into his spirit.

"Good. Especially you, Briar." Collins paused and crossed his arms, taking a step back from Martin. He lowered his voice and continued. "They want you bad, Briar. You're not the kind of man they'll kill at first chance—they will torture you. They want that sweet, sweet gift you have, and if they have to rip it out of your organs, then that's what they'll do."

This moment ten weeks ago had forced Martin to dedicate his life to the training program. He didn't know if the things Collins said were true, but he did know Chris wanted him, whether out of revenge for fleeing, or for being a Warm Soul.

Today was day 70, the final day of the training program, as Martin lay in the mud. They expected him to maintain his new figure, and he had every intent of doing so. Martin felt the best he ever had in his life. He slept better, ate better, was never tired, and no longer craved alcohol. He was now a middle-aged man with a chiseled physique and the skills to murder a man with his bare hands.

"Everybody up!" Collins grumbled, intentionally kicking mud in the faces of those slow to rise. Despite the cramping spread across his entire body, Martin jumped to his feet within two seconds. His mental strength had developed even more than his body, in his opinion. "To the rifles!"

The group of three men and two women dragged themselves out of the mud pit where they had just completed a twenty-minute round of army crawling. At least the rifles didn't require any further physical strength, but rather mental will.

A gazebo housed the rifles one hundred feet away. Martin ran to it, grabbing his rifle and a bandolier to sling over his shoulder. Every day ended with a quick session on the shooting range.

"Start us off, Briar," Collins shouted. They all had to watch each other shoot, a way to practice in the spotlight.

"Learn to shoot under any circumstance. There will be times you feel like you're dying, maybe you *are* dying, but you have to shoot on. Kill every last Revolter until you no longer can."

Another inspirational line from Staff Master Collins.

Martin obliged and took his post. Ten rubber dummies stood across the open field, ranging from fifty to five hundred yards in distance. He focused on his breathing, inhaling deeply through his nose and exhaling steadily out of his mouth. He dropped his head to see into his scope and started firing.

He shot the first nine in rapid succession, his hands gliding from side to side as each dummy rocked in its place. The tenth and final shot required extra concentration as it stood 500 yards away. He'd heard the stories of Andrei Morozov's long distance shot on Chris in Alaska. Even though the shot didn't end up deadly, it was still touted as the greatest shot in the history of the Road Runners. Martin had the opportunity to meet Andrei at the beginning of their training program and received a few tips from the pro, including the breathing technique used when lining up the long distance shots.

He drew his breath and fired the shot, watching the dummy's head rock back. His fellow trainees ruptured into applause at witnessing his performance. Maybe once a week someone would have a perfect outing and hit all ten targets; this week was Martin's turn.

"Nice shooting, Briar," Collins said in the closest tone he had to a normal voice.

Martin stepped back and joined the rest of his team, who all offered slaps on the back and fist bumps for his stellar performance.

"Can I have a word with you?" Collins asked as the next trainee stepped up with their rifle.

"Sure."

They dropped back a safe distance where their voices couldn't be overheard by the others. Collins spoke in a low voice, just above a whisper. "They want me to report back what I think your best role would be. Now, by the looks of it, you have all the tools of a front line soldier. That would mean you'd barge into Revolter hideouts and kill everyone in sight, help with ambushes, and kick ass in general. But I get the sense that doesn't really excite you—you don't have the killer mentality that most soldiers have."

Martin nodded. "I'll go wherever I'm needed."

"Get off your high horse, Briar. Just tell me what you want to do."

"I honestly don't care. I just want to get this medicine for my mom. Whatever happens after that I'm fine with. I do want to kill Chris."

"Well, get in line. We already had a task force assigned to kill him, and they failed."

"The mission failed; they did not. Andrei landed that shot."

"Precisely. You may not have all the knowledge of someone who's been with the organization for years, but I feel you have the smarts to figure out a way. Combine that with your Warm Soul, and you might be the person who brings down Chris."

Martin had never thought of himself as smart. He got by in high school, never went to college, and bounced around jobs as a mid-level manager for various companies. Now with the Road Runners, more and more people had been praising his thinking ability, when all he thought he was doing was giving honest feedback.

"I don't even know what my ability means—I've never even seen it in action."

"There'll be a special session for you with some of our scientists. I think you'll be heading there the day after tomorrow."

"Can't wait."

"Don't be a smart-ass, Briar, I'm trying to help you."

"I know, and I appreciate it." Collins had never shown his compassionate side, and Martin wasn't sure what to do with it as the others in his group howled and cheered for each other on the shooting range. "I have my sights set on one thing at a time, and for me, it's getting that medicine."

"I respect that, but you can't lose sight of the future. Especially around here – you have to be ten steps ahead."

The two men stood in silence as an ugly gray cloud moved above them.

"I know. Honestly, I'll trust your recommendation for whatever position you think is best."

"I only recommend, but Commander Strike has the final say. She's checked in with me every day about your progress."

"What have you told her?"

"I told her there's something burning inside you, something that's pushing you to do the impossible." Collins paused and kicked the dirt with his heavy boot. "I'll be honest with you, this program is not meant for fifty-year-old men. It's designed for kids in their twenties, in their physical prime—like them." He nodded to the rest of the trainees. "I didn't think you'd make it past day one, but you've proven all of us wrong. That's how I know there's something driving you; I've never seen a transition like yours."

The Road Runners had put Martin through a rigorous rehab for his legs before starting the training program with Collins. Through that, he felt a motivation to not let Sonya's cowardly actions define the rest of his life. They thought he'd have a new limp after coming out of his cast—he didn't. They said his knee would never bend the same way again, leaving him no flexibility—they were wrong. The weakness in his shot knee tried to creep up at times, but he followed the rehab program to the last detail. The Road Runners' doctors may have not had medicine from the future, but they had knowledge from it, and applied it to his rehab to make his legs stronger than before.

"I appreciate the compliment, and I'm sure Commander Strike will have a talk with me before deciding anything. I assume a lot will depend on how these tests go with the scientists."

"I suspect that, too. Either way, it's food for thought. If you ever need to talk about things, just let me know. I'll be here."

Collins stuck out a hand for Martin to shake. He had never shown his human side, and by doing so, showed Martin how highly the Road Runners thought of him. Collins thanked him for working so hard over the last ten weeks and wished him the best in whatever he'd end up doing for the organization.

An hour later, Martin was officially free to return home after living on the training base for the last ten weeks. Granted, it was only ninety minutes away from his house—and had all the luxurious accommodations he'd come to expect of anything hosted by the Road Runners—but he wanted to sleep in his own bed and see his mother in person instead of the brief phone calls they had at night.

He'd have to drag himself to the car to begin his long drive, but the prospect was enough to spark a new wave of energy as he left the hardest chapter of his time as a Road Runner in the rear view mirror.

Get Bad Faith on Amazon today!

Acknowledgements

I've got a great team now, this being my sixth novel. There's a lot of work that goes into the production of a book, a lot more than just the actual writing of it. I'd like to first thank Arielle and Felix for being the daily reminder to keep moving forward. It's not easy working to create a life outside of the "norm" but you two make it worth the effort every day.

Thank you to my editor, Stephanie Cohen, your changes are always appreciated and I know working on a series is a whole other beast, so thank you for putting up with me for many more books to come in this Wealth of Time universe.

Dane Low for creating the best covers in the business.

Big thanks to my Advanced Readers team. Your excitement is felt and I'm blessed to have you all as some of my biggest fans. You've all done so much in making every book launch a huge success.

Writing is a lonely process and can often feel like you're stranded on an island screaming for help. Thank you to the Dizzy Dragons for being there and offering support. We are "coworkers" in a sense, and I know not every writer has that support group to lean on.

Lastly, as always, thank you to my wife, Natasha. I'll say she the most honest critic, to put it nicely, but it's very much needed to make a book as best as it can be. We're getting so close, and now is the time to double down and make the dream come true.

Andre Gonzalez
    August 10, 2018 – April 25, 2019

Also by Andre Gonzalez

Books are listed in order of most recent publication:
Bad Faith (Wealth of Time Series, Book #3)
Snowball: A Christmas Horror Story
Road Runners (Wealth of Time Series, Short Story)
Revolution (Wealth of Time Series, Short Story)
Warm Souls (Wealth of Time Series, Book #2)
Wealth of Time (Wealth of Time Series, Book #1)
Erased (Insanity Series, Prequel) (Short Story)
The Insanity Series (Books 1–3)
Replicate (Insanity Series, Book #3)
The Burden (Insanity Series, Book #2)
Insanity (Insanity Series, Book #1)
A Poisoned Mind (Short Story)
Followed Home

About the Author

Born in Denver, CO, Andre Gonzalez has always had a fascination with horror and the supernatural starting at a young age. He spent many nights wide-eyed and awake, his mind racing with the many images of terror he witnessed in books and movies. Ideas of his own morphed out of movies like *Halloween* and books such as *Pet Sematary* by Stephen King. These thoughts eventually made their way to paper, as he always wrote dark stories for school assignments or just for fun. Followed Home is his debut novel based off of a terrifying dream he had many years ago at the age of 12. His reading and writing of horror stories evolved into a pursuit of a career as an author, where Andre hopes to keep others awake at night with his frightening tales. The world we live in today is filled with horror stories, and he looks forward to capturing the raw emotion of these events, twisting them into new tales, and preserving a legacy in between the crisp bindings of novels.

Andre graduated from Metropolitan State University of Denver with a degree in business in 2011. During his free time, he enjoys baseball, poker, golf, and traveling the world with his family. He believes that seeing the world is the only true way to stretch the imagination by experiencing new cultures and meeting new people.

Andre still lives in Denver with his wife, Natasha, and their two kids.

You can connect with me on:

🌐 http://andregonzalez.net

🐦 http://www.twitter.com/monito0408

📘 http://www.facebook.com/AndreGonzalezAuthor

🖋 http://www.instagram.com/monito0408

Subscribe to my newsletter:

✉ http://andregonzalez.net

Made in United States
Orlando, FL
15 August 2023

36107612R10167